I dedicate this book to Brayden, Mason, Madden and Zayne. Some of you have forsaken me, but I still love you more than anything in this world. And, as always, to my Sarah.

Chapter One

At two thousand, one hundred eighty feet, Poke-O-Moonshine was not part of the New York forty-six. To be considered a part of that group of mountains, the peak needs to be higher than four thousand feet. Poke-O was still a decent hike, with many challenging spots, especially for the casual hiker. The ranger trail was just under four miles long round trip, having several spots where there were natural steps and scrambles.

Kim and Steven Reynolds had hiked a few trails in Vermont, where they lived. They had heard about the group known as the Adirondack Forty-Sixers and wanted to join. Never having experienced any trails that challenging, they had decided to start with a smaller mountain.

Kim was thirty-five and relatively new to hiking. Steven had hiked most of his life and had introduced Kim to it when they started to date. She was in decent shape, though she felt that she could lose twenty pounds. Her red hair and pale skin made hiking the perfect outdoor activity as most of the time she was under the tree canopy, thus protecting her sensitive skin from the sun.

Steven was five years her senior and had been told he had the body of a Greek god most of his life. He never had to work to attain the muscle definition that he started to get as a teen. By fourteen he had a six-pack and had never done any crunches or sit-ups. He looked very much the part of an outdoorsy man, with long black hair that was always in a ponytail and a beard that went down past his chest.

Their honeymoon was spent on the Long Trail in Vermont, and that was where they had come to the decision to try and join the Forty-Sixers. On the one-month anniversary of their September wedding, they made the hour-long drive from Burlington over to Chesterfield, New York to begin their hike. Poke-O was rated more difficult than anything in their area, so they had figured it would prove to be a good starting hike.

The couple had arrived at the parking area on Route Nine just before seven in the morning. They found the lot empty, exactly as they had hoped, and reached the summit shortly after nine.

The pair unstrapped their packs, placed them on the ground and looked at the fire tower that stood before them. The tower stood roughly sixty feet above their heads, with five flights of stairs leading up to the entrance.

Without the need to speak aloud their desires, Steven led the way up to the top. He was tired and sweaty from the hike but knew that the view from inside the tower would be well worth the additional climbing.

The landing after the fifth flight of stairs formed a sort of balcony with the entrance to the tower at the far end. The aluminum bar and wooden plank construction seemed sturdy enough, but the tower swayed slightly with strong wind gusts. Kim was happy that the air at the summit was relatively calm on this day.

As Steven reached the last step, he smelled something that reminded him of days old garbage that had sat in the sun for too long. Having spent a lot of time in the woods, he had come across dead, rotting carcasses quite a few times, and his mind told him that that was what he now smelled. He thought that a squirrel or perhaps a raccoon must have climbed into the tower and died.

The enclosure at the top of the tower was made from wood. It was all held together by large bolts and nuts. The windows that were cut into the walls did not contain any glass, so it would be easy for an animal to have gotten in. The couple was so enthralled by the view of the area around them, that they failed to notice the source of the smell until it was too late. As Steven entered the enclosure, he tripped over the body that was lying on the floor.

Kim heard her husband grunt and hit the floor. Turning her head towards the commotion, she let out a scream when she saw the body that was now partially covered by her husband. It had been there long enough that it was difficult to say if it was a woman or a man, what age they had been or really anything else.

The sight and the smell were too much for her, so Kim turned and vomited over the railing. Steven clambered to his feet and took a wide path around the body to rejoin his wife. When he reached her, he pulled out his cellphone and was relieved to find that there was a strong signal on top of the mountain. He said a quick, silent thanks to Verizon Wireless and dialed nine-one-one.

The phone rang only once before the operator picked up. "911, what is your emergency?"

Chapter Two

The parking area for the trailhead for Poke-O-Moonshine was located on Route Nine just south of Keeseville. There was a building to the right of the entrance that was no longer used. It was a remnant from when people used to camp there and had provided the caretakers a weather-proof place to live. The building was kept up and it appeared as though the brown paint was fresh.

The entrance into the parking area was blocked by a state police car, the sun bringing out the deep blue color of the paint. Besides the emergency vehicles, there were only three vehicles in the parking area when the lead detective arrived, two belonged to the field techs and the other most likely to the hikers.

Sarah Barney had been with the New York State Police for sixteen years. She had graduated with a criminology degree from SUNY Canton and been hired right out of college. She was short for a trooper at only five feet five inches but made up for what she was lacking in stature with a superior intellect. She kept her black hair short, in a sort of bob cut and her deep brown eyes missed nothing.

Sarah had been given the rank of lead detective in the Plattsburgh area five years ago. There were not a lot of murders in the area, thankfully, but she had solved every case that she had investigated, with a ninety-eight percent conviction rate. As luck would have it, Sarah was a member of the forty-sixers, having just received her badge last month. She lived in the hamlet of

Keeseville, just over seven miles away from the trailhead to Poke-O, so she hiked it at least once a year.

Her partner was a junior detective named Brian Sloan. Brian was not a hiker, he was more of a video gamer, as was typical with a lot of men these days, even in the police force. He lived in Plattsburgh but pulled into the parking area a minute after she arrived. Sarah gave out a belly laugh when he showed up at the trailhead wearing his usual suit and tie. Brian was quite tall, at just over six feet seven inches. He kept his brown hair cut in a military style and his face was always clean shaven. He had eyes that were the color of the sky as the sun was setting.

"Brian, it's Saturday," she said. "And, we have to hike up a mountain. Why the hell are you in that suit?"

Brian looked around at the pair of paramedics and the two forensic techs that were there, as well as at Sarah. They were all wearing shorts and some kind of athletic shirt. He also noticed that they had packs, where they were probably carrying their forensic tools and the clothes that they would need to wear to protect the crime scene. He shook his head at his own short sightedness and looked at his feet, further realizing that he was woefully under prepared for the hike. His wing tipped shoes would be slippery at best.

One of the techs said something that he could not quite hear, and he looked at Sarah in askance.

"He said that there is no way you will be able to keep up," she said. "In fact, he is quite right. I want you to head back to the barracks, interview the people that found the body and start the paperwork."

Brian started to protest, but Sarah did not wait to hear whatever he wanted to say. She knew that the hike would be especially arduous this time because she and her team needed to get to the summit before anything else got to the body and site. Her best time for reaching the summit was in just over an hour, she hoped to make it in forty minutes today. Without a word, she assumed the lead position and the team fell in line behind her.

As she made it to the first set of natural stairs, Sarah felt a smile spread across her face. It was a beautiful day, and she was getting paid to do an activity that she loved. Sarah was not callous enough to forget why she was there but saw no harm in taking some enjoyment from the hike. The temperature was hovering around seventy and the humidity was low as was typical, but under the protection of the canopy, the air felt cooler. The crunch of last year's leaves under her feet and the rustle of the rapidly changing leaves on the trees presented her with her favorite soundtrack and before long, Sarah had left the techs in her wake.

Thirty-five minutes after she began her hike, Sarah found herself at the point on the trail where the old ranger house had been. Many years ago, exactly when differs depending upon whom you asked, there had been a cabin where the forest fire ranger had stayed. This made more sense than having to make the hike up the trail daily. In an epic turn of irony, the house burnt to the ground, leaving only the foundation and chimney, which still stand to this day.

Most people, not just the highly observant, can tell when they are being watched. To someone like Sarah, with her heightened powers of observation and what seemed to others to be a sixth sense, she instantly knew if someone glanced in her direction. As she walked past the lean-to that was on the trail before the remnants of the cabin, she felt the familiar tingle at the nape of her neck that alerted her she was not alone.

Sarah stopped and her right hand reflexively went to her hip, finding her sidearm. All her senses started to analyze the information that they were collecting. There was a slight scent of wildflowers mixed in with the damp smell of decaying leaves in the air. From some distance behind her, she could hear the voices of the techs and the light crunch of leaves beneath their feet. Her eyes scanned the myriad tree trunks that surrounded her, but she could not make out the shape of anyone watching her. A puzzled look crossed her face, and she wondered if perhaps she was just a bit on edge today. Still, she lingered, unsure about how to proceed.

Sarah wished that Brian was not such an idiot and had dressed properly for the hike. She would have found the entire situation a lot less stressful if her partner was here to watch her back. She sensed that the techs had caught up to her before one of them spoke.

"Something wrong Detective?" asked John Tibbits.

John was a career tech, having been with the department twenty years. He was now pushing forty and still in great shape. John competed in mountain bike racing in the area, which helped him maintain a lean, muscular body. He did not look the part of a police forensic technician though. He was five feet, seven inches tall and his blonde hair was almost touching the ground. He had stopped getting it cut years ago to protest a new policy that the department had passed and never got it cut again. Besides the long hair, his general appearance was unkempt, his clothes were always wrinkled or stained. He was always proficient at his job though, so the department tended to look the other way.

The second tech was Charlie Franks. She was twenty-two and had just moved to Plattsburgh from Jackson, Mississippi three months ago. Her father was white, and her mother was black which gave her skin the color of coffee with cream. She had a few other genetic anomalies that gave her an unique appearance, which combined with her southern drawl made all the men she worked with vie for her attention. She was a natural blonde, which ran counter to her skin tone, and she also had heterochromia, a genetic mutation that caused her to have two different colored eyes. Her right eye was a blue so pale it was almost white, and her left eye was a vibrant green.

"Yeah," Sarah replied trying to ignore her uneasy feeling, "you two are slow. Try to keep up, huh?"

With the two techs now directly behind her, Sarah pushed on to reach the summit. As she got closer to the remnants of the cabin, her skin began to crawl in earnest. It was a sensation that she hated and soon she was covered in goosebumps. Her eyes repeatedly scanned every inch of the stone foundation and chimney, yet there was nothing that seemed out of sorts. Still, she could not shake the feeling that there was a set of eyes watching her every move.

Chapter Three

The ruins left by the total loss of the ranger's cabin afforded those that desired and knew how to find them, many a hiding spot. They had discovered several such spots many weeks ago when they began to plan out where to leave the body. It was in one of those spots that they had secreted themselves when they heard someone approaching.

The chance of getting caught was always part of the thrill with what they did. The couple that had discovered their latest body had almost discovered them when they went to view it, and now someone else was coming. They felt a slight thrill when the woman came into view. She was dressed in hiking apparel but was clearly a cop. The gun on her hip was a dead giveaway. They knew this cop and she was very good at her job. They also knew that it would be she that would get assigned to the case. It would seem that the game was afoot.

They shifted ever so slightly in their position to try and get a better look at the cop when she stopped walking. They froze, uncertain if they had given away their position. They watched as the cop scanned the area, her hand on the butt of her pistol. There she stood until two more people joined her. They recognized the pair as a couple of techs. These would be the people that would collect any clues that would lead this lady cop to their door. They could barely contain their excitement.

The male tech said something imperceptible, and the lady cop answered. They strained their ears but could not make out what was being said. When the lady cop was finished talking, she started her ascent once more and the pair of techs followed behind her. The cop's eyes never left the spot where the cabin once stood. It was evident that she knew on some level that they were there. They stayed hidden away in their secret spot for several minutes after the trio vanished from view.

Slowly, they extracted themselves from hiding and came out by the chimney. They knew that they were smarter than the cop could ever be and had already demonstrated that fact many times over. She was the cat to their mouse and for once the mouse would win. They hoped that she enjoyed the gift that they left behind. They knew that it was perhaps a bit predictable and slightly childish, but they wanted her to know that she was being challenged, maybe even dared to come find them.

They turned to leave the mountain, deciding the best way off was via the lesser used observer's trail. This would allow them to avoid the police that were most likely stationed in the parking area for the ranger's trail. As they walked away from the foundation, they began to prance and whistle a happy little song, Don't Worry, Be Happy.

Chapter Four

With her pace having been slower so that the techs could keep up, Sarah did not reach the peak in a personal record time. She knew that that was not what was important here, but her competitive side could not help but be upset. The top of the mountain was empty of people, and she took a moment to close her eyes and live within it. This was her haven, the one place where she felt connected to nature and the world. The air was a lot cooler here even though the sun was out in full force. There was not a cloud in the sky. There was also a slight breeze that caused her hair to dance.

Whatever serenity she found on this day was shattered by the sound of John dropping his pack to the ground.

"Time to get into our work clothes, I suppose," he said.

Charlie mumbled her reply and set her pack down on the ground with a lot more care. The pair began the arduous task of pulling on their clean suits over sweaty bodies.

Sarah would not need to don the clean suit like the techs because she would not be getting that close to the body until after the pair had processed the scene. She would concentrate on sweeping the area around the fire tower for clues. In order to keep the risk of contaminating the scene to a minimum, she placed a pair of booties over her hiking boots.

The peak was surprisingly large and flat. The tower was set back about sixty feet from where the mountaintop fell away and there were a lot of rocky surfaces for hikers to sit and relax after summiting. In some spots between the rocky areas were green patches with signs asking hikers to refrain from walking there. Sarah was happy to see that the conservation effort was still alive and well.

Sarah slowly and meticulously covered every inch of ground that made up the peak, doing her best to avoid walking in the green oases. Unlike any movie or television show, the discovery of clues was not an easy task. They rarely jumped out at you. Instead, it took time and a lot of patience to ferret out anything that might prove of use, especially atop a mountain where the wind and elements could get to anything that a criminal may have left behind.

After over an hour of crawling around and combing the area, Sarah had not discovered anything that would prove useful. This was looking more and more like a case of accidental death. It was possible that whomever that person was, had died right where they were found.

As she was heading back to the fire tower, she noticed a small rock pile that must have been left behind by a hiker that had summited before. It was all the way to her left, next to a drop off and in one of the vegetated areas.

Sarah was always bothered by those structures, and even though she had work to do, she could not leave it standing. The pile itself was one of the better that she had seen. Whomever the architect was, they had a decent knowledge of balance. Unlike most of these that she had seen and demolished before, this one began with the smallest rock on the bottom and the largest on top.

They had built the pile close to the spot where the summit ended, and that was a dangerous endeavor all on its own, the wind here had a tendency to whip at high speeds. Leaving the pile standing in that location invited others to go look at it and risk them falling to their doom. She approached the pile with caution, not wanting to fall to her death. Almost in answer to her caution, the wind picked up suddenly. The gust of wind caused Sarah to notice that there was something stuck between the fifth and sixth rock in the pile. As she closed the gap to within a foot it became obvious that it was a bunch of pictures.

Sarah was now intrigued, both on a personal level and as a police detective. Why would anyone leave a stack of pictures on top of a mountain? She started to reach out and immediately recalled her hand. Her detective instincts shining through, Sarah pulled on a pair of blue nitrile gloves that she had placed in her right, front pocket. She gripped the stack of pictures in her left hand while pushing the pile over with her right. The rocks tumbled to the ground, though Sarah hardly noticed the brief crescendo of noise it caused.

Sarah stood back up from a crouching position and started to leaf through the pictures. She felt her blood run cold and the hair on the back of her neck stood at attention. Every picture was a close-up shot of a person, and that person was her. In each of the pictures, she was in the middle of destroying similar rock piles on top of various mountains. She reflexively spun around and scanned the area for anyone that might be watching her. She saw no one, but that fact did not put her at ease.

Sarah stood there, on top of a mountain, the one spot where she had always felt free and able to be wholly herself, afraid and uncertain. Someone had been watching her for a very long time, some of these pictures were five years old. She did not know what fact bothered her more, that she had been being spied on or that she failed to notice.

She unslung her pack and secreted the pictures in one of the pockets. They may or may not have something to do with this case, but until she determined if they did, then there was no need to share them with anyone.

"Sarah," called out Charlie.

There was a sense of urgency in her usually calm voice. Sarah slung her pack and jogged over to the stairs on the fire tower. She ascended the flights with both speed and ease. Sarah found Charlie and John standing next to the body. They had moved it into a body bag, and it was from under the body that they had found an object that caused them to be so excited. Charlie held out her hand towards Sarah. Sarah did not take what was offered and neither did she need to look at it. The size and shape told her all she needed to know.

"That is a picture of me, hiking somewhere and destroying one of those stupid rock towers," she said.

Chapter 5

Jessica Momsen had only been the chief of the Plattsburgh barracks for six months. In fact, she was still the interim chief. The title interim never sat very well with her, she found it almost demeaning. She was the first person to be awarded the position with that qualifier. She was also the first woman to be the chief, interim or not.

While it was true that at five feet tall, she was far from intimidating, she was a damned good cop. She had shoulder-length red hair and a pale complexion that was dotted with freckles. Her eyes were slightly almond shaped and a bright green. She was your typical ginger, complete with the fiery attitude. That was half of what had made her such a good cop. The other half was that she hated to lose.

She had been bugging the commissioner to remove the interim and make her the permanent chief. She had actually just gotten off the phone with him when Sarah Barney knocked on the glass door that led from her office to the larger area where all the cops under her had their desks. Jessica knew that from the look on Sarah's face, this was not going to be a happy conversation.

She waved, indicating for Sarah to enter. Her office was small for someone in her position. Besides her desk and chair there was only enough room for an additional pair of chairs for visitors. Three of the walls were made of glass, so the only personalization that she had been able to give the office was a picture of her daughter that sat on the corner of the desk.

Jessica had lost both her husband and daughter on the same day, in different accidents. Her husband, Tom Momsen, was also a cop. He had pulled over a BMW that was doing well over one hundred miles an hour on the Northway. As he approached the vehicle, the passenger jumped from the car and shot him in the head.

Before he was shot, Tom had called in the plates, and it came back as being owned by an older gentleman. Unbeknownst to Tom, the car had been stolen twenty minutes prior and had not yet been reported. The two men that had killed her husband were still out there. The only reason that they knew as much as they did was because of the cruiser's dash cam. The shooter had been just far enough away that their heads had been out of the frame, so it was not possible to identify them. The car had been found three days later in a small town in Pennsylvania, burnt to a crisp. No trace of either man was found.

Her daughter, who even at eleven could almost have been Jessica's doppelganger, had been on a school field trip. Her class had gone hiking on Rattlesnake Mountain, so named because there were always a lot of timber rattlers to be found there. It was one of those foul creatures that had taken Hailey from her. Hailey had been posing for a selfie and lagged behind the group. The teacher had found her lying on the ground in the midst of an anaphylactic attack. She never made it to the hospital.

The M.E. had found what looked to be a wound that was consistent with a snake bite, and they had found enough venom in her blood to take down an elephant. Some juvenile snakes have a difficult time unlatching once they bite and end up delivering far more venom than one would receive from a normal bite.

It had taken Jessica six months to return to work after her dual tragedies and six years to be able to place the picture of her daughter on her desk. In her grief, she had burned all of the pictures that she had of Tom, somehow blaming him for getting shot. She knew that it was not logical, but everyone grieves in their own way, and hers was to blame Tom.

Sarah entered the office and did not take a seat, and neither did she say anything. Instead, she placed a stack of pictures, all in individual bags on the desk. A look of confusion played across Jessica's face, but she picked them up and leafed through the stack. As she reached the last picture Sarah spoke.

"These were all at the crime scene," she said.

This statement only served to increase the level of Jessica's consternation. "Sarah, some of those look like they are several years old," she said.

Sarah nodded. "The one where I am wearing the red hoodie is from my first high peak, five years ago."

Sarah could see that Jessica began to digest the information that she had just been given. They were very likeminded people, and she was confident that her boss would come to the same conclusion as she, that the killer was making this personal. The only concern that Sarah had was that she did not want the chief to pull her off from the case.

"So, this guy has been watching you for at least that long," said Jessica. "That is creepy as hell! Whoever it is that did this clearly has an odd infatuation with you. This seems like a challenge to me, extended towards you to catch the person responsible. Logically, it would also mean that you are his ultimate target. I want to send a unit over to your house and make sure that there is no one laying there in hiding."

Sarah could find no reason to object, so she simply nodded. She felt a chill run down her spine. Someone had been watching her and watching her closely for at least the last five years. Again, Sarah found it heavily disquieting that she had failed to notice someone watching her. It was not like the peaks of mountains afforded anyone ample spots where they could hide from view.

Jessica's voice broke Sarah's reverie. "Sarah, hello?"

Sarah looked at Jessica and nodded that she was listening.

"This case is now your only case. I do not care what else you already have or what else comes across your desk. This case is where you are going to live until we catch this person."

Sarah let out a sigh of relief. Not only was she staying on the case, but the chief also knew the importance of solving it and solving it fast. She thanked the chief, left her office and headed down to the office provided for the detectives. She hoped to talk things over with Brian and see if he had any thoughts.

Chapter 6

Corporal Dan Clemmens had been a patrol cop since coming onto the force four years ago. He enjoyed the job. He got to ride around in a car, take in the scenery and enforce traffic laws. On the odd occasion, he was summoned to a domestic or some other crime.

Dan was six feet tall and very muscular, the result of him spending three hours a day in the gym. His blonde hair was kept in a high and tight, part of the job requirements. His bright blue eyes sparkled when he smiled, a fact that made him popular with the ladies. That was an unfortunate because Dan was gay. He had not yet found the courage to come out, even though there was a lot more support for people in the community than there used to be. He was afraid that he would lose any respect that he had earned as a cop.

He was on interstate eighty-seven trying to catch speeders when his radio popped to life. "Dispatch to car thirty-seven."

Dan grabbed his radio and answered. "Thirty-seven to dispatch. Go ahead."

The voice came back across the radio and Dan felt his heart sink a little. This was going to cut into his Netflix time. "We need you to head to eighteen Hill Street in Keeseville and do a security sweep at Detective Sarah Barney's house. Be advised that there might be someone there, armed and dangerous."

Dan pushed down the button on his mic, "Roger dispatch, I am on my way."

He put the car into drive and turned on his red emergency lights. Traffic was light so he pulled right out onto the interstate and headed south towards exit thirty-four. He was just over a mile away from exit thirty-five for Peru, so he was less than six minutes away from Keeseville.

It was not an emergency, but he still took the cruiser up to one hundred miles an hour. He had always loved the feeling of speed and being a cop made it legal. Before he knew it, exit thirty-four was rapidly approaching and he let off the accelerator.

Saturdays in Keeseville were pretty mundane and there was never a lot of traffic on the roads. He turned right at the end of the exit ramp and headed into town. At just over one mile from the ramp, he turned left onto Liberty Street and then again onto Hill Street.

Eighteen Hill Street was around a quarter mile from the turn. It was a small, two-story house that was sided with tan vinyl. The driveway sat directly in the front of the house and was made of black crushed stone. The driveway was empty, so he pulled in and shut off both his lights and the engine to his cruiser.

Dan picked up the microphone and keyed it on again. "Dispatch, this is car thirty-seven. I am at the residence and about to do my sweep."

The response from dispatch was immediate. "Copy that thirty-seven. Proceed with an abundance of caution."

Dan knew that there had been a body found at the top of Poke-O this morning, but he could not understand why headquarters was so worried about Sarah and her house. She was a detective with the state police. She had just as much, if not more training as him.

He got out of the car and walked down the small sidewalk that led to the front porch. It was painted a soft blue and covered by an attached green roof. The color scheme did not quite work, but who was he to judge? With one hand on his gun, Dan reached out and opened the storm door. It moved with some protest and the hinges squeaked a bit. He did not think it was loud enough with all the ambient noises to alert anyone that he was there.

He used his body to hold the storm door open and tested the bronze-colored knob on the wooden main door to see if it was locked. As he expected, it did not move. He looked in the small, square window that was centered in the door and could only see the outline of a few pieces of furniture through the slightly transparent curtains.

Dan allowed the storm door to close slowly and moved across the porch to the only window on the front of the house. This too was covered from the inside by a curtain, but it was slightly open. He had a good view of the living room but saw nothing of interest.

There was a tan, three-cushion sofa, a pair of end tables and a coffee table made of cherry. The last piece of furniture in the room was a large unfinished bookshelf that was full of books. He found it odd that there was not a television set to be seen. He always found Sarah to be cerebral on the few times that they had interacted, but no TV was just weird to him.

He had no access to the interior of the house from the front door, so he decided to circle around and try the back door. If that one was also locked, he would radio his dispatch to get permission to forcibly enter. On his way to the back of the house, Dan passed two more windows. These were covered by blinds and offered him nothing.

He rounded the corner to the back lawn. He was surprised to find a small, inflatable pool there. Sarah lived alone so he could not imagine her swimming. Sarah, it turned out, was full of surprises. He slowly circled the pool to ensure that there was no one behind it. As he did so, he lazily dragged his left hand through the water. He found the temperature to be quite pleasing despite the crispness of the autumn air, and even toyed with the idea of jumping in for a quick swim. Dan thought the better of it and made a direct path to the back door.

The wooden steps leading to the back door were in need of some TLC. They looked like they had been constructed from pressure treated wood and just left untreated after they were in place. The wood had taken on that deep brownish black hue that signaled rot was setting in. There were three in total, including the landing. Every single step squealed under his weight. If someone was in the house, they definitely knew he was there.

Dan knew that he had to finish his check, so he reached out with his left hand to grab the knob. With inches left between his hand and the gleaming gold colored knob, the hair on the back of his neck stood at attention. Dan did not have the time to wonder why. He felt a sharp pain in the right side of his neck as a hypodermic needle found his corroded artery. Before he could mount a counterattack, Dan felt his body go limp and his grasp on consciousness slip away.

Somewhere in his sedated mind, Dan knew that he was in mortal danger. He could not do anything about it and instead embraced the warm sensation that his body was experiencing.

Chapter 7

The phone on Jessica's desk rang. She was deep in thought and was going to ignore it. Something made her hand seek out the receiver after the fourth ring. The black plastic was cold and hard to the touch. Before her mind could catch up to her involuntary movements, the earpiece was touching her head, and she was speaking.

"Momsen," she said curtly.

"Captain," said the voice of Lieutenant Jeff Ratta. He was the head of the dispatch department and had been with the force for just over twenty years.

"We have not heard back from Clemmens in over a half an hour. I was going to send over another car but wanted to check in with you first."

Jessica felt her mouth go dry. Dan was not a rookie and certainly not prone to making mistakes, like not checking in when on a call. This meant that something went wrong.

"Jeff do not send anyone else out there. I will get Sarah and we will check it out ourselves." She hung up the phone and rose from her chair. She could feel the rush of adrenaline hit her bloodstream as she rounded her desk toward her office door.

The barracks were not large by any means. The office that the detectives shared was a one-minute walk down the hall from Jessica's office. The hall itself was fairly plain, the walls were painted a soft shade of off-white, and the floor was covered in an industrial grey tile. She passed the restroom doors before arriving at the black metal door that led to the detective's office. It was closed, which meant that Sarah or Brian was probably working on the paperwork from this morning's case. Jessica entered without knocking.

Sarah looked up with a look of annoyance on her face at the sudden interruption until she saw that it was the chief. Her expression went swiftly to one on concern. She knew that if Jessica came in without knocking that something drastic must have happened. Sarah got to her feet and was about to ask Jessica what happened, but the chief spoke first.

"It has been more than thirty minutes since Clemmens reported in. You and I are going to go check things out. Put on your vest and meet me at your car ASAP."

Jessica turned and left without waiting for a response, leaving Sarah with more questions and an uneasy feeling in the pit of her stomach. If something had happened to Clemmens, she would blame herself. She could not get her mind around what was happening, why this killer had such a hard-on for her, but she was determined to find out who it was and why they did.

She was alone in the office, so she quickly removed her shirt and put on her bulletproof vest. Once it was secure, she pulled her shirt back on and started to leave the office. She paused at the door and returned to her desk. On her hip sat her police issued Glock 21. It was a forty-five-caliber pistol that held thirteen rounds. She also had a spare magazine with an additional thirteen, but she did not want to take any chances. She opened the top right drawer in her large metal desk and removed two more magazines.

Satisfied that she had sufficient ammunition, Sarah exited her office and walked down the hall at a brisk pace. The hall led directly to the doorway leading to the back parking lot where she typically kept her car. As Sarah opened the door, she saw that the chief was waiting at the passenger side door for her.

Sarah drove a brand-new Dodge Charger that was modified for police use. It was all black with heavily tinted windows. Because she was a detective, it lacked any rooftop lights. Her emergency lights were instead mounted in the front grill and at the bottom of the back window. When Sarah got close to the car, it detected the FAB in her pocket and unlocked. Both women entered the car at almost the same time.

The barracks was located under a mile from exit thirty-six in the southern end of Plattsburgh. At normal highway speeds, it would take around ten minutes to travel exit to exit. Sarah was determined to make it in under five. This was the one thing about Sarah that the chief was wishing would change, the need to always race against the clock. She pushed the start button and the engine roared to life.

Without waiting for Jessica to buckle her seatbelt, Sarah threw the car into drive and toggled the switch that would start her emergency lights. She raced out of the parking lot and onto the short stretch of Dunning

Way. When she got to the stop sign where Dunning met Route Twenty-Two, she barely slowed down. Her tires screamed in protest as she turned left at almost forty-miles-an-hour.

"Jesus," muttered Jessica. That was the only form of protest she spoke though. She too wanted to get to Sarah's house and find out what might have happened to Clemmens. The entrance to the interstate was a half cloverleaf with a posted limit of thirty-miles-an-hour. Sarah was doing fifty when she started on it, and she did not slow down. It was just past midday on a Saturday and there was a fair amount of traffic. Luckily though, the entrance ramp was empty because Jessica was quite sure that Sarah would have driven through anyone that was in their way.

The top speed of Sarah's car was one ninety and she took it to that speed in an alarming period of time. There was no margin for error on her part, so she was thankful that Jessica did not speak. Sarah encountered light traffic just after exit thirty-five and was forced to slow down to one fifty so she could weave around the cars that did not move out of her way fast enough.

Once at exit thirty-four it was a two-minute drive to her house. As they neared Sarah's driveway, they saw that Clemmens' car was there with all four doors open and the emergency light on top strobing.

Sarah shut off her lights and pulled in behind the cruiser. She had her gun in her hand as she exited her vehicle and saw that Jessica did as well. Without speaking, they both flanked the cruiser, Sarah on the driver's side and Jessica on the passenger. They both cleared each door and found the car empty. Jessica reached in and turned off the emergency lights before following Sarah toward the house.

Sarah used hand signals to indicate that she would circle the house to the left and that Jessica should go to the right. Jessica nodded and the women split up, meeting in the back of the house. Neither of them found any sign of Clemmens or anything out of place.

Sarah climbed the back steps and was not surprised to find the door unlocked. This door opened to her kitchen. The white tiles that made up her floor were just as clean as when she had left this morning. There was nothing to indicate that someone had been walking on it, though she knew that someone had.

Sarah scanned the room to see if there was anything that looked out of place. The kitchen was spacious with walnut cabinets, a granite countertop and stainless-steel appliances. Sarah was a fastidious housekeeper, an easy feat when living alone, so she immediately noticed the piece of paper that sat on her counter.

Sarah looked at Jessica and pointed at the paper before walking over to it. She pulled out a pair of gloves from her back pocket and slid them on before reaching for the paper.

She held a note that was written with remarkable penmanship. Jessica walked up behind her to listen as Sarah read it aloud.

"I know you and you know me. Who is most clever? That we shall see. You like to hike mountains, oh what fun. Now your police friend is on top of one. You have six hours to find him, oh what a pain. Hurry, hurry and bring a cane."

Both of the women wore looks upon their faces that were a mixture of worry and confusion. Sarah reread the note several times, trying to deduce the meaning to the riddle. Sarah started to pace from one side of the kitchen to the other.

"Clearly, he has taken Clemmens up another mountain, but what the hell does a cane have to do with it?" asked Sarah.

Jessica grabbed the paper and started to pace as well. "This riddle, or clue, or whatever you want to call it, it rhymes. Granted I am not grammar wizard, but I think that too is a clue."

Several minutes passed, the women continued to pace and think. Jessica kept looking at her watch, dreading each minute that passed.

"Hurry cane, hurry cane," said Sarah. Then a light turned on in her mind. "Hurricane, as in Hurricane Mountain!" she all but shouted.

"Aw hell," said Jessica. "It is pretty thin, but that is the best lead we have."

"That is just under a six-mile hike," said Sarah. "My best time is five hours, and this guy must know that. I am heading out now."

Sarah turned to leave, and Jessica pulled out her cell phone. "Go!" she all but shouted. "I will call for a ride and to see if I can get a chopper to fly over there as well."

Sarah barely heard what was being said. Her anxiety was through the roof, and she was not an anxious person. All that she knew was that she had to save Clemmens. She jumped in her car and only then realized that she had the note in her hand. She placed it in the glovebox before starting the car and heading south on Route Nine toward Keene. That trip usually took about forty minutes and being a mostly rural trip, she did not know if she could shave much off from that.

Chapter 8

Dan Clemmens was having some very weird dreams. There was one recurring theme to them all, he could not close his mouth. It felt like there was a desert in there and nothing he could do would alleviate that feeling. In one dream, he was surrounded by cups of water but each time he tried to take a drink, the liquid would pour from his mouth, soaking his shirt.

Slowly, the world started to reform before him. He felt the sun on his body, but he was slightly cold. He realized that it was probably from the constant breeze. As he regained consciousness, however, he began to understand that he was also sitting on something very cold.

He did not fully yet understand that he was on top of Hurricane Mountain. In October, snow and ice started to form at the peak. Dan tried to turn his head to take in his surroundings but found that motion was not possible. He could not move his head up or down either so he took in as much as he could with his eyes. He was outside, somewhere high. All he could see was the horizon and a couple of pine trees to his sides.

There was something cold and hard in his mouth that was keeping him from closing it fully. He ran his tongue across it and discovered that it was made from rusty metal. He was sitting on the ground but neither his hands nor his legs were bound. There was nothing preventing him from standing up. Dan slowly reached up towards the contraption that was attached to his head when he detected movement from his periphery.

A strange sounding voice came from that direction, and it only took Dan a moment to understand that the person speaking to him was using a device that changed their voice.

"Uh, uh, uhhhh," they said. "I would not touch that were I you. What you feel on your head and in your mouth is a timed trap. If you or anyone touches it in any spot other than the point where it can be disarmed, or should you run out of time, then the trap will open with enough force to rip your jaw from your head. Not original, I know. I saw it in a movie that I rather liked and had always wanted to try it."

"Traps are not my thing usually. I am more of a kill them outright kind of person. But then, you just happened to be in the right spot at the wrong time. Oh, and in case you were wondering, there is also a piece of fishing line attached to my trap, so if you were to try something foolish, like say, get up and try to walk to safety, well then you will never have to worry about chewing ever again."

Dan's assailant let out a small chuckle before continuing.

"I gave your friend Sarah six hours to find you, and that was almost five hours ago. I would love to stick around and watch in person to see if she is in time or not, but I do so hate to dawdle."

Dan heard the sound of retreating footsteps before the person spoke again, their voice growing fainter with distance. "Oh, please do not take this personally. This is really between me and that Sarah bitch. You are just collateral damage."

With that, Dan was alone. He tried to call out but did not dare to open his mouth more than it was and his voice came out muffled. He knew that he had around one hour to escape or be rescued, but he held out little hope for either. He did not even have any hopes that a hiker would chance upon him. He was certain that the person that had done this was smart enough not to put him somewhere heavily traveled.

The cold that was seeping into his body from sitting on the frozen ground had started to cause him to go numb. He almost hoped that he would become hypothermic before the hour passed. It would be a more humane way to go. As the minutes ticked away, Dan became more and more resigned to his inevitable fate.

Chapter 9

As they sat hidden along the trail to the top of Hurricane Mountain, their mind began to drift back to the first time they had met Sarah. It was the first day of second grade. Sarah was one year their senior, and cooler than anyone they had ever met before. They were instantly infatuated, but because Sarah was older, the feelings were not reciprocal. It was almost as if they did not exist. They ignored this slight though and spent the entire school year trying to befriend Sarah.

They had become so desperate that it did not take long for all of their classmates to notice, and the relentless bullying began. It all came to a head in late May, with just a few weeks left to the school year.

They had been hanging out in the general area where Sarah was playing cops and robbers at recess with her best friends. There was a play area that was constructed from split rails and formed a square pen. This was being used as the jail and this was where they had sat next to. No one understood the glory that they felt just basking in the presence of Sarah. It was transcendental and addictive.

After sitting there for about ten minutes, their mind almost was convinced that they too were a part of the game. They were dragged back to reality by their biggest bully. Looking up they saw Tommy Thompson standing above them.

"Why don't you ask her to marry you, freak?" he spat out.

This was his typical go-to and not particularly funny. That did not stop his legion of cronies from erupting into laughter. When they looked over at Sarah and her friends, they noticed that she was ignoring the whole situation, as usual. A kick to their thigh made them look back at Tommy.

"I'm talkin' to you freak. Why doncha answer me?" he asked, speaking as loud as possible.

They knew that this would not end well, so they stood and started to scan the area for a teacher. There was not one within sight and they felt their heart fall a little bit. This always went the same way, relentless teasing followed by something embarrassing like a wedgie as the final act.

Being small for their age, their flight instinct greatly outweighed their fight instinct. They scanned the crowd of ten kids that stood in front of them and, finding a small hole, made an attempt to run away. It was a valiant effort but failed. Tommy grabbed them by the back of their shirt collar and threw them to the ground.

"Oh, you would rather run than talk to me, your best friend?" he asked, a voice dripping with sarcasm and malice. They lay there on the ground, their backside complaining about the rough handling. They started to slide their elbows down so that they could sit up when the first blow struck them on the nose.

Blood and perplexion both flowed heavily. Tommy had never hit them before, so surely this must have been a mistake. It did not take long for the next blow to come, this one on their temple. The speed and ferocity of the blows grew in intensity until they lost count of how many times they had been hit. From somewhere in the distance, they heard the bell that signaled the end of recess which was followed by the sound of footsteps retreating.

Bloodied, they slowly climbed to their feet. They were disoriented and could not really see. They turned towards where they believed the school to be and started to shamble in that direction. They fell several times along the way and after the fifth time remained on the ground. They were exhausted, confused and scared. How could Sarah have allowed this to happen? How could anybody? It was in that moment, as they lay there bleeding and face throbbing, that infatuation changed to abject hatred. They knew that they would no longer worship Sarah but would instead work towards causing her to fail in everything that she attempted. It was a sinister and lofty plan for one so young, though that did not lessen the level of commitment that they would put towards making it a reality.

They were both kids though, and summer vacation began before they were healed enough to return to school. Although they went to the same school and Keeseville was a small town, they did not live near enough to Sarah to interact over the vacation. When the next school year started, they avoided Sarah at all costs, lest Tommy and his crew single them out for additional beatings. This did not keep them from constantly daydreaming about how best to ruin Sarah. Time would be both their ally and enemy.

As they aged, they began to experiment on small animals, cliché they knew. There was no better way to test how much abuse a body could take before failing. It was easy for them to find animals upon which to experiment, starting with mice and eventually escalating to stray dogs. They were careful to dispose of the bodies in the mountains so as to not draw any unwanted attention. By the time of their sixteenth birthday, they were proficient in killing.

Still, they waited to make the logical leap to people until they turned eighteen. They had traveled to Vermont late one night and gone to Burlington. Burlington was the largest city in the tiny state and had plenty of trusting people inhabiting it. The murder rate and overall crime rate in the city and state were both very low. People in the smaller surrounding towns still left their homes unlocked.

They remembered the first kill with such fondness and could recall it with ease. It was just after two in the morning and the bars had just closed. Plenty of people were walking home, most of them in groups. What they needed was a single person. Male or female it mattered not. They happened upon a lone female that was nearing the University of Vermont. They surmised that this must be a college girl heading back to her dorm after a night of drinking.

A quick scan of the area showed them that there was no oncoming traffic, motorized or pedestrian. They pulled the car to the side of the road a few feet in front of the girl and pulled out a map to pretend that they were lost. The New York plates would surely help sell the lie. As the girl passed by, they rolled down the passenger window and called out.

"Excuse me, I was wondering if you could help me find a street?"

The girl paused and looked warily at them and their car. It could be their years of victimhood or their slight build and unthreatening manner, but the girl looked almost instantly at ease. She approached the open window and leaned her head in.

"What street you lookin' for?" she asked.

They had already planned for this part of the ruse and had a street name ready. They answered without pausing. "I need to get to Ocean Avenue."

The girl looked thoughtful for a moment before climbing into their car. This was proving to be easier than they had hoped. The girl sat in the passenger seat and reached over to take the map. As she studied the map, they pulled a syringe from their pocket. In a blur of motion, they plunged the needle into the girl's neck. Her fate was now sealed and as she lost consciousness from the drug that was streaming through her circulatory system, they reached over her body and closed the passenger door. They pulled out into the road and drove calmly and by the laws back to their home.

The sound of footsteps tore them from their memories. Given their rapidity, they concluded that it could only be one person. They were suitably impressed.

Chapter 10

Sarah had made it to the parking area for Hurricane Mountain in just under twenty minutes. There was a sheriff's car parked there when she had arrived. They had arrived in advance of her to prevent anyone from hiking the mountain and possibly getting into harm's way. No one thought that the killer would be foolish enough to come down from the mountain and walk through the parking area.

She did not speak to the deputy and immediately started her hike to save Dan. The whole time she was driving she could not stop blaming herself for everything. Had she simply gone home herself, he would not be in peril. It was a mistake she would not repeat. She would not put anyone else in danger while this killer was still free. She was thankful, and not for the first time, that she did not have anyone in her life that she held important. Sure, she had a few close friends, but her parents had died in a freak accident a few years ago. She had yet to meet a man that complimented her enough with whom she could enter a serious relationship.

Once she had saved Dan, and save him she would, then it would truly be a battle of wits between her and whoever it was behind everything. The hike was arduous at best but that was mostly because of the fact that she was almost running up the mountain. There were many scrambles and switchbacks along this trail as well as what hikers referred to as stairs. Stairs were the spots where the people who made and kept the trails had placed rocks to form graduating steps in spots where hiking would otherwise be more difficult. Some of them were natural and enhanced, but the majority were definitely man-made.

Sarah knew that she should be focusing her senses on any possible attacks, but she could not stop replaying the events of the day. She always started with the discovery of the pictures of her on top of Poke-O and ended up back on that riddle at her house. This person clearly thought that they were smart. They also thought that they were smarter than her, but the riddle was not that difficult to decipher. Sarah went back and forth between hoping that it was not a test and hoping that it was. As wrong as it seemed because there were lives at risk, she was enjoying the challenge. None of the crimes she had investigated in her tenure had even come close to being this challenging.

Sarah reached what she knew to be the halfway mark and took a short break. This being her second hike up a challenging mountain in the same day, her strength was waning. She also had not found the time to eat anything except for a granola bar before she had climbed Poke-O. What she really wanted right now was some water. Her leg muscles were starting to cramp from the dehydration that was setting in. She had drunk a lot of water after her first hike but the exertion she was putting forth to ascend Hurricane in record time was causing her to sweat profusely.

Sarah knew of various tricks for finding water when stranded without any, but she did not have to time to employ any of them now. She had silently ticked off five minutes and resumed the hike. Dan needed her after all. For as long as she could remember when she was faced with exhaustion, she had joked that she would get plenty of rest when she was dead. Today was no different.

Sarah was also finding it difficult to find a happy pace that was just shy of reckless. It would not be a good idea to misstep and twist an ankle. Not on this mountain and not with a killer that was most likely watching her every move. At just under three-thousand-seven-hundred-feet, Hurricane was not a part of the forty-sixers either, but it was still a very tall mountain. Even under the best of circumstances one risked a leg injury when hiking the trail.

Fatigue, thirst and worry were her constant companions as she pushed herself harder than ever before. She never took a glance at her watch because she did not want to know how little time remained. Every sound around her gave her brief twinges of panic. She was not wearing her vest anymore and was an easy target for anyone that might choose to take a shot at her. It was not like she was silently moving along the trail. Her hurried pace made her sound like the proverbial bull in a China shop.

Sarah wished that there had been someone at the barracks that could have kept pace with her. At the very least, she wished her partner Brian was with her. That thought almost made her stop dead in her tracks. She had not seen Brian since sending him back to the barracks this morning. He should have been in their shared office doing paperwork when she arrived, but she had not seen him. Sarah was so distracted by the discovery of the pictures that she had not even thought to look for him.

She became immediately suspicious. Where could he have been? Could the fact that he was overdressed this morning be coincidence or was that on purpose? Sarah started to run through every memory she had of Brian and every interaction that they had shared. She could not decide if he was capable of such atrocities or not.

Unproductive or not, these thoughts made time pass more swiftly and before she knew it, Sarah was approaching the summit. She slowed her pace and began to look around the surrounding area. She doubted that the killer would make it as easy as finding Dan at the peak. She was less than five minutes from reaching the peak, so this would be where she would start looking for signs of someone leaving the trail.

There were spots where ice and snow clung to the ground. The air was moving slightly, and the relative coolness combined with the fact that she was soaked with sweat gave her chills that ran to her bones. Sarah could feel time slipping away and she began to think that she would not find Dan in time.

As she scanned the ground, a familiar sound from somewhere in the distance caught her attention. It sounded like a chopper. Sarah turned her attention to the horizon to see if she could spot it. Off to the east she spied an object that was rapidly getting larger. That must be the chopper. She was beyond excited to see it, though the timing was terrible. Had she known it would arrive at the peak at the same time as she, she would have ridden it to the summit.

The sensation of her phone vibrating in her left pocket startled her. She reached into the pocket and retrieved the phone. The caller ID showed her that it was not a number she knew. Sarah thought that it might be the pilot of the helicopter and answered.

"Barney," she said.

"You are so close," said a heavily disguised voice. "Don't stop now. Your police friend has less than five minutes left."

The phone went dead, and Sarah's mouth became the Sahara Desert. Her suspicions were confirmed, she was being watched. The fact that the killer also had her number did not bother that much. It was her department issued phone and her number was on her business cards. Dispatch was also instructed to give out the number to anyone calling for a detective if she was away from her desk.

When the phone vibrated a second time, she almost screamed and threw it. Sarah composed herself and looked at the ID. It was Jessica calling this time.

"Chief, you in that chopper?" she asked.

"Sarah, yes," replied the chief. "What's your twenty?'

"I am minutes from the peak. Listen chief, the killer just called me. He said that Dan has less than five minutes left," she said.

"Alright, we are going to circle the summit and see if we can spot him," Jessica replied. "Hold on."

Sarah could not just stand around and wait, so she continued to scout the ground for signs of someone deviating from the path. After a minute, she spotted what looked like a partial footprint with a drag mark next to it in the snow. That was it though, every other trace of someone walking through that spot was gone. The killer had taken the time to double back and erase any signs that they had left or been good enough not to leave any at all. Either they were careless in leaving this one mark, or it was left on purpose, another part of their twisted game. From what little Sarah knew of the killer, she doubted anything that he left behind was done with anything except purpose.

Sarah did not waste any more time dwelling on the issue. She practically ran through the scrub brush that made up the majority of the vegetation atop the mountain. The trees were pretty thin up this high, so the greenery was comprised of gnarled looking bushes and sparse grasses.

A moment after she started down the path where she thought she would find Dan, the helicopter passed over her head. Jessica started talking to Sarah again.

"I see you, Sarah. I also just saw Dan. He is about fifty yards in the direction that you are going. He has some sort of contraption wrapped around his head and he is just sitting on the ground. It looks like he can move if he wants, but he is too afraid to do so."

Sarah was concentrating all of her energy on reaching Dan before time expired, so she did not reply to the chief. When Jessica had told her how far from her Dan was, she had broken into a run. She stumbled and fell a few times, tripping over rocks or exposed roots, but none of that mattered to her.

Sarah saw a large boulder ahead and started to round it. Halfway past it she saw the back of Dan. He was sitting on the ground in a patch of snow and shivering, but otherwise unmoving. She called his name, and he sat a bit more erect but did not make an attempt to stand.

Abandoning all caution, Sarah closed the distance to him and began to examine the device that was attached to his head and inserted in his mouth. It looked like a modified bear trap, set to spring open if triggered. She guessed that the aim of it was to remove his jaw and ultimately kill him. The metal from which it was constructed was rusty and old looking, but otherwise sturdy. Sarah reached out to try and free Dan's head and he swatted her hand away.

"Ithhh you touth the wrong thingth, I am deadth," he said as best he could around the trap.

It took a moment for Sarah to fully comprehend what it was that he had said to her. Understanding dawned on her and her hopes began to sink. She circled him to try and find a way to remove it without setting it off. On the right side of Dan's head, attached to the device was a small digital clock that was counting down. The readout indicated that there were only twenty seconds left.

Sarah knew that she was out of time. She finished circling Dan and was about to give up all hope when she noticed a small cotter pin on the left side of his head. With less than ten seconds left she grabbed the pin in her right hand and placed her left on his shoulder.

"Forgive me if I am wrong, but we are out of time," she said to Dan.

Sarah yanked on the pin and the contraption fell apart. The metal pieces clunked as they made contact with the solidified snow and rock. Sarah quickly went to the front of Dan and pulled the trap's teeth from his mouth. Dan tipped over with obvious relief and lay prone. Sarah was about to bend over and tend to him when she noticed a piece of paper that had fallen from somewhere in the trap.

Lacking any gloves, she snatched it up before the wind had a chance to blow it away and turned to tend to Dan. Sarah placed a hand on his forehead and noticed that it was cool to the touch. He was most likely in the beginning stages of hypothermia. She pulled her phone back out and called Jessica. She answered on the first ring.

"Great job!" she exclaimed.

Sarah did not acknowledge the praise. "Chief, we need to get Dan down from the mountain, now! He is just about hypothermic, and I do not think I can guide him down the trail."

Jessica said something that Sarah could not understand, presumably, to the pilot before speaking to Sarah again. "He has a basket on board. He is going to set the autopilot in hover mode and lower it to you. Get Dan in there and we will get him to the hospital."

As Sarah watched, the side door on the helicopter opened and a basket was slowly lowered towards her. When the wind gusted, the basket danced like a fish on the end of a line. Despite her misgivings about the safety of letting Dan be rescued in this manner, when the basket was at eye level, she grabbed it and guided it to the ground. She used all of her strength and helped Dan get into the basket and then watched as he was reeled up into the helicopter.

Once Dan was secure inside, the pilot returned to his seat and the helicopter turned to leave. Sarah stood there and watched it go, getting smaller and smaller until it vanished from sight. She was left alone on top of the mountain in the growing darkness, with more questions than answers. That trap was far too easy to disarm. She stooped down to get a better look at the remnants. She did not want to touch any of it and contaminate things worse than they already were, but it did not even look like it would have worked if time had expired.

The wind gusted suddenly and the paper that she still held in her right hand fluttered, causing Sarah to remember that she had grabbed it. She stood back up and read what was written on it, clearly in the same hand as the riddle that was in her house.

"You think you are so smart, but I just made you jump through hoops and for nothing. I am sure you have not figured it out yet, but that trap was never meant to go off, your police friend was never in danger. Come and find me, I am watching you. Oh, sorry that this one did not rhyme, but you did make it in time!"

Sarah read and reread the note several times before letting out a scream of frustration. She had been played, she had been tested, and she had failed. This guy now knew that she would perform whatever task he asked of her without question if it meant saving a life. She felt defeated and flopped down on the cold ground, a tear streaming down her face. She pulled her phone out and called dispatch. They answered on the third ring.

"This is detective Sarah Barney. I need someone up on Hurricane Mountain to collect evidence." She did not wait for a response and hung up. She needed time to think and there was no better place to do that than where she was. She reached behind herself and grabbed a handful of snow. It was not a good idea to eat ice or snow as a source of water, but she had little choice at the moment.

Chapter 11

They watched as Sarah read their note and screamed. The joy they felt at her frustration was the best feeling in the world. She was now their toy, and they would play with her to the point of breaking her before they ended her life.

They were certain that if they desired to, they could leave the spot from where they watched Sarah and kill her now. No time would be easier but there would be no sport in it.

They sat there and watched her suffer, chewing on snow and rereading their note over and over for the next several hours. It was not until darkness had fully taken over the sky that they grew weary of watching Sarah. They knew that the forensic team would soon be arriving, and they did not want to chance one of them encountering them.

They were a superior hiker and mountain climber. As a child, they had sought out the woods and mountains as a place of solace and solitude. Not that they needed to go into the wild to be alone. They had had no friends and their parents hated them. They never said as much but their actions and lack of affection spoke volumes.

Because of their comfort and ability in the woods, they knew that they could hike down the mountain far enough away from the main trail with relative ease, even in the dark. The hike down the marked trail would take the average person six to seven hours, but they figured that they could make it in around three.

The hike down was quite difficult in some spots. While the actual trail was packed down from so many people walking over it, the way they chose was not and it proved impossible to tell if they were setting a foot down on something that would give way under their weight. Since the descent would be slower this way, they used the time to revisit their memories once again.

The college girl had taught them so much more than any animal could have. People react to pain far differently than animals. Some prey animals, like rabbits for example, will not give any signs of being in pain. It is a survival tool that they evolved. The coyote might be more apt to cover a great distance to chase a rabbit that was acting like its leg was broken after all.

People on the other hand seem to want you to know when something hurts, even if you are the one causing that pain. The college girl had begged for mercy, and they decided that they enjoyed people begging very much. They had made her beg for weeks before ending her suffering. In the end, they had decided that they were not so much a person that enjoyed torturing people but more so one that enjoyed ending their lives. It was intimate as they stared into your eyes with their life draining away.

They now had to figure out what to do with the body. It was not like they could bury her in the front yard. Luckily, upstate New York was an area with many wooded spots. West of town, just past the interstate was a vast area of woods where they had spent a great deal of time hiking. They knew that this would be a great place to hide a body.

They had gone out after cleaning themselves up and hiked around that area for several hours before finding the perfect spot. Less than a mile in, they had discovered what was either a large sinkhole or an underground cave entrance. Whichever it was mattered little to them. It was a deep spot, so deep that they could not see the bottom.

Darkness was settling in, so they knew that this would be the perfect time to dispose of her. They hiked back home and dismembered the girl for easier transport. It ended up taking them three trips into the woods, but as the sun began to rise on a new day, they had gotten rid of the body and any evidence that she had ever been in their home.

That first victim had taught them so much and they had applied all that they had learned in the years that followed. One thing that they knew without having to be told was to never hunt where they lived. The police would take notice if too many people from one area vanished. They had taken to traveling outside New York state as well as cities and towns on the opposite side of the state.

By the time they had reached their car, a two-thousand-twelve Jeep Wrangler, the blackness of the night was absolute. Clouds had come in and hidden the moon and stars. The Jeep was a two-door and all black. There were no accents on it. They thought that the less flashy their car was, the less attention that it would draw. The Jeep made perfect sense for them to own as they often went into the mountains on some pretty rough roads.

They had parked far enough away from the parking area for the mountain that they knew they could drive away unnoticed. It was the perfect escape from another perfect crime. They knew that Sarah and her friends would not be able to catch them, so they did not try to be sneaky as they had walked to the Jeep. There was also no traffic on the road this late at night.

As they drove away from the mountain and the frustrated police, they began planning their next murder. This one was a long time in the making and would be quite satisfying to commit. A smile spread across their face as they pictured him begging for his life as they plunged a knife into his heart. They knew that they needed to wait a few days in order to allow the police time to relax and think that this was over. They felt like a kid eagerly awaiting Christmas morning.

Chapter 12

Tommy Thompson had been a bully his entire scholastic career. There were always kids that were smaller and weaker than him, and they needed to be toughened up. He saw what he did as a service to them.

He really blossomed when he reached high school. The school he attended was seventh through twelfth, and as he ascended through the grades, the school constantly replenished its supply of younger kids for him to help.

Tommy had always been big for his age. By the time he was a freshman, he was over six feet tall. He also was very muscular, spending many hours a day with his home weight set. The coach for the football team had begged Tommy to play, but even though he would have excelled at the sport, his grades were never good enough to qualify for extracurricular activities like sports.

Tommy somehow ended up as one of the most popular kids in school, a fact that was a mystery to most. He was tall and strong, but his face was not pleasing to anyone. His left eye was slightly lower than his right which gave the appearance that his head was always tilted. His brown hair was never combed or washed regularly for that matter. He never dressed nicely, preferring clothes that were stained and full of holes. It was most likely fear that had propelled him to the top of the higher echelon of students.

Upon graduating, something he only accomplished because of the no child left behind act, life changed for Tommy who now went by Tom. He had not gone on to higher education and had never developed a respect for authority. As a result, he had found it difficult to find and keep gainful employment. This meant that even though he was in his thirties, Tom still lived with his mom.

His first job was as a bouncer at one of the hottest nightclubs in Plattsburgh, The Rave. His height and build made him perfect in the role, but his temperament negated the positives. After only one week on the job, a fight had broken out between two of the male patrons. The fight was caused when one man stepped on the other's shoes accidentally. The reason did not matter to Tom, his job was to stop it. He was not always the smartest person in a group, but he did understand that it was the best idea to eliminate the largest person first.

Tom grabbed the biggest guy in a full nelson. The guy was a regular named Scott Delaney. He was just under six feet tall and lifted daily, so he was a mass of muscle. Scott was a lady's man, with a thick head of blonde hair and bright blue eyes. It was his smile that usually won the women over though. The fact that Scott was such a looker made Tom hate him from the first second he saw him. This fight would be the perfect opportunity for Tom to knock Scott down a peg or two.

Scott struggled as Tom started to drag him to the door. There were over two-hundred people in the club that night, so it was slow going. Although Tom was strong, Scott proved to be stronger and freed himself halfway to the door. He turned on Tom, rage all over his face. Scott pulled back his fist to swing at Tom and that was all the motive Tom needed.

Scott was stronger but Tom had grown up fighting. His reaction to Scott's raised fist was instant. Tom's right hand slammed into Scott's nose palm first, shattering the bone. Before Scott could react, Tom's left hand struck him in the stomach, forcing all of the air from Scott's lungs. This level of violence, while extreme, could have been overlooked by the bar's owner and the police. Scott did try to hit Tom first. Tom did not stop there though.

As Scott started to double over from the blow to his stomach, Tom caught him with an uppercut directly in his left eye. There was so much power behind that hit that Scott's orbital bones fractured. Scott became airborne and slammed to the floor on his back. Tom had won the fight but did not stop there. Instead of walking away, Tom pounced on top of Sott, using his knees to pin Scott's shoulders to the floor. Tom rained lefts and rights down onto Scott's face with all of his strength, knocking out seven teeth in the process as well as breaking both Scott's jaw and right cheek bone.

It took six of the largest people in the bar to pry Tom off of Scott. Scott spent a few weeks in the hospital and Tom was fired for the first of many times. Tom was also awarded his first criminal charge, aggravated assault and placed on probation. He was ordered by the court to attend anger management classes, though those had little effect.

Tom jumped from job to job for several years. He worked in factories and fast-food places alike. The end result of each was a termination due to anger issues or a lack of respect towards his boss. Tom ended up working for a private contractor, where he was one of three employees. He never had to interact with anyone besides the owner, a man named Steve Cadieux, and Steve always treated Tom like a brother. This helped keep Tom's anger issues from interfering with his job and he had been with the company for five years.

Tom was earning a regular paycheck but had developed a taste for liquor. He ended up drinking his salary by the middle of the week. He was never without his flask and although Steve knew that Tom was drinking on the job, he ignored it because Tom's work was so good.

It was a Friday, almost a week after the body had been found atop Poke-O, and it was quitting time. Tom did not have a license, he had never bothered, and so was dependent on his mother to bring him back and forth from the job sites. Steve and the other guy, Hank Hefford, had already left but there was still no sign of Tom's mom.

As he waited, Tom pulled out his flask. It was made of pure silver and gleamed in the sun. He unscrewed the cap and lifted it to his mouth to take a pull. His heart sank when no vodka found his tongue. Damn, he was out, and his body was screaming for a taste. This caused his frustration to grow. He was at least six miles from the closest store, so he could not even walk to one and get a beer to hold him over.

Tom sat there for over an hour, fuming and growing more sober. He realized that she was not going to show up and pulled out his cell phone. He was using the straight talk phones that you could buy at Dollar General because he was as reckless with his phones as he had been with everything else in his life. This one was some kind of LG flip phone because it was all they had in stock after he had demolished his last one in a fit of rage.

He punched in the number for the house phone and heard it ring. After the seventh ring, he knew that no one was home and ended the call. He tried his mother's cell phone next. This yielded the same result, except her voicemail picked up after six rings. Tom screamed at the sky and ended the call. He knew that he needed to try to get ahold of his father, but he was more than reluctant to do it.

Tom's father, Senior as everyone called him, had walked away from the family when Tom was eleven. Since then, communication between the two had been sporadic at best. The fault lay with Tom more than his father. Bad relationship or not, Senior would be the only one that would be willing to come and get Tom. All of the popularity that he had enjoyed in school swiftly faded once he had graduated. Tom was a man with no friends, and he was now desperate.

Tom dialed the number and Senior picked up on the first ring.

"Junior," he said. This was a nickname that Tom had despised his whole life, though his father still called him that. "To what do I owe the pleasure of this call? Looking to catch up, son? It has been seven months."

"I need a ride," came Tom's curt reply.

"No hello, no how are you? Just a demand?" asked his father.

"Listen, if you want, we can make nice while you bring me home, I am pissed at ma for flaking on me. You gonna come or not?" Tom replied.

"Junior, of course I will come. Where you at?" asked his father.

"4599 Route Twenty-two," Tom answered and then ended the call.

He knew that his father would come, and he also knew that since his father was coming from Plattsburgh, he would have around a thirty-minute wait. He was angry but there was no one or nothing that he could visit his anger upon. That fact made him even angrier.

Tom decided that pacing would help pass the time, but after only three minutes of that activity, he became bored. The crew was building a garage at the residence on Route Twenty-two while the owners were away on vacation.

Tom was never one that made good choices in life, and boredom coupled with anger always made him make progressively worse choices. The expression "while the cat's away, the mice will play" ran through his mind. He knew that the owners of the house did not have a security system. They had given Steve a key so the guys could use the bathroom as needed.

During his trips to relieve himself, Tom had taken note of several items that he figured he could pawn for some quick cash. It was only because of the fact that he was never left alone at the property that he had not yet taken anything. Today would be a different sort of day though.

The property had a neighbor, but they had a stockade fence separating the two lawns, so Tom knew that he could enter the house unseen. He did not want to risk being seen from the road, so he circled to the back of the house. The house was a raised ranch, clad in blue vinyl siding with a lighter shade of blue shutters.

A raised ranch house is built with the foundation set higher in the ground so that the basement is fifty percent above ground. A lot of people turn this space into additional living space. This meant that the windows to that area were close to the ground. A fact that made for easy access, should one be brazen enough to use one.

Tom approached the window on the east end of the house, nervously looking around. He knew that there was no way anyone could be watching him, yet he could not shake the feeling that there were eyes on him. This did not dissuade him though. Tom pulled back his right hand in a fist before stopping. He knew that he could punch through the glass, but that would open him up to the risk of getting quite the gash. Instead, he decided to see if the owner had left the window unlocked.

Luck was on his side this day. Not only was there no screen or storm window in place, the window itself slid up without any effort. Tom took one more furtive look around the area before entering the house.

He lowered himself the four-and-one-half feet to the floor and turned to look at where he was. Though it was dark in the basement, there was enough ambient light from the window that he could make out his surroundings. He was in a game room. The floor was covered with an industrial grey carpet. He assumed the owners had used this because it was cheaper to replace than most anything else if the basement flooded.

There was a full-sized pool table and what looked like a foosball table as well in the room. He could just make out a dark board hanging on the far wall, though it was encased in shadows. The white walls seemed to absorb the light, but Tom chalked that up to paranoia, this being his first home invasion. There was a doorway off to his left, so he headed in that direction.

The doorway led to a landing at the base of a wide set of stairs. The first part of the staircase was short and led to a landing and the front door of the house. Tom knew that there was another staircase off to one side and out of his field of vision. He had come in the front door many times before. In front of him was another doorway, the room beyond was darker than the one he left. Tom assumed that there were curtains or blinds covering the windows. He did not want to turn on any lights. His goal was to leave no fingerprints on the lower floor. If they turned up upstairs, well he could reason that away with the fact that he was using the bathroom.

He decided to forgo the searching of that room and headed up the stairs. As he turned away from the door, a hint of motion caught his eye. Tom felt his heart skip a beat. Did these people have someone staying here that he did not know about? He would not be able to give a good reason as to why he was creeping around the basement at this hour. He stopped and held his breath, straining his ears for any noises that would indicate that there was someone else in the house.

The only sound that reached his ears was the rushed thumping of his heart and a clock ticking away from somewhere on the main floor. He stood there, silent and still for as long as he could manage before chalking up what he saw to nerves.

Tom knew that his father would arrive soon, so he rushed up the two flights of stairs and found himself in the living room. These people were loaded, and they liked to flaunt that fact. The carpet was new and lush, a deep blue that stood out against the pale wood that made up the walls here. Their furniture was all clad in black leather. On the largest wall was mounted what must have been a one hundred twenty-inch flat screen television. If Tom was driving himself, this would be the first item he took.

Set into the wall below the television was a set of four shelves upon which sat the various devices that operated with the television. Tom recognized one as a surround sound system. The rest of the items were either cable boxes or Blu-ray players. All of them were too bulky to fit into his pack. Set in various places where the wall met the ceiling were small speakers that must go along with the sound system. Tom counted eight in total.

There were a few paintings by artists he did not know hanging on the walls. Tom found it odd that there were no family portraits anywhere in this room.

He decided to head toward the master bedroom which was right next to the bathroom that he had used. He was certain to find many valuables in there. As Tom took his first step towards the doorway leading out of the living room, he felt a prick on the left side of his neck.

Surprised, Tom turned around with alarming speed, his right fist leading the way. As he completed the turn, his fist found nothing but air. His eyes, however, found a person of small stature standing a pace back from him, a smirk on their face. Tom could feel his consciousness fading away, but something in the back of his mind told him that he knew this person, though he could not figure out from where.

As Tom's body lost the fight over the drug that had been introduced into his system, they closed the gap and loomed over his prone body. This one would be almost as enjoyable as killing Sarah would prove to be.

They had been wanting this for a very long time. Not only would they kill Tom, but they were also going to make sure he suffered. They decided against the knife in the heart idea.

Chapter 13

The days passed since Sarah rescued the trooper atop Hurricane Mountain with no leads or activity. She and Brian had analyzed everything that was found at both crime scenes, which was not a lot, plus the note left at her house. The only fingerprints that were found belonged to her, Jessica or Dan. Her suspicions and the killer's admission that the trap would not have gone off were confirmed by the state crime lab. The trap had been hastily constructed from an old leg trap and the modification to get it around a person's head and in their mouth had rendered it useless.

The notes hinted only that the killer was educated, though at what level remained a mystery. The whole case was confounding and frustrating. What was proving to be most frustrating was the total lack of evidence at all three locations where she knew the killer had been. The footprint and drag mark that Sarah had seen on Hurricane Mountain was several weeks old, there were no fibers left behind in her house that proved useful, no DNA had been left behind on anything. It was almost like the killer was a ghost.

Dan was unable to provide anything of any use to them. While he had interacted with the killer. He had been standing so far away and at Dan's periphery that he had no description to give anyone. The only bit of useful information that Dan provided was that the killer had used something to alter their voice. Sarah already knew this from the phone call she had received.

Sarah had no immediate suspects, with the exception of her partner Brian. He had explained his absence on the Saturday everything happened by saying he had left to bring the couple back to their car at Poke-O. There were no troopers available, so he had taken it upon himself. While this did provide a reason for him to have been away, it was not the strongest of alibies.

As the days ticked by, Sarah began to lose hope that she would catch a break in the case. The lack of activity on the part of the killer also caused her to worry. She knew that whatever his plan was, the killer was not done playing his twisted game.

The news was also having a field day with the case. They were painting the department as a group of inept fools, especially since one of their own had fallen victim to the killer. The department had left out the information about the sedative the killer had used to subdue Dan. This would prevent any copycats from throwing them off the trail of the actual killer.

Since his rescue, Dan had been placed on leave. He was also assigned a pair of troopers to shadow him everywhere he went. Jessica was not certain, but there was always the chance that the killer would try to actually finish the job that they had started with him.

Though it was late in the afternoon on a Friday, Sarah was still at her desk. She was once again combing over the evidence that had been gathered, including the pictures of her. She knew that there was a clue hidden in the pile of papers in front of her, she just did not know what it was.

Sarah both hoped for and dreaded the call that the killer had struck again. The police did not know who to warn to be vigilant, as there were no similarities between the two victims. The body had ended up being identified by dental records. In life, she had been a twenty-five-year-old mother from Watertown, New York. That was just over three hours away from Keeseville. Amber Smith had been reported missing by her husband three weeks before her body was discovered. The M.E. had put her time of death around a week before she was found, which meant that the killer had held her for two weeks before killing her. There were no signs of sexual trauma, so no one could wrap their minds around why she had been taken or why she had been killed.

Dan was of course a young and very strong state trooper. He was a local resident and taken from Sarah's house. Jessica, Brian and Sarah had all agreed that his was a crime of opportunity. That left them with nothing. Nothing but a stack of pictures and a few handwritten notes. Sarah had made copies of them and sent those to the state lab for analysis, however the results were inconclusive. This left Sarah with more questions than answers.

Chapter 14

When Tom senior had arrived, there was no sign of his son. The first thing he did was try to call his cell phone. As Senior sat in his truck, he could hear his son's phone ringing from somewhere outside. Curiosity caused him to get out and search the area for the phone. He had to call it several times, but eventually followed the sound to the mailbox by the road.

Senior felt a sense of unease as he reached for the door on the box. Where was his son, and why was his phone in the mailbox? Curiosity had turned to horror as he found three fingers in the box next to his son's flip phone.

It had taken the first state police officer ten minutes to show up but another twenty for the detectives. Tom knew them both, if only by name because of the news. When he saw Sarah and Brian, his heart sank. Could the person that had left the body atop of Poke-O and kidnapped that officer be responsible for his son's disappearance?

Both of the detectives were dressed in suits. Brian all in black with a red tie being the only splash of color in his outfit. Sarah wore a white blouse with a navy jacket and navy pants. They looked like the stereotypical police detectives that Tom had seen countless times on television dramas.

The detective walked towards Senior and Sarah introduced herself and Brian. She left the two men alone and went to check out the area. Brian would take the father's statement and allow him to go home while she sought out clues. The techs had also arrived, and it was the same pair that had worked the body on top of Poke-O. They were both working at the mailbox, John was busy dusting for finger prints while Charlie was bagging the phone and fingers. They both looked up and nodded at Sarah as she closed the distance between them.

"Nothing to report yet boss," said John.

"No pictures in the box, in case you were wondering," Charlie added.

Sarah felt a miniscule amount of tension leave her body. She knew that Tom Junior was not a well-liked individual. He had a rap sheet and most of it was from various assaults. She also remembered that he was quite the bully in school, for as far back as she could recall. This could have been a revenge attack and if that was the case, the suspects would be pretty much limitless.

She stood in the driveway, unsure as to where to begin. There was a lot of area to cover, and it was not like the top of the mountain. Here the grass was well kept but in need of mowing because the owners were away. As she was formulating a plan of attack, she sensed that Brian had walked up beside her.

"The owner of the property is away on vacation. Reach out to Cadieux and see if he has their cellphone number," she said to Brian. "We need to let them know what happened and that we will be entering their house to look for clues."

She looked at Brian and he had a look of reservation on his face. "What is it?"

"You don't think that Tom went into the house, do you?" he asked.

"I don't know anything for certain," she replied. "What I can tell you is that there is only one neighbor, and their view of the property is covered by a stockade fence. That gave whoever did this absolute secrecy. Perhaps they ambushed him outside, from some location on the property. Or perhaps they had broken into the house and hidden there waiting for their opportunity. Either way, we will need to look inside the house."

Brian nodded and walked over to the corporal that had arrived before them. Corporal Hays had been on the force for three years. He was the very picture of a trooper, tall and strapping. There was not a part of him that did not look like it was not chiseled from rock. He had dark eyes and even darker skin, with a square jaw that looked like it could absorb any punch thrown at it.

Sarah started to walk toward the house, mindful of keeping her eyes on the ground. She reached the transition line where the driveway met the lawn and pulled on her protective foot coverings. She also had a pack with her that contained little yellow flags that she would use in any spot that she thought would have evidence.

She only made it two steps onto the lawn where she found a spot that looked to be soaked with blood. She slowly squatted and placed a flag in that spot. Sarah turned and called out to John, pointing to the flag. John waved at her, signifying that he understood what she wanted. Sarah got up from her crouch and continued towards the house.

As she approached the front door, Sarah slipped on a pair of gloves. She reached out and tried the knob, finding it unlocked. Sarah's brow furrowed with confusion. Surely, the owner had not left the house unlocked while they were away on vacation. The hair on the back of her neck stood instantly at attention and a chill ran down her spine. Sarah looked over her left shoulder to locate Brian. He was leaning against her car on his phone. Sarah waved her left hand at him to try and catch his attention. If there was someone in the house, she did not want to do anything to alert them that she was on her way in.

Brian saw Sarah waving her hand at him and cut the conversation short, ending the call and pocketing his phone. He hurriedly put on his protective booties and gloves before jogging over to her. Halfway there he noticed that her gun was in her right hand, so he pulled his as well.

When Brian had reached her side, Sarah pushed the front door open. The door moved without sound and stopped when it was three-quarters of the way open. Brian felt his pulse quicken with the dawning of understanding. The perp or maybe the body of Tom Junior could be within the house at this moment.

Sarah made motions with her hands to signal that she would go first, and Brian should watch their backs. He nodded and then put both hands on his gun, aiming it at the floor. Sarah entered the house and decided to go down the stairs first. It was dark in the stairway with the sun setting outside, so she plucked a flashlight from her inside breast pocket on her jacket. The beam cut into the darkness but showed them nothing of interest. There were two large rooms in the basement, one used for storage and the other was a game room.

The storage room had little of interest besides piles of boxes. The game room had nothing of note either, though Sarah did make a mental note of the fact that all of the windows were closed and locked. Neither room featured any closets, so the search was fairly easy.

The pair made their way back upstairs and searched the five rooms there. None of the rooms had anything of note, there was no one hiding under any of the beds, and nothing looked as though it was out of place, though only the owner of the house would be able to let them know for sure.

Sarah started back down the stairs, a feeling of frustration building within her. The fact that the front door had been unlocked must have meant something, but what that was escaped her. She walked out the front door, holstering her gun and placing her flashlight back in her pocket. She stood on the front step, waiting for Brian to join her when she heard him speak from the doorway.

"What the hell is this?" he asked.

Sarah turned and went towards Brian. He was standing a foot inside the house. The front door was halfway closed. Whatever he had found was behind that door. Sarah entered the house again and it only took a second for her to find what had caught his attention. Taped to the back of the door was a picture. She was again the subject of the picture, but the composition was different. She felt as if someone had poured ice on her very soul.

Sarah reached out and plucked the picture from the door to look at it closer. She knew exactly when and where this picture had been taken. It was from Saturday when she was hiking up Poke-O in response to the call about the body. The picture had been taken at the exact moment when she had stopped, feeling as if someone was watching her.

Brian looked at the picture and then back at Sarah. She had gone white as a ghost. "This guy is good," he said.

Chapter 15

Consciousness slowly returned to Tom and with it came pain. His right hand throbbed and he could not figure out exactly why. He slowly opened his eyes and was met with darkness. Wherever he was, the absence of light was absolute, the darkness so deep that he almost thought he was blind. He also noticed that his arms were bound behind him and that there was what felt like a metal pole tight against his back. He was trapped.

Lacking the ability to see where he was, he tried to ascertain his location from his other senses. The ground underneath him was firm yet soft, as if made of packed dirt. The air had a musty, damp smell to it and there was a slight cool breeze. If he strained his ears, he could hear the sounds of birds singing from very far away, or it could just be his imagination. He could not be certain which was true.

Tom started to test his bonds and found that they had no give. He could not move his arms more than a fraction of an inch. Whatever was used to keep his arms where they were was as strong as steel. He tried to reach out with his fingers to figure out what was used, and shock struck as he understood why his one hand hurt so much. He was missing at least three fingers. Tom felt a wave of panic wash over him, a new feeling for him. He was so used to being the alpha, the one in control that he did not know what to do in this situation. He had been robbed of the thing that made him who and what he was, his strength. With the loss of that strength came a vulnerability that he had never really known.

The minutes stretched into hours, at least that was how it seemed to Tom. In truth, he had no way of measuring the passage of time. The only facts he knew for sure was that both his thirst and need to empty his bladder grew. As the pain in his lower abdomen grew to a point he could no longer take, Tom urinated in his pants. As the warm fluid soaked his clothing, any hope that Tom had held onto was washed away. He was now at the mercy of whomever had captured and restrained him.

Before long, fatigue took over and Tom fell into a restless slumber, plagued by dreams of being buried alive. He was awoken sometime later by a sharp pain in his right hand where his fingers used to be. Reflexively, he tried to yank his hand away from the pain but was unable to do so. His slight and sudden movement caused something behind him to snarl. Tom understood that there was some animal chewing on his wound.

The snarl quickly turned into the familiar chirping sound of a raccoon. Tom knew that although many people found them cute, raccoons could be vicious animals. The single chirp became several and pain exploded up his arm as multiple animals began to feed upon his flesh.

Tom began to beg to a God that he had never believed in. He did not want to die by being eaten alive. The bites began to grow in ferocity, and he could feel large chunks of his flesh being removed from his arm. In desperation, he let out a scream, crying out for help.

In answer to his cry, a blinding light turned on less than six inches from his face. His eyes stabbed with pain because of the sudden change from absolute darkness. It felt as if he had looked directly at the sun for too long. He blinked several times, but all he saw was spots wherever he directed his gaze. The light had frightened off the nursery of raccoons that were feasting upon his flesh.

Despite being scared out of his mind, Tom found some bravado and spoke. "I don't know who the fuck you are, but when I am free, I will kill you."

There was no reply, though as the spots in his vision started to clear, Tom could almost make out a shape standing off behind the light source. Fear filled his very soul and all he wanted was to be free of his bonds to strike back at this person.

The person behind the light started to clap, a slow, mocking sound and then chuckled. This caused the fear Tom had been feeling to be replaced by rage.

"Tough to the last," the person said. It was a voice that was neither feminine nor masculine. All Tom knew for sure was that he had never heard it before.

"I swear to fucking god, you are a dead man," Tom spat out.

"Oh, of that I have no doubts, but it will not be you that kills me," replied the mystery figure. "I had so many plans for you, but it seems that nature has given me a better answer. As I sat here watching you for the last few hours, I noticed that nothing struck as much fear into your cold, dead heart as being feasted upon. So, in order for you to experience what it was like for me and many like me, I am going to leave you here, fodder for the animals until you expire."

With that, the light went out and Tom found himself quite blind once again. He heard the sound of footfalls approaching and then the searing pain of something sharp slicing across his bicep on his left arm. A grunt of agony escaped his lips, though he did not want to give this person the satisfaction. Tom felt several more slices across his body, ending on his shins. Blood flowed from the wounds, forming small puddles around where he sat.

"Ahhhhh, not too many cuts and not too deep," said the voice. "We would not want you to bleed out, but we do want to attract our small woodland friends once more. I will return in a few days to collect what is left of you so that I can display it for the world to see."

Tom heard the person start to leave and once again panic flooded into his system. "WAIT!" he screamed. "Don'tchu fuckin' leave me!"

The footsteps paused and the voice said, "Oh, don't worry. I will be watching you die. I shan't deny myself that pleasure."

The footsteps resumed and faded away into nothing. Tom was alone but he knew that that would not last.

The raccoons or something worse would soon find him. The scent of his blood was sure to attract something.

He started to struggle at his bonds in earnest but all that that accomplished was causing his muscles to cramp. He was defeated and he knew that death was not far away. His fear grew so much that his bowels released.

As Tom sat there in his own filth and blood, he heard the sound of a mouse or rat squeaking nearby. He shouted to scare it away but that was in vain. The scent of his blood was too strong in the air for his impotent shouts to dissuade anything that had a hunger. He felt the teeth of the rodent on the wound on his left shin. Small pieces of him were removed and consumed. The rodent fed for a while before it was satiated and left.

Tom was thankful for the reprieve, but it was not long lived. From somewhere behind him, he heard the racoons returning. This time, it sounded like there were at least a dozen of them. They soon arrived and began tearing at his body and he screamed for all he was worth, hoping against hope that someone would find him.

As they exited the cave on Wight Peak, they heard Tom screaming in agony. A small victory smile spread across their face. They knew that he would most likely be dead before they returned home to watch, but they had their video set up to record. They would be able to relive the moment he expired as often as they wished. They unslung the pack they were wearing and placed the set of night-vision goggles safely within it before returning the pack to their back.

They were still tired from the exertion of dragging up Tom's limp body in the middle of the night. Wright Peak was just over four-thousand-five-hundred feet tall and the cave that they had discovered was almost at the peak and far from any groomed trail. They knew that no one ever came around this part of the mountain, so it was the best spot to torture someone. The subject of their ire could scream until they lost their voice, and no one would ever hear them.

As they began the hours long descent down the back side of the mountain, they started to whistle their favorite song, Don't Worry, Be Happy. This song seemed especially fitting today.

Chapter 16

The day after discovering the picture of her on Poke-O, Sarah returned with Brian and the photograph. She needed to know where the person had lay hidden to take it and she felt at her core that it would shed some light on the case. There was no clever note found at the house to give them a hint as to Tom's location, so Sarah decided to try to focus on the larger case at hand.

Studying the picture, she had Brian stand in the exact spot where she was when it was taken. Sarah proceeded to circle him until the background lined up. It only took her a couple of minutes to locate the exact angle. She did not know what they would find, so she pulled her gun and had Brian do the same. Slowly they moved forward towards the area where the killer had to have been in order to take the picture.

They inspected every tree and bush that they passed, finding nothing of interest. Eventually they closed the distance to the stone foundation.

"Of course," she said. "How could I have been so blind?'

"Sarah," said Brian. "Don't beat yourself up. There was no way for you to have known that you were being watched, or that the person watching you was hidden over here."

Sarah brushed off his attempt to placate her. She had no time for platitudes, no matter how sincere they were. She started to crawl over the foundation, seeking anything that might be a clue and Brian started at the opposite end.

Brian was over by the chimney when he called out to Sarah. She got to her feet and jogged over to where he was. Brian pointed to a space that was large enough for a small adult to crawl into. He was too large, but it looked like Sarah might fit. She pulled off her pack and removed a flashlight before placing her face in front of the orifice.

"Be careful," he said as she started to crawl into the space. "This could be an elaborate trap."

It was cramped but Sarah managed to get into the crawlspace and proceeded forward. It led her to a spot that featured a large crack. That crack looked out onto the area where she had been when the picture was taken. She felt angry and ashamed. She knew better than to ignore her gut, yet she had on that day and now the killer was free and had most likely killed again.

There looked to be another four or five feet of crawlspace in front of her, though it was tighter than where she was now. Still, she would not leave it unexplored. She knew that it would be tricky trying to back out from that area but went forward. She was happy that she had listened to her gut this time. At the very end of the space was a Ziplock bag that contained yet another note.

With her prize in her hand, she began the arduous task of crawling backwards and out of the space in the foundation. She got hung up several times before Brian grabbed her ankles and assisted her fully out. She was filthy, covered in spiderwebs and dirt but she was smiling.

Sarah shut off her light and showed Brian the note. His eyebrows raised in surprise. Sarah sat on the foundation and held up the note for Brian to take. She found that if someone else read something to her, she absorbed it better. Brian took the note and began to read.

"You are not very good at this, are you? I thought you would prove to be a challenge, but thus far I am almost a mile above you. I do hope you enjoyed the peak, though we both know you will never be right. My next victim will never be found, that is unless I cave in and tell you where they are. Worry not though Sarah, your time is coming soon."

Sarah had him reread the note five times. When the killer had kidnapped Dan Momsen, the note that they had left had clues hidden within it and she was certain that this one did too. He seemed to have a thing for mountains, so she started to run the names of all the local mountains through her mind.

"Sarah," Brian said, interrupting her thoughts. "It looks like there is a hair in the bag with the note."

Sarah grabbed the bag from Brain's hand and looked at it intensely. He was right, the killer had left behind a hair. It looked as though it was blonde, though it was not possible to tell if that color was natural or chemically enhanced. This was the first actual piece of evidence that was found, though Sarah knew that if it was left behind, it was completely on purpose. She doubted very highly that this guy would make such a mistake.

"Good catch," she said to Brian. "First things first though, we need to try to figure out where the clue lies within that note."

Brian looked at the note again and said, "Okay, let's see if we can pick this apart. I think that the first clue might be in the phrasing of almost a mile above you. People usually say miles ahead of you."

"Good, that's good," said Sarah. "This perp seems to have a thing for mountains, so let's assume he means one that is just under a mile high at the peak."

Brian started to pace. "Well, that is just about every mountain that qualifies as a forty-sixer."

"True," replied Sarah. "But it would have to be fairly close. I would also say that we can discount Hurricane, I doubt he would revisit the same mountain."

Brian stopped mid pace and looked at Sarah. "You keep saying he. We have no empirical evidence yet that this is a guy."

Sarah looked at Brian with a mix of confusion and pity. "Statistically, serial killers are men. Also, it would take someone with a lot of strength to haul these fully grown, unconscious men to the top of these mountains."

Brian was still not convinced. "I am sure that you are right but let us not discount anyone at this point."

Sarah conceded the point. "Alright. They would most likely not revisit the same mountain. So where does that leave us? What was that part about enjoying the peak?'

Brian reread that line from the note. The two of them closed their eyes to think.

"The phrasing there is all wrong as well. Why would I not be right about the peak I was supposed to enjoy?" asked Sarah.

They both fell silent again for a moment. Almost in unison they both blurted out, "Wright Peak!"

Sarah pulled out her cellphone and dialed the chief. Jessica answered on the first ring.

"Tom is on Wright Peak," she said. "Most likely in a cave. We need some kind of topographical map of that mountain."

"Get your asses back here, I will have one waiting," said Jessica.

Sarah got up from her seat and ended the call. She pocketed her phone before looking at Brian. "You better be able to keep up with me."

With that said, she took off at almost a run. The trip down the mountain could be dangerous for those without a lot of hiking experience. Sarah had that in spades, but Brian did not. He managed to keep pace with her and avoided rolling his ankle several times.

They both knew that time was running out before Tom went from kidnap victim to murder victim.

They reached Sarah's car in under thirty minutes and threw their packs in her trunk before getting into the car. She turned on her lights and siren and sped away at an almost reckless speed. She meant to be at the barracks in twenty minutes or less.

Sarah was almost on autopilot as she drove back towards Keeseville and the Northway entrance. She was deep in thought about the note and the hair. Could the hair belong to the killer, or was it from the next victim? She hoped that to whomever it belonged, they were in a DNA database.

The car rounded a turn in the road at almost one hundred. Neither Sarah nor Brian saw the spike strip that had been placed across the road. Normally, when a car drives over a spike strip, all four tires will go flat, and the car becomes inoperable at high rates of speed. This was not a normal set of circumstances, however. The car was traveling at such a speed, and due to the turn in the road, Sarah's car immediately slid sideways and then began to roll.

The whole accident was over in under ten seconds, but to Sarah and Brian it seemed to go on forever. When the car stopped rolling, it had traveled just over one thousand feet and settled on the roof. Neither of the passengers were lucky enough to remain conscious through the entirety of the crash.

Sarah came to, unsure of how long she had been out, and found herself alone. Her first thought was that Brian had been ejected during the crash. A quick inspection of his seatbelt told her she was wrong. It had clearly been sliced and someone had taken him.

Sarah reached for her radio, hoping that it still worked. "Dispatch, there has been an accident, I repeat there has been an accident."

It took twenty minutes for both the police and paramedics to arrive. By that time, Sarah had dragged herself free from the wreckage. She was in a lot of pain, which was to be expected from such a serious crash. There were two paramedics, both men in their mid-thirties. Sarah did not know either of them.

The name tag identified one as Smith. He had hair down to his shoulders and a full beard, both dark brown and run-through with grey. His blue eyes were kind and his voice, while deep, was also soft and reassuring. The other's nametag identified him as Yang. His dark black hair was cut short, and his dark brown eyes were hard, like he had seen much in his job.

The two men attended to Sarah's injuries and got her stable enough to move to the hospital. They figured that she had fractured her collar bone and three fingers on her left hand. She also most likely had a concussion. There were no signs of internal injuries, but they started a saline IV and put her on oxygen just to be safe.

Jessica hovered over Sarah like a mother hen the entire time that the paramedics were tending to her.

She even went as far as to hold Sarah's hand. As they were loading Sarah into the back of the ambulance Jessica spoke for the first time.

"Sarah, did you find anything up on the mountain?" she asked.

In all of the confusion, Sarah had forgotten about the bag with the note and hair. "Shit!" she exclaimed. "I hope it did not get thrown from the car. There was another note. It is in a Ziplock bag and there is a hair in with it."

Jessica raised her eyebrows in surprise. She gave Sarah one last pat on the hand before turning to go search for the bag. Both of them knew that they needed that hair.

Chapter 17

They had watched with satisfaction as Sarah's car went into a barrel roll. They knew that she would be traveling at an ill-advised speed and the car would crash. They had not anticipated that the crash itself would be so spectacular.

Once the car had settled on the roof, they approached with caution. The last thing that they wanted was for one of them to see them, that would end this game far too soon. They were correct in their assumption that both of the detectives would be unconscious.

They stood over the shattered driver's side window, gazing down at Sarah. How easy it would be to end this whole thing right here, but why would they want to rob themselves of all the fun that was to come? They bent into a crouch and looked at her face. It was so peaceful right now.

"You think you are so smart," they said to her. "Who is the one in the position of power now? Oh, I have such plans for you. Not yet though. It is much too soon. But, before long, you will be mine to do with as I please."

They stood back up and walked around to the other side of the car. They looked at Brian. Who knew that Sarah herself would deliver their next victim so nicely? They pulled a knife from the sheath at their side and bent over to slice the seatbelt. Brian fell from where it had held him, his head banging off the roof. It took a lot of their strength to pry him from the wreckage as the car was partially crushed on this side. The window was now barely wide enough to allow his body through.

When he was free and lying on the road, they injected him with their special mix of drugs to ensure he would be out for twelve hours. Leaving him there, they sprinted over to where their Jeep was hidden off the road and drove it over. Work smarter, not harder, they always said.

They lifted Brian's limp body from the road and poured it into the back of the Jeep. Before getting back behind the wheel to drive away, they went back to Sarah and slid a note into the pocket at the back of her pants, not an easy task considering how she was positioned. They did not want anyone to find it too swiftly though, and that seemed the best place to put it. They knew that Sarah would be too discombobulated to notice it was there. They also knew that the hospital staff would undress her upon arrival and her clothing would most likely get tossed into a bag.

Note deposited, they took off in the Jeep towards the next mountain. The trail head was just over an hour away and the sun would be setting by the time they arrived. Given the time required to hike that mountain, they were fairly certain that there would be no one there to see them arrive.

The hike to the peak was Just over five miles. Lugging Brian along with them would take around seven hours. They were about to miss another night's sleep, but it was worth it. There was a spot atop the mountain that was all rock and set above the rest of the summit. It was there that they would deposit the good detective.

They made sure to drive within the speed limit on every road. They needn't get pulled over in their haste, that would only complicate things. As they suspected, when they arrived at the trailhead parking area, the last remaining car was pulling out. Dusk had turned into night, though there was a full moon that was bright enough to illuminate the surroundings well enough that they noticed the driver wave as they passed.

Now would begin the arduous task of getting Brian to the summit. They went around to the back of the Jeep and opened the door and lifted the glass. They reached in and with a hard yank, plopped Brian on the ground. The back seats were folded down and that was where they kept the sling that they had created. It resembled a backpack that parents used to carry their babies on their back. This one was much larger, and it secured a person across their shoulders in a fireman's carry. It also had a compartment built in for them to carry food, water and whatever tools they might need. If there was a lot to bring up the mountain, they would stash the pieces close to their destination the day before.

The method of killing Brian was simple and required very little, so it all fit in the compartment. Once they were certain that they had all they would need, they went about the task of strapping Brian in and then hoisting the entire sling on their shoulders and back. Lastly, they put their headlamp on and started up the trail.

While Brian was slightly smaller and lighter than Tom, this mountain was more challenging than Wright Peak. Thus, they began to tire more rapidly than anticipated. They knew that they had trained for nights like this though, so they knew they would summit before sunrise.

After the first twenty minutes of the hike, they entered the mindset that they called, "the zone". This was where they shut down everything in their mind and only focused on the destination and getting there. Nothing else mattered, not the pain they felt, not the scenery, nothing. As dawn approached on a new day, they reached the summit, soaked with sweat and tired. They unstrapped the sling and allowed it to fall to the ground with a thud. Bending over, they pulled a water bottle and granola bar from the compartment and consumed both with shocking rapidity.

Once they had slaked both thirst and hunger, it was time to get to work on Brian. The trap, for lack of a better term, that they had devised was simple. There were several mechanisms built in that would trip it and send him falling to his death. There was also only one way of disarming it once set. Essentially, it was a no-win situation. No one could attempt to free Brian, except for them, without tripping the trap. There would be no saving of this man's life.

The trap itself was very simple looking and constructed of short pieces of steel that they had fastened and welded together. It assembled in less than ten minutes. They secured the trap in the exact position upon the rock where, once tripped, Brian would begin a free-fall to his death. They used paracord because they knew it would be strong enough to support the weight of both man and machine. When they were satisfied with the placement of the trap, they dragged Brian up the rest of the way and placed him in it.

As a final thought, as if to add insult to injury, they stripped Brian of all his clothes before setting the trap. He would be humiliated before he died. Petty, they knew, but when one held all of the power, then one should do whatever they wanted.

The sun began to rise on a new day, and they knew that Brian would soon wake. They took up a position behind him where he had no hope of seeing them and waited. He slowly began to stir but snapped to fully conscious upon seeing where he was.

"What the fuck!" he shouted. "Help, someone help me!"

They placed the voice changer over their mouth. "Ah, poor Brian. There will be no one to help you. I have placed you in a mechanism that, no matter what anyone does, will cause you to plumet to your death. Should you struggle too hard, should someone approach you wrong, or should someone attempt to free you, the trap will trigger, and you will die. Do not take it personal, you just have the unfortunate luck of being her partner."

"What is that supposed to mean?" asked Brian. He received no response. "Hello?"

Brian gathered several facts from the brief encounter he had just had with the killer. They were overconfident, they were intelligent, and they were afraid of anyone knowing who they really were. If Brian was truly in an escape-proof trap, then why hide and disguise their voice? Brian would not give up hope.

As he lay there waiting for someone to happen upon him, he was happy for the rising sun. His naked skin was rapidly losing heat in the cold air atop the mountain. He could not tell upon which mountain he was, but he knew he was high up.

Time became a presence to him, unwilling to move as he wished. It became oppressive and no matter what he did he could not take his mind off how slowly it passed. Brian tried many tricks to lessen his focus on the slow passage of time, from working through what he knew about the case, to how he was secretly in love with Sarah, something he did not realize until just this moment. He also tried to focus on the pain he felt from the various injuries he sustained from the crash. He hoped that the pain would keep his mind focused. The freezing cold breeze and the growing thirst and hunger he felt would cause him to think instead about his own mortality.

Brian was certain that he would either freeze to death or tumble into madness before he was found. He figured that only two hours had passed since he was left to die when he thought he heard the sound of people approaching.

He called out, "Hello?"

There was a pause in the noise he had heard but no response. He called out again, putting more urgency in his voice.

"Is someone hurt?" the unknown person called out.

Brian felt his heart soar and his spirits lift. "I am a cop. I have been kidnapped and I am being restrained up here. Call 911!"

Chapter 18

Rebecca Francios just turned seventy yesterday. She had long been a member of the forty-sixers and still hiked the high peaks. She hiked every day, though she did not always do a high peak. Her husband had died two years ago, so she spent her alone time doing what the couple had loved.

To look at her, one would think she was barely fifty. Her long, braided hair had never turned grey, so it was just as black as ever. Her mocha-colored skin was still free of wrinkles and her muscles were still tight, a result of an active lifestyle.

She had decided that, to celebrate her birthday, she would take on Wolf's Jaw. This was the last mountain that she and Dave, her late husband had hiked. She had not revisited it since he passed, and it was way past the time to do so. She had also decided to bring Dave's ashes with her, to scatter them atop the last peak he ever saw.

Rebecca had always been an early riser, something that had only gotten worse as she aged. She was now lucky to sleep past three in the morning. This allowed her to get an early start on her days. She always looked to the positive sides of things like that. As she lived only thirty minutes from the mountain, she had started her hike at four. The sun rose at just after seven these days and the crisp air made for good hiking weather. She was enjoying the foliage through the light her headlamp provided, but it became even more spectacular as the sun rose.

She had reached the halfway mark by the time the sun had reached a high enough point for her to remove her headlamp. The air was brisk, and she had dressed accordingly before leaving the house. Her navy sweatpants and shirt had kept her warm enough, but the spot on her back where the pack she carried sat was soaked with sweat. She felt so very alive, and she loved it.

Rebecca found a rock upon which she sat to enjoy her breakfast. She unslung and opened her pack and removed a bottle of Dunkin's coffee, it was one of the Girl Scout flavors, Thin Mint, and a white chocolate, macadamia nut Cliff's bar. She took her time with both, as time seemed to be the one resource that she had in spades these days.

Around her, the trees had started to come to life. The birds were singing, and the squirrels and chipmunks were scurrying around the fallen leaves. It was, to her, the song of the mountain, and it was her favorite song.

She was finishing off the last bites of her bar when she heard the sound of someone approaching. They sounded as though they were descending the mountain, which given the hour, seemed odd to her.

Rebecca had long been one to mind her inner senses, and something about the situation gave her goosebumps. She had read somewhere about a body found atop one of the mountains. She started to scan the area for a place to hide, though she felt foolish. There was a large rock formation to her left, so she headed there as fast as her legs could carry her. The person coming was making enough noise that she did not worry about her own. Rebecca rounded the rocks just in time. The person passed by, seemingly unaware that she was hiding there, singing happily to themselves. She could not quite make out the words, but thought she heard "don't worry".

The person was dressed all in black, with a hood covering their head. Rebecca could not get a look at their face. They were slight of build and short, around five feet, four inches she guessed. They wore an odd-looking pack around their shoulders. She wondered what it was meant to carry.

She waited behind the safety of the rocks until there were no more sounds to be heard and the song of the mountain resumed. Feeling safe again, she resumed her hike. She spent the remainder of her ascent thinking about who that could have been and why they were coming down the mountain at such an early hour. Could they have camped on the peak? Could it have been the killer? She started to feel foolish and chided herself for acting like a frightened child.

As she neared the peak, she had all but calmed down enough to enjoy the last quarter mile. The air was warming, and the birds were singing. This was going to be a good day; she would be sure of that.

The last part of the hike was quite challenging, so she focused all of her energy into completing it. There were a few spots where she had to use her hands to help gain purchase, something she did not have to do as a younger woman. With the peak in sight, she slipped and sent some loose rocks tumbling down. This made more noise than she would have liked and silenced the few animals that lived so high on the mountain.

To her shock, Rebecca heard someone call out. Her blood ran cold, it was a police officer and he had been taken by someone. She pulled off her pack and retrieved her cellphone and dialed 911.

Chapter 19

John Clemmens had been a state trooper for twenty years. In all of his life, he had never hiked. He was athletic enough, having played both baseball and football in school. He stood at just under six five and was broad in the shoulders with a barrel chest. He was dressed in his uniform but did not have the hat or boots on. John was in charge of leading the group of state police, sheriffs and volunteers up one of the more challenging mountains in the area to look for a cave where they might find Tom.

He looked at the group before him. Most of the police officers there were in uniform but like him, had donned footwear more suitable for hiking a mountain. Most of the people, both police and civilian were in good enough shape, though there was a handful that looked like they liked their beer more than anything. He decided then and there that everyone would team up, he did not want anyone to get lost or injured on the hike.

As he was about to address the group, one of the civilians approached him. He looked to be about one hundred years old. His thin hair was all grey and his slim body was bent slightly forward, as if he had carried the weight of the world for most of his life. Where his skin was exposed, it hung slack from the bones that were no longer covered in dense muscle.

"My name is Larry," said the old man as he peered at John over his glasses. "You can call me Tiny though. It is an old nickname. I have been grooming these trails for longer than you have been alive. I know this mountain better 'n anyone an' I can tell you, there ain't no cave anywhere near the main trails. In fact, I only know of one cave 'n it's almost at the tippy top."

John listened to everything Tiny had to say and decided that they would team up, though he was not sure the old man could keep up with him. He nodded at Tiny and stepped forward to address everyone.

"Folks, for those that do not know me, I am Lieutenant Clemmens. You may all call me John though. We are all here to find Tom Thompson. He was abducted from a house he was working on in Keeseville and is believed to be in a cave somewhere on this mountain, held against his will and most likely in mortal danger. I want everyone to pair up, and I do not want any of you civilians to be without a cop at your side. The person that took Tom is clearly dangerous and we do not need anyone else falling victim to them."

From towards the back, a cocky looking man spoke up. He was clearly in his early twenties and a hunter given the fact that he was dressed in blaze orange from head to toe. His mop of hair was covered with a hat and his brown beard was kept short and it did not hide the smirk that he wore. "Excuse me John, but wasn't one of the people this guy kidnapped a cop?"

John swallowed down his annoyance. He knew that they needed every last person that showed up that day to help find Tom.

"Why, yes, yes it was," he said as nicely as possible. "So, if a fully trained state police officer can fall victim to this guy, what makes you think that you would be better off without a cop at your side?"

The smirk fell from the man's face as his buddies chuckled at him. John paused to allow what he had just said to sink into the thicker heads in the group.

"I do not want any heroes here. This killer likes to set traps and we do not know if there will be one waiting for someone that is trying to rescue Tom. Also, if you see anyone on the mountain, do not approach them. Every last policeman here had a radio, use it. Alright, we are moving out in five."

"Tiny," he said turning to the old man, "you are with me."

"'Swhat I figgered," Tiny said in response.

The group slowly broke up into pairs. When they were ready to move out, there were thirty groups of two.

"I want us to spread out so that we just lose sight of the others before moving up the mountain. Once you cannot see a team on either side of you, start climbing."

"There salot o' places where ya gonna find ya cannot climb," Tiny said. "Dunna waste yer time, go 'round."

The people in the group that knew who Tiny was nodded with understanding while those that did not know who he was looked questioningly at John.

"You heard the man," he added to back Tiny up.

Tiny led John to the spot where he thought the ascent would eventually lead the pair to the cave. John did not wait for the other groups to vanish from his sight. He looked at Tiny before speaking.

"You might want to take the lead; you know better than me where we are going."

Tiny did not need to be told twice. He took off like a shot, with a speed that shocked John. After only five minutes at the pace that Tiny had set, John found himself breathing hard and sweating profusely. This was looking to be one long day.

Chapter 20

Sarah was leaving the hospital and on her way to the taxi when her cellphone rang. She was not in the mood to talk to anyone but answered it anyway when she saw that it was the chief.

"Jessica?" she said.

"Sarah, someone found Brian. He is alive but in some sort of trap. He told the person that found him to not come any closer, that it would trip, and he would fall to his death."

Sarah felt the bag of her belongings fall from her hand and her heart skipped a beat. It took her so long to compose herself that Jessica said her name, thinking that the call had been dropped.

"Where is he?" asked Sarah.

"Upper Wolf's Jaw,' replied Jessica. "I know that there will be no keeping you from going up there. I have a car enroute to pick you up and take you there."

"Good," Sarah said and ended the call. She went up to the taxi and handed the driver a twenty and apologized for wasting his time. She then went back and picked up the bag of her clothes that the hospital staff had removed and opened it. She wanted to put on her hiking boots before the trooper arrived.

The boots were at the bottom of the bag, and it took her longer than she would have liked to don them. She could not move as freely as she wanted given the fact that her left arm was in a sling and her fingers were bound together to help the three that had broken heal.

With her boots on, she started to go through the bag to locate her gun and instead found a piece of paper that she did not recognize. Was this with her the whole time, or did the killer sneak into her room and leave it? With uncertainty, she unfolded it. There were only two lines of written text on the paper. "Speed kills. So sorry for your loss."

Sarah was now being taunted by this person and it caused her anger to boil over. How was it possible that this person had spied on her for five years, taken pictures of her and remained at least one step ahead of her? She was better than that.

Sarah was done playing defense. She did not know how, but she was going to get the upper hand and find this asshole and put them in the ground. She knew that she would not arrest them, she was going to kill them.

A police cruiser pulled to a stop in front of her, breaking her from her thoughts. She got in the front seat and was surprised to see Jessica was driving. Sarah said nothing though and the car took off as soon as she had closed her door.

Jessica glanced over at Sarah and saw the note in her hand. She raised her eyebrows at Sarah.

"It is little more than a taunt. There is nothing to learn from it," she said.

"That note that you found on Poke-O with the hair, vanished," Jessica said.

Sarah simply shook her head in resignation. Their only solid clue was gone.

The trip to Wolf's Jaw went by mostly in silence. Both of the women were deep in thought about Brian and the killer. Jessica was also worried about Sarah. She knew that Sarah would do whatever it took to catch this guy, even if that meant putting her own life at risk. The issue at hand was that the killer was always several steps ahead of them. He had them looking left when he had already made four moves on the right.

"Who do you think is doing this?" asked Jessica.

Sarah was silent for a minute before she answered. "I have no clue. It is clearly someone that has it in for me. It could be someone I arrested in the past, but they have been watching me for a while now. They seem to know a lot about me."

Jessica nodded in agreement about the last statement. "Have you given any thoughts as to who you arrested and could be out now?"

"I have, but any of those people would be on parole and would not have the freedom to move about like this person. Also, they would not have been able to surveil me constantly like this person has."

Jessica noticed that Sarah did not refer to the killer as a he. "You think it could be a woman?" she asked.

Sarah was impressed by her perceptiveness. "I am not ruling it out. Brian brought up the fact that we were limiting our field of suspects by doing that."

They pulled into the parking area for Wolf's Jaw and Sarah was exiting the car before it had fully stopped. Jessica knew better than to say anything. Sarah would want to get to the peak as soon as possible.

She shut off the engine and exited the car and hurried to catch up to Sarah. She was going to do her best to stay at her side the entire way up the mountain. A light rain had started to fall, adding a somber feel to the day.

Chapter 21

John was winded and soaked with sweat by the time he and Tiny had scaled most of the mountain. Tiny on the other hand was just as fresh as he had been at the start of the hike. John was impressed with both his stamina and knowledge of the mountain. It was obvious that Tiny had spent the majority of his seventy-five years on the mountains in the area. John also learned a lesson about judging books by their covers.

"We are getting close now," Tiny said. "You might wanna radio the others and get 'em here."

Each of the members of the force wore GPS devices when they went on searches in wooded areas. It helped them find each other and keep people from getting lost. If John were to call in the rest of the party, they would be able to find him and Tiny with ease.

"You are certain that this is the only cave around?' he asked.

Tiny just turned and looked at him. The expression he wore translated to disbelief that John would even question his knowledge. Per protocol, the police members of each two-person team checked in every fifteen minutes. No one had found anything, and it looked like Tiny was correct about the location of the cave.

"Alright, alright," John said as he turned his head towards the microphone he wore on his left shoulder. "Attention all search members, come to my location. We are minutes away from the cave."

He received numerous replies with agreements that they would come to his GPS location. There was a tree that had recently fallen next to where Tiny stood. John went over to it and sat. He needed to rest while they waited for the group to rejoin them. John did not ask Tiny to join him, he knew the old man would not sit down.

"Ya think he's alive?" asked Tiny.

John really had not thought about it. He had been given the task of finding Tom and had not thought much past that. Almost in answer, a light rain started to fall. It was as if nature was setting the mood for them.

"I'm not sure," he answered honestly. "Let's hope that he is."

The pair waited for thirty minutes before the majority of the search party met up with them. Seeing that around eighty percent of the group was standing around not really doing anything, John decided to finish the ascent.

"Alright everyone, let's get moving," he said. "Tiny, take it easy on these guys."

Tiny chuckled but moved forward at a slower pace. The group reached the mouth of a cave in less than fifteen minutes. In that time, more of the party had joined up with them.

John, being a state trooper, had a rudimentary knowledge of first aid. He hoped that one person in the group would know more than he.

"Anyone here certified in first aid, or maybe work as an EMT?" he asked.

One of the sheriff deputies stepped forward. Her name tag gave her last name of Dawoud. She was slim and pretty, almost model material, not what one would expect in a deputy. Her skin and eyes were dark enough to peg her as someone from an Arabian country.

"I was an EMT before I joined the sheriff's department," she said.

John nodded and waved her to the front of the group. He also waved up two of the larger troopers that were there, Collins and Thompson. Both were cookie cutter troopers with clean shaven faces, short bristle hair, a tall build and large muscles.

"These three will be joining me," he said. "The rest of you please wait here. We are thankful that you helped in the search, but we do not even know if Tom is in here, or what is waiting for us."

John plucked a flashlight from one of the pockets in his pants and headed into the cave. The other three followed suit, with the exception of Dawoud. She did not think to bring a light.

After a few feet, the cave turned to the right and the ambient light from outside vanished. Were it not for the three flashlights, the group would not have been able to see a thing. The cave itself was damp and musty. It was also silent, except for the sound of water dripping from somewhere outside the reach of the lights.

All four of the police officers had their guns drawn and they moved forward with slow, deliberate speed. Their eyes and lights were constantly scanning their surroundings. It had not taken long for word to circulate about how Clemmens had been rigged into a deadly trap, so they did not know what would be waiting for them.

They had walked for well over one hundred feet when Dawoud stopped and touched John's shoulder. He looked down at her in question and she pointed to her ears. The three men all strained to hear what it was that Dawoud heard. Slowly, John detected a faint noise from just ahead of them. It sounded like an animal was chewing on something that was quite wet.

John moved forward and held up his hand to indicate he wanted the others to wait where they were. He shined his light as far ahead of him as he could. After he took five steps, his foot kicked a large stone, causing it to hit the rock wall. The sharp clack of rock against rock swiftly echoed through the cave. The sound of chewing stopped, and his light was suddenly reflected back at him from around twenty sets of eyes. One of the creatures made a noise that John recognized belonged to racoons. A group comprised of so many of them would cause them to be bold, so he waved the others forward and broke into a run, yelling incoherent words at the racoons in the hopes that it would frighten them off.

The other three joined in with the shouting and the eyes vanished as the racoons fled from the threat.

John's light found Tom's body, or what remained of it, and he stopped so abruptly that Collins ran into him at full speed. John was barely able to keep his feet under him. He heard a gasp from Thompson when he saw the body.

Tom's head was the only part that had not been gnawed upon. His skin and muscles over his abdomen were gone, as were the organs that they once concealed. Most of the flesh on his arms and legs was also gone. But his face was still pristine, and the look Tom wore upon it was one of pure agony. John knew that face would haunt him the rest of his life.

He pulled the microphone from his shoulder and keyed it on. "Dispatch, this is Clemmens. We have located Tom Thompson. We need the coroner and a team of CSIs at my GPS coordinates ASAP."

Chapter 22

Sarah and Jessica made it to the peak of Upper Wolf's Jaw in just over three hours. Sarah had to fight with herself to keep a pace that the chief could handle. Jessica ended up surprising her with how quickly she managed the hike, considering she was a novice. As they neared the peak, the light rain transitioned into snow, making the ground even more slippery.

There were already three troopers up there awaiting their arrival. Upon seeing the women, one of them walked over. Their nametag identified them as Riviera.

Riviera was short and stout, her long black hair was in a ponytail and tucked under her hat. Her eyes were a deep brown and full of compassion. She had thick, full lips that were turned down in a frown.

"Chief, Detective," she said. "He was doing alright until it started to snow. The colder temperature combined with the snow started to cause him to shiver. Brian said that the killer warned him that if he were to struggle too much, it could spring the trap. Three of the lengths of paracord that were holding him in place snapped. The killer also warned him that if someone were to approach from the wrong angle, then that would trip the trap as well."

"That explains why no one offered him a blanket," said Jessica.

Sarah barely heard any of what was said, her gaze was fixed on the large rock where she knew her partner was suffering. They had only been partners for a little more than a year, but that still made them family. It did not help lessen her guilt remembering how she had considered him a suspect.

"I'm going up," she said as she walked away from the pair.

It only took her thirty seconds to get to the top of the rock. There were lengths of paracord tied off to anything that would serve as an anchor. Sarah studied them and where they were hooked onto the trap and surmised that those were just there to prevent someone from getting close enough to Brian.

Brian looked to be unconscious. His skin had taken on a slightly blue hue and his body continuously shivered. He was soaked from the snow and clearly almost hypothermic. Hypothermia would probably have been a blessing though. Once a body becomes hypothermic, it stops shivering. Sarah got closer and circled the trap, trying to figure out a way of saving her partner. The killer had forty lengths of paracord attached to random areas of the trap, it was impossible to tell which one was the trigger.

"Hey partner," Brian said weakly.

Sarah drudged up her most sincere smile, though it was fake. "Hey yourself. You're in quite the predicament."

Brian smiled back but ignored the statement. "I knew that you would make it here before it was too late. That's a pretty nice sling."

Sarah glanced down at her left arm. "Yeah, the hospital spared no expense. It is just a broken collar bone."

"I did not get a look at the guy, and they used a voice changer when they spoke to me. They are coming after you Sarah, you need to be vigilant."

Sarah frowned. "This sounds like goodbye to me. You are gonna be around to watch my back."

Brian's body gave a hard shiver as he shook his head no. "We both know the only way I am getting down from this mountain is via the express elevator. Stop lying to yourself."

A tear traced its way down Sarahs right cheek. She knew that there was no time to save him. By the time she could figure out a way to disarm the trap, he would die of exposure. It was a miracle that he had not already succumbed to it. She was a mixed bag of emotions, frustration, anger, sorrow, regret, and fear.

"I am gonna get this guy," she said. "I am gonna find him and I am gonna fucking kill him."

Brian tried to calm her down. "Hey now, easy. That would mean your badge. I want you to find him but put him behind bars where he belongs."

Sarah was never very good in these moments. She had always played her emotions close to the cuff. She shifted nervously, unsure of what to do next. Sarah carefully stepped around the lengths of paracord and got as close to the trap as she dared. She bent down to take Brain's hand, and as she did so, he shivered more violently than she had ever before seen. With that shiver came the sound of something snapping and Brian fell away from her view, their fingertips brushing together as he went. Sarah stood there in shock as she heard his body impact the side of the mountain some unknown number of feet below.

Almost in answer, the snow started to fall in earnest, soaking her to the bone as the cold flakes melted from her body heat. Still, she stood there, lost and afraid. It was the fear that she felt that surprised her the most. Sarah had never been afraid of anyone or anything. Yet now, it held her firmly in place.

Sarah did not even notice that Jessica had joined her and was now taking her by the shoulders to lead her down from the rock. The CSI team of Tibbits and Franks had shown up and needed to process the scene. It took Jessica's coaxing and the help of the three troopers to finally get Sarah down.

Along with the techs, two EMTs had arrived. Seth Haskins and Bob Grundel had been called in because they were both hikers. There would have been no way to get them on top of the mountain via helicopter, so the fact that they both hiked was perfect.

Seth was in his late thirties and completely bald. He shaved his head so close that it was impossible to tell if his complete lack of hair was by design or nature. He had piercing green eyes that went with the red hair of his eyebrows and pale skin nicely. He was single and all of the women swooned at him.

Bob was not a man that women swooned over. He was just barely five feet tall and had a head of tight black curls. His eyes were a welcoming shade of hazel, but his face gave off the impression that he was always angry.

Seth had an emergency blanket that he wrapped around Sarah. The two men coaxed her off to the side and checked her over to be sure that her state of shock was not adversely affecting her. As a precaution they strapped an oxygen tube to her face. Sarah did not acknowledge that any of this was happening.

"I am not sure we can get her down in this state," Bob said to Jessica.

Jessica looked at Sarah like a concerned parent. She knew how deeply this would hurt her. Sarah cared deeply about those that were within her circle, which was odd for a woman that on the outside seemed to not want any personal relationships.

"Chief," said Charlie, breaking Jessica's line of thought. "We are done up there. Nothing much useful, the snow saw to that. What we did manage to figure out was that there was no way to save Brian."

"What do you mean?" asked Sarah, shocking everyone.

Charlie looked at her with sympathy. "I mean that the trap had no way of being disarmed. Once set, the only outcome was for it to cause Brian to fall. The bastard that set this trap knew what they were doing."

"What about materials?" asked Jessica. Anything special about any of them?"

John answered these questions. "Nah, what was used to construct that could have come from any hardware or box store. Shit, Walmart sells paracord."

"So, we have a dead detective and nothing to go on, is that what you guys are telling me? You are all supposed to be the best in your field, that is why you were called in. What the actual fuck are you guys doing?" Jessica stopped. She realized that she had been yelling and had not intended to.

"I am sorry," she said. "This whole thing has me stressed out. I have never been faced with an adversary like this."

"None of us have chief," said Sarah softly. "But I am going to catch the sonofabitch."

Sarah's gaze lost focus and it drifted off towards a small stand of pines behind the group. The wind gave a sudden gust, blowing the vegetation. Sarah caught a glimpse of something metallic from one of the small pines. She stood and shrugged off the blanket and pulled the oxygen line from her nose, walking over to the tree.

"That sick bastard," she pulled a camera from the branches. "They have been watching us and most likely listening the whole time."

Charlie ran over to Sarah and took the camera from her and examined it. "It has a cell transmitter on it. They have definitely been watching us."

Jessica pulled out her cellphone and dialed a number. "Hi, I need a trace on a cell signal, and I need it now."

Chapter 23

They had been sitting in their Jeep, parked on the side of the road several miles from the parking lot at the base of Wolf's Jaw watching. The camera they had left hidden in the small pine tree was linked to the burner phone in their hand. It had taken much longer than they had anticipated for Sarah to arrive.

It was unfortunate that the camera did not afford them a view of the top of the rock where Brian was secured. They had missed the look on Sarah's face when he had fallen to his death. That did not detract from the enjoyment they got when she was pulled back down. The look on her face gave them such pleasure, it was almost orgasmic.

Sarah was defeated. Despite all of her intelligence, her confidence, and her immeasurable success as a detective, they had beaten her. It was only a matter of time before Sarah would find out that Tom had died as well. They were so very pleased with how things were progressing, but all of these deaths had failed to slake their desire to kill. They knew who their next victim would be, and plans were already in motion to trap them.

They were pulled from their thoughts by the sound of voices. One of the two CSI technicians that had worked the scene atop Poke-O was telling Sarah and Jessica that their trap had not had a way to be disarmed. This only served to further prove that they were far more intelligent than the entire police force. There had been a failsafe built in, lest the trap trigger while they were setting it. The unintelligent swine could simply not figure that fact out.

They listened intensely to all of the conversation. There was no such thing as knowing too much. They felt their heart sink as Sarah looked directly at the camera and got up, walked over to it and plucked it from the tree. It was time to move on, their mode of spying had been discovered.

They turned the key in the ignition and the Jeep's engine fired up. As they rolled down their window, they heard the chief asking for a cell trace. They extended their hand out of the window and dropped the phone to the ground before pulling away.

Let the cops chase after the phone. They would be wasting their time, for when it was finally found, they would be miles away.

As they drove, they started to work out the details for their next trap. Over the course of the last year, they had bought a steady supply of disposable razors and had dismantled them all. They kept the blades and had around two thousand. Up until this time, they had no idea what they would use them all for. Now they knew that these would be used in a future trap, ensuring an agonizing death for their next target.

It was odd how they had decided who would be next to die. This person had no ties to Sarah, but they were a public figure. There had not yet been enough news coverage about them and that was unfortunate. They had authored a letter and sent it to the local news stations, only to be ignored thus far. They knew that by killing a member of the media, they would cease to be ignored.

Tomorrow would be the day they caught that person and placed them in their trap. It had been almost two days since they had slept. Although they could go for long periods of time without sleeping, eventually they would need to succumb to fatigue. They made a turn that would lead them back to their house where they would spend the next ten or twelve hours sleeping.

Chapter 24

Sarah had headed home to rest after her failure atop Wolf's Jaw. The chief had spent the entire trip trying to console her, stating that it was not her fault. In her mind, there was no denying the fact that it was completely her fault. If Sarah had not done whatever she had done to cause this madman to target her, then those around her would be safe.

Immediately upon arriving at her house, shortly after two in the afternoon, Sarah had climbed into bed. She needed to be alone and comfortable. Her intent was to spend her time in bed thinking. Instead, she had fallen into a deep sleep. Her sleep was not restful though. It was plagued by dreams of Brian falling to his death. She had cared for him more than she was willing to admit. Losing him cut her deeply.

Sarah awoke a little after six in the morning to her cellphone stating she had missed over forty calls. She scrolled through the numbers and did not see a single one that she recognized. She also had ten voicemail messages waiting for her.

She set the phone back down on her nightstand, not willing to deal with any of it at the moment. What Sarah needed in her life more than anything was a shower and coffee.

Her bedroom was large despite the fact that the house was just under fifteen hundred square feet. It had been the selling point to her when she bought the house. In it resided her king-sized bed, three dressers and a desk. This still left plenty of room for her to move about without worrying about running into something. The walls in here, like the rest of her house, were bare and white. She was not much of a decorator, something she always promised herself she would work on.

The second-best feature of her bedroom was that it came with an attached bathroom. In the northwest corner of the room was a door that led to her second haven. Sarah walked into the room and, as it always did, it relieved some of the stress she felt instantly.

The entire bathroom was covered in small tiles that formed a mosaic pattern on the floors and walls. They were varying shades of blues and purples, her two favorite colors. To the left of the doorway was a large shower. It was framed on two sides by the wall and the other two by glass, with a sliding door for entrance. The shower had fifteen different heads that you could have on all at once or select which ones you wanted to use. Her absolute favorite part of the shower was the bench seat that it contained. She had often sat there after a long day and let the steaming hot water pummel her worries away.

On the far side of the shower was the toilet and vanity with a sink. The sink itself was the color of huckleberry and shaped like a seashell. The toilet was the only oddball part of the room, the former owners having chosen white.

Sarah slipped out of her sling and clothes, careful not to move her left arm too much and disturb the break. She slid open the glass door, leaned in and turned the shower on so that all of the heads were running. It did not take long for the water to reach a pleasingly scalding temperature and she climbed in. Sarah sat upon the bench as the water jets rained down, and she could feel herself relax even more. She sat there for over thirty minutes, thoroughly enjoying the hot water on demand feature.

Once she was out of the shower, she dried and dressed and went to her small kitchen to make some coffee. The kitchen was like the rest of her space, containing only the essentials. Upon her black granite countertops sat a toaster oven and a Keurig. From the pantry, she removed a k-cup and placed it in the machine. When she pressed the button to activate it, nothing happened. It would be her luck; the damned machine had died. It looked like today would be a Dunkin kind of day.

Sarah was essentially stranded at her house, with her car having been destroyed. She was good friends with her neighbor, Jerry Connel, and knew that he would allow her to use his truck. The nearest Dunkin was one town over in Peru, so she could make the trip in around thirty minutes. He never left for work before eight, so that should provide her with plenty of time.

Sarah put her shoes on, a pair of Nike cross-trainers and went to her front door. She opened it to a circus of reporters that all seemed to spring to life upon seeing her. She was in awe of the number of cameras and microphones that were pointed at her.

"Ms. Barney," a female reporter that she recognized as Monica Trudeau screamed louder than everyone else in the throng. "Do you have any leads as to who killed your partner?"

Sarah did not answer. She just stood there like a deer in the headlights, unsure of how to proceed. She could go back inside and avoid these people, but she would need to leave her house eventually. She also knew that the killer would be the biggest piece of news in the area, it was uncommon. They would certainly not leave until she gave them some sound bites.

Sarah composed herself, cleared her throat and shouted over the barrage of questions. "People, people, listen."

This silenced the group. They all stood there, silent, with their cameras recording or snapping pictures and their microphones and pens at the ready. It looked like all three networks had sent someone as well as every paper in the surrounding area.

"I will give you my statement, but I will not answer any questions. Brian Sloan was my partner and friend, and I am deeply saddened by his loss." As if to help drive that statement home, Sarah felt tears start to slide down her cheeks.

"We currently do not have any leads on the identity of the killer, nor do we know what their motive is. Their selection of victims is random at best. The police department would like to caution everyone to always travel in pairs whenever possible and avoid anyone that you do not know. That is all."

When Sarah finished talking, the reporters resumed firing questions at her. She did not listen to any of them and closed her door. She retreated to the implied safety of her living room and sat on the couch. As an afterthought, she pulled her cellphone from her pants' pocket and listened to the voice mail messages. As she suspected, they were all from reporters.

She hung up and dialed Jessica. She would be needing a ride. Jessica answered on the first ring.

"Sarah, how are you holding up?" she asked.

"Despite the fact that every bloodthirsty reporter is camped out on my front lawn, pretty good," she replied.

"They have been calling the barracks all night," said Jessica. "I assume you want a ride in?"

"Yeah, if it is not too much trouble," said Sarah.

"I will send two cars with three troopers. One car will be left in your care and the troopers will be there to safeguard your way out of your house," said Jessica. She hung up without another word.

Sarah felt like a child of divorce waiting for her father to show up for a visit. She stood vigil at the front door, peeking through the blinds, hoping against hope that the cruisers would show up soon. The throng of reporters were still out front, some were talking at the cameras while others were on the phone, no doubt recounting the brief impromptu press meeting that just happened.

Her stomach rumbled, reminding her that she had not yet eaten or drank anything. Sarah remembered that she had bought a package of breakfast sandwiches, so she turned from the door and went into the kitchen to her freezer. She was still distracted by the encounter with the reporters as she reached for the handle to open the door, yet something screamed out at her, stopping her hand.

Her refrigerator was free of any sort of ornamentation. The only magnets she had were attached to the two chip clips she kept there. Sarah rarely ate chips, but when she did, she wanted the clips to keep them from going stale. The green clips almost mocked her distracted mind because what they held made her blood run cold.

Each clip held a polaroid picture of her sleeping, taken at some point last night or early this morning. The one on the right was innocent enough, just a simple close-up of her face. The one on the left however, almost caused a panic attack. The person that took these pictures was holding Sarah's own gun to her temple.

Panic was replaced by rage, a rage that was so powerful that Sarah did not know upon what to focus it. She pulled the pictures from the refrigerator and ripped them to sheds. She began to pace when a knock from her back door sounded. The knock seemed to focus her back into the present and she was shocked to realize that her gun had found its way into her hand, and she was currently aiming it at the door.

Sarah holstered her gun and walked with caution to the door, opening the blinds to the face of the same three troopers that had been on Wolf's jaw with her the night before. Sarah opened the door and Riviera smiled weakly at her.

"Your escort has arrived," she said.

Sarah looked out at the two cruisers and saw the other two troopers were doing their best to keep the reporters at bay.

"Guess we better get going," she said, exiting her house. She did not bother locking her door, she no longer saw the point in it.

Chapter 25

Monica Trudeau had just gotten done doing her live report when the two cruisers left Sarah's house. Sarah was alone in the lead car and the second held three troopers. She was upset at the timing, because that would have made an excellent closing shot to her report.

Monica had gotten her job with the local Fox affiliate on her looks alone, lacking any sort of education in media. She had moved to Vermont from Montreal five years ago, fresh from secondary school, better known in the states as high school. She was the result of a black man marrying a Chinese woman and had gotten the best genes each parent had to offer. Her skin was just slightly darker than white, her hair was black, and it cascaded from her head in light curls. Her dark brown eyes were almonds set in a flawless complexion. She was just under six feet tall with a figure most models had to buy. With her stunning looks had come a ton of confidence, so she had few problems with public speaking, and she loved being in front of the camera, perhaps a little too much.

Everyone had skeletons in their closet, and she hoped hers never found their way out. She wanted to make it to the network news, not remain where she was. She would be mortified if anyone ever found out that in order to finance her immigration, she had posed nude for some pictures. She had found the person on craigslist, and they were offering four thousand dollars to photograph a nude woman in a voyeuristic manner.

Monica never met the guy. He had given her a location, some closed restaurant in a small border town called Blackpool. Monica had entered to find an envelope and a note awaiting her on the counter. The envelope contained forty one-hundred dollar bills and the note instructed her to strip and walk about as naturally as she could for thirty minutes.

Four grand being four grand and Monica being just eighteen and in need of funds had done just that. At the end of the thirty minutes, she had dressed and left the establishment. As she was walking out, another woman was about to enter, though Monica could not understand why anyone would want to see this one nude. She was short, perhaps just over five feet tall. The way she dressed informed Monica that she was shy. She was wrapped head to toe in black sweats and her hood was up, covering her mousy brown hair. The new girl did not look up from the ground, so Monica was unable to give her a solid assessment. Her build was so slight that, dressed as she was, she could almost pass for a teenaged boy.

Now, five years later, she had no idea what had happened to the pictures of her. They could ruin her chances of ever going national. She had discussed the existence of the pictures and the threat to her future with her boyfriend, David. He had brushed off her concerns, bringing up the vast number of actual celebrities that had had their nude pictures leaked online with no negative impact on their careers. Some of those celebrities have even enjoyed greater success from the leaks. This helped assuage her fears, but only a little.

She no longer saw any need to stay at the house, the only lead having just pulled away. Monica turned to her camera man David Crane, who also happened to be her boyfriend. David was built to be behind the camera for sure. He was not traditionally attractive, in fact, Monica had initially been repulsed by him. He had long brown hair that he kept in dreadlocks. His beard was also quite long and most people that saw him outside thought he was homeless. His clothes, while clean, always looked like he had lived in them. His eyes were a dull shade of brown. And his five-foot seven-inch frame housed a huge beer belly. David was beyond intelligent though and also possessed a rapier wit and sense of humor. It was his mind that had drawn Monica to him.

"Babe," she said. "I am going to head back to the studio."

"Alright," David replied while leaning in for a kiss. "I think I will hang behind for some stock footage."

Monica kissed David and walked over to her black Kia Sportage. It was far from her dream car, but it handled the weather in the area well enough. The darkly tinted windows also kept her from being recognized. She might currently only be a minor celebrity, but she was still a celebrity.

The engine fired up and she put the SUV into drive. Her phone started to ring before she could pull out of the parking spot. She did not recognize the number, but it was a New York cellphone, so she answered it.

"Leaving so soon?" asked a heavily disguised voice.

Monica was puzzled and intrigued all at once. "David, is this you?"

"Not David, I am afraid. Though I think you will find me infinitely more interesting," said the voice.

"Okay, I will bite, who is this?' asked Monica.

"I am the stalker in the night. I am the cold breath you feel when you are all alone. I am the taker of lives," the voice taunted.

"Listen," Monica said sharply. "I am in the middle of the story of my life. I certainly do not have time for games from....".

"Oh," the voice interrupted. "I just thought you might want an exclusive interview with the person that has been killing all of these people. There are more deaths to come too."

Monica felt her heart skip a beat. She had heard of this happening before, where a serial killer reached out to a member of the press to tell the story from their point of view. Could this really be happening?

"I am sorry," she said. "I just thought this was a prank phone call."

"I see that I have your attention," said the voice. "Good. You will slowly drive away from Sarah's house and return in twenty minutes. That will give the others time to leave. Once you return, come to the back door and let yourself in. You must be alone. I will allow you to use your cellphone camera to record our interview."

The killer hung up the phone, leaving Monica in a state of shock. This would be her way to the networks, she knew it. She was almost giddy as she pulled away and drove down the street. She had twenty minutes to kill, so she would drive to Peru and back. If she did the speed limit, it would take almost the full twenty minutes.

Monica also understood that this would be too good for the local Fox station. Last year, she had met the head of the network at a Christmas party. Susan Day tried to make her way to a different affiliate once a month. They had hit it off, making small talk over drinks. Monica was embarrassed when Sue had propositioned her. No one knew Sue was gay and Monica had never been with a woman. Ever the person eager to advance her career though, Monica had made an excuse to David and gone to Sue's hotel room that night. They had exchanged numbers the next day. Over the months that had followed, Sue would text Monica playfully, but they had never discussed her ambitions.

Siezing the opportunity, Monica called Sue who answered on the second ring.

"Mon, baby," she said excitedly. "Are you taking me up on my vacation offer?"

Monica hated being called Mon. She had also forgotten about Sue's proposition to spend a month in Jamaca with her. She shrugged off both things and began to talk rapidly.

"Sue, no, sorry. Listen. There is a serial killer on the loose up here in the Plattsburgh area. The guy has killed at least three people so far, one of them a police detective. He also kidnapped a trooper but that one was saved. He just called me and offered me an exclusive interview with him. I think this is too big for the local station. I want to go on the national news with it tonight."

Sue was quiet for so long that Monica began to think she had overestimated how close she and Sue really were. "Mon, I honestly never took you for a national news reporter," she said breaking the silence. "After our night of sex last year, I watched scads of your stories, hoping to move you up to the network so we could be closer. But this, yeah, this is too big for the local station. You've got good instincts. I will give you that. When are you meeting him?"

Monica felt her heart flutter with excitement. "In twenty minutes."

"Great," said Sue. "I am getting on my private plane in ten minutes and heading your way. I am four hours from you. We will meet when I land, take your tape to the station for editing. Your story will run right before Fox and Friends."

Monica could almost cry, she was so happy. "Perfect Sue," she said. "You will not regret it."

Monica hung up the phone and realized she was in Peru. She had been so excited that the trip had taken only six minutes. She would just have to pull into a store's lot and kill time. She was about to make the biggest career move ever. She started to think about some good, pointed questions to ask the killer.

Monica sat in the Stewarts' parking lot with her engine idling for ten minutes before heading back toward Keeseville. She thought that she had come up with some very good questions for the killer, making certain that none of them would seem like they were a trick for him to reveal his identity. She most certainly did not want to become his next victim.

Monica made the turn onto Hill Street and was relieved to see when she reached Sarah's house that the rest of the reporters were gone. She pulled into the lone spot in the driveway, put her car into park and shut off the engine. She took a moment to look at herself in the rearview mirror to be certain that her make-up was still on point. Satisfied, she exited the Sportage and crept around the back of the house.

She climbed the three steps and was almost surprised to find the door unlocked. Monica warily entered the house, fully aware that she would soon be face to face with a cold, unfeeling killer. As she closed the door behind herself, she pulled her cellphone from her purse and started to record her surroundings. She was perplexed by Sarah's stark decor, at least in the kitchen.

As Monica gazed into the living room, she felt her pulse quicken. Hanging on the walls were poster-sized pictures of her. Some were from the last few weeks, some from much further and some were from the day she posed nude for the stranger. Could this killer and the stranger that was seeking nude images be the same person?

There would be no denying these pictures were of her. Sure, her hairstyle was slightly different, and she had aged slightly in the five years since, but that was definitely her face. Still, she recorded it all. There was a reason why the killer had set the house up this way. The couch had clearly been moved from where it normally sat. In its place were two wooden chairs, most likely from the dining room table. Neither chair was set in a place where the occupant would be facing either of the main entrances. Monica chose the one that put her back to the majority of the house. She wanted to show this man that she trusted him not to hurt her.

"Do you like my photography?" asked a voice from somewhere behind her. She recognized it as the same from the phone call.

"You have quite the knack for taking pictures when people do not know it," she answered.

"Yes, yes. An artform you helped me perfect," they replied. "Who would have known our paths would cross again, and so soon too? Don't feel like you need to answer that, we are here to talk about me after all."

The killer came out from behind her and sat in the chair opposite Monica. He was short and slight of build, not at all what she had expected given the fact that he lugged large men to the tops of some very high mountains. Perhaps he had a partner, she thought.

The killer was dressed in camouflage, with a very expensive looking pair of L.L. Bean hiking boots. His head was covered by a hood and a mask that looked like the one worn by the protagonist in the movie V is for Vendetta.

There would be no gleaming anything about how he looked from this. Monica pointed the phone at him and asked, "Shall we begin?"

They nodded slightly. "My dear, this began years ago, for both of us, but yes, we may begin the interview. I do have some ground rules. There will be no questions asked that might hint where I live, work or who I might be, other than that, feel free to ask me anything."

"I guess the first question is the most obvious," said Monica. "Why?"

The killer shook their head. "Oh, you disappoint me. Perhaps I chose the wrong person to tell my tale. Nevertheless, a question asked is one that shall be answered. If you were hoping for a tragic story from my past, my mommy did love me enough, I did well in school, I was never molested. The answer that I have for you is perhaps not what you might expect. You ask me why, I tell you I do these things simply because I can, and there is no one that can stop me."

"You think that you are uncatchable?" Monica asked.

"Clearly the evidence points to that fact," they replied. "I have kidnapped two policemen, killing one. I know the police have told you that the first one that fell into my web was freed from one of my traps, but to be perfectly honest with you, he was never meant to die. He was simply a distraction for my pursuer."

"So, you meant for him to live. Is there anyone else in your list of victims that will share that fate?" she asked.

"Your queries are getting better. Indeed, besides our poor friend the detective, anyone I capture and set in a trap can be saved. It is all on the police to solve my riddles and find that person in time. Poor, poor Tom. Had Sarah not been so intent on catching me, well she could have saved him. Sure, he would have had a few physical scars, but he would have lived."

Monica felt her back straighten a bit at the news that Tom was dead. This had not been released yet by the police. "So, Tom is dead too?" she asked.

"Oh yes. That is still being kept a secret by our beloved friends in blue," the killer said. "Yes, he expired long before they stumbled upon his body."

Monica pressed on. "Why the traps then? Why not just kill them outright?"

"An excellent question," they said. "The first person I killed, well the first one that I left to be found, let's be clear on that point, I killed with my own hands. It was our police friend that I allowed to live that set me on this new path. The whole idea behind placing him in that trap was to give me time to execute the capture of my next victim. The chief had sent him someplace he should not have been, and I was close to being discovered. So, I needed time. The trap allowed me that time. Upon watching Sarah try to work against time to save the young lad, well that gave me a pleasure I had not yet experienced and birthed my new way of dispatching people."

Monica did not miss a beat. "You killed before that person that was found on top of Poke-O-Moonshine?"

"I have been taking lives for the last twenty years, yes," they said. "None of those people will ever be found though. Where they lie will go with me to the grave."

"Is there an endgame here?" asked Monica.

"You mean, do I have a goal, a quota or something? Do I wish to be famous?" asked the killer. "My only goal is to settle an old debt, owed to me by Sarah Barney."

"What did she do to you?" Monica probed.

"Oh no, no, no, no. That would violate my ground rules. If I answered that question, then it would be easy to figure out who I was," they said. "This interview is over."

Before they could rise, Monica fired away one more question. "I am sorry, but please, you said there would be more victims, who is next?"

"For someone that is paid to gather facts, you are not very good at it, are you?" they replied.

Before Monica could understand what was going on, the killer lunged at her with astonishing speed, plunging a needle into her neck. As the liquid mixed with her blood, Monica felt her consciousness fade and she went limp in the chair.

They picked up the phone from the floor that had fallen from Monica's hand and looked at the camera. "This interview is now truly over," they said before turning the phone over and stopping the recording.

Luckily Monica did not have some kind of security measure set up, so they could access her phone with ease. They went online and downloaded a program that would compress the video. They then went to Monica's e-mail program, entered Sarah's and the television station's addresses and sent the video. They then placed a note upon the chair that they had just vacated and scooped Monica up, carrying her to the back door. The game was afoot once again.

Chapter 26

Sarah had stopped at the Dunkin' in Peru before heading to the office. She desperately needed the coffee as well as the time to sort out everything in her head. She did not have the beginnings of an idea as to who might be gunning for her. The fact that they could come and go from her house made things all the worse.

She knew that she was missing something, some vital clue that would inform her as to the identity of the killer, but she could not get the time to think on that. This guy was always so far ahead of her that she was stuck running every which way to try and save the people they trapped.

The young woman working in the drive-through handed Sarah her blueberry crisp iced latte and she took a huge swallow of the intoxicating beverage. It was like pure heaven crossing her lips, flowing over her tongue and down her throat. With the coffee came a jolt from both the caffeine and the massive amount of sugar it contained.

As Sarah pulled out from Dunkin's, her phone chimed, alerting her that she had received an e-mail. She ignored it, deciding that she would check it when she got to work. The entrance to the interstate was a quarter mile from the restaurant, Sarah turned left onto the ramp that would take her north. Her phone rang and she cursed because it was not set-up to the Bluetooth in this car.

She knew it was not legal, but she answered it anyway. "Barney, who is this?"

"Sarah? It's me, Beth Allard," said the voice.

Sarah was taken back decades by that name. Beth had been her friend since first grade, though they fell out of touch when Beth left the state for college.

"Beth? Oh my god, how are you? It has been forever," said Sarah.

"Far too long," echoed Beth. "I hope you don't mind, I got your number from your dispatch person. I had to lie and say it was about the murders."

"No, my goodness, it is fine. It is damned nice to hear a friendly voice," Sarah gushed. She felt like a schoolgirl once again.

"I am back in town visiting my folks and I saw you on the news this morning," said Beth. "You looked like you were in rough shape. How are you doing?"

Sarah gave a humorless chuckle. "That is a conversation for another time. I am on my way to the office and really do not have the time to get into anything."

"Understood," said Beth. "Can we catch up soon though?"

"I would love that," said Sarah. How about dinner, tomorrow night?"

"I can do that," answered Beth. "You will come here. My parents are worried about you too."

"It's a date then," said Sarah. "I'll be there around six." She ended the call and felt a smile spread across her face for the first time in days. Maybe today would be a good day after all.

Sarah arrived at work ten minutes after leaving Dunkin'. There were no reporters waiting in ambush as she had expected. That meant that they had either gotten their pound of flesh this morning, or the chief had had someone chase them off. At this point, Sarah did not really care.

She entered the barracks and went directly to her office. She was now the sole detective employed at the Plattsburgh base, so for all intents, it was her office. She sat at her desk, logged on to her computer and opened the e-mail program. There were fifty unread messages awaiting her, including the one that had chimed on her phone just a short while ago.

The name of the sender gave Sarah the chills and she almost deleted it. It was the subject line and the fact that there was a compressed file attached that made her open it. The subject read, "Must see". She selected the file and began to decompress it. The blue progress line had made it halfway when Jessica walked in.

"Thought you could sneak by me?" she asked.

"Not at all," Sarah lied. "I just have a bunch of e-mails to go through and a ton of thoughts to sort out."

"What is that?" Jessica asked, nodding at the fully decompressed file on her computer.

"Why don't you pull up a chair and find out with me," Sarah replied. "It came from that reporter, Monica Trudeau from Fox Forty-four."

That had piqued Jessica's interest enough for her to grab a chair and pull up a seat next to Sarah. Sarah hit play and felt her mouth go dry. It was her living room. It seemed like anyone that wanted could just enter her house.

Her slight anger faded as the video progressed. Sarah knew at once from the pictures on the wall who it was that had really sent her the video. "The killer has Monica," she said.

The pair watched the video three times before Sarah stood. "I need to get back to my house. There will be a clue there."

Jessica stood as well. "You are not going alone. I am coming and so are our three friends from this morning." She picked up Sarah's desk phone and dialed dispatch, instructing them to send those three troopers back to Sarah's and sweep the exterior. They were to then await her and Sarah's arrival.

Sarah and Jessica made their way to the cruiser as fast as Sarah's tired and battered body would allow them. The return trip to Sarah's home took eleven minutes, Sarah deciding not to speed as much as she had previously done. It seemed that the killer was having an effect of her, making her less reckless when heading to a crime scene.

They arrived in advance of the three troopers and decided without words to await their arrival. No one knew what they would find and the more eyes there, the better. Five minutes ticked by. The whole time Sarah was visually surveying the area.

She assumed that the black SUV in her driveway belonged to Monica. Assumption was the mother of all mistakes though, so she radioed dispatch to run the plates.

"Dispatch, this is Sarah. I need you to tell me who owns the plates ABZ147, New York reg," she said.

"Roger that Sarah, running now," said the voice of Tim Allard.

While she waited for dispatch to get back to her, Sarah watched each window to check for movement. She knew that they were being watched and most likely that was by a camera. She could not find where it was located though. When there was nothing to be seen in the windows, she shifted her attention to the surrounding area.

"Sarah, come back," said Tim via the radio.

"Go ahead," she answered.

"The vehicle is a black Kia Sportage, registered owner is Monica Trudeau."

"Thanks, Tim," she said as the cruiser with the three troopers pulled in behind her. The two women exited their car and walked over to the other cruiser as the three troopers were getting out.

Riviera had been driving. Jones was in the passenger seat and Smith was behind the driver. Both Jones and Smith were tall and very dark complected. The whole barracks joked that they were brothers separated at birth because their complexion was not the only thing that was strikingly similar. They were both six feet and five inches tall, broad at the shoulders with a barrel chest. They both shaved their head bald, and their eyes, nose and mouth were almost identical in shape and color. People often confused one for the other.

"Jones, you and Smith are to sweep the interior of the house," Jessica said. "Be watchful for anything that might look like a trap, and do not touch anything. Riviera, you are to stay right here beside Sarah while I sweep the exterior."

Sarah started to protest when Jessica held up a hand to silence her. "Listen, this guy is gunning for you. I want you to be guarded from here on out. Someone has to sweep the grounds so that leaves me. You two stay put. I will call out if I need help."

The three moved out as one, Jessica breaking off when they reached the front steps. Jessica went to the left to search the back lawn. As she passed by the windows, she could see the troopers in the house. She slowly made her way to the backyard. It did not take her long to search the shed and around the pool to determine that there was no one there.

Jessica rounded the far side of the house, slowly making her way back to the front. There was a large pine tree that she took time to search. She was hoping to find a camera. The last one had led the police to the discarded burner phone, but that did not mean that would prove to be the case this time. Finding nothing of interest in the tree, Jessica rejoined Sarah and Riviera by the cruiser. The troopers came back out of the house shortly after, finding nobody hidden.

"Well, I suppose we go in," Sarah said.

Sarah headed towards her house with the other four following. She headed directly to the living room where she found the pair of chairs, Monica's cellphone and a note. She went immediately for the note, knowing that within it, she would find a clue to where Monica had been taken.

She read it aloud. "Poor little Sarah, always playing catch-up. I am keen for us to meet again, face to face. Am I black, or am I white? Perhaps I am named after a peanut, or perhaps not. I cannot tell you these things, for there is power in discovery. I could give you one thousand, eight hundred thirty-seven hints, yet I doubt you would know me still. You will find Monica all alone. You have nine hours."

"Could he be more cryptic?" asked Smith.

"He used the word face twice and the word white, do you think it is Whiteface?" asked Jessica.

Sarah chewed on her bottom lip in thought. "He also said keen. There is a town nearby called Keene. And, what about the peanut reference?" said Sarah.

"Could that be just to throw us off?" asked Rivera.

"Peanuts, maybe like in Charlie Brown," said Jones. "Wasn't one of the kids in the group named Marcy? Mount Marcy is in Keene."

"Well shit," said Sarah. "We have two mountains, in opposite directions and nine hours."

"Each problem has a solution," said Jessica. "There are five of us here right now, so we split up."

Sarah was about to agree when something in the note made her pause and take out her phone. She called up her web browser and typed in "mountain 1837 NY". The search result told her all she needed to know.

"He took Monica to Mount Marcy," she said. "I am certain of it. Mount Marcy clicks off three of the hints he gave us. Keene, peanuts and eighteen thirty-seven. That was the first time it was recorded as someone hiking to the top."

"Aw hell, she's got my vote," said Smith.

Instead of answering, Jessica pulled out her phone and dialed a number. "Dispatch, this is Momsen. I need troopers with hiking experience sent to Whiteface Mountain. They are looking for Monica Trudeau. She may be on the peak."

She hung up the phone and ushered the group out of the house. Riviera, Jessica and Sarah all got in one car while Smith and Jones got in the other. They turned on the lights and sirens and drove away from Sarah's house at the fastest speed they could manage safely.

"Riviera, what is your first name?" asked Sarah.

"It's Luciana," she answered. "Listen, the note he left said we had nine hours, and I would imagine it would take at least six or seven hours to hike Mount Marcy, why are we driving so fast?"

Jessica chuckled at the question despite the lack of humor in the given situation. "Because he starts his clock from the moment that he takes his victim. We are already down one hour. That is a very beautiful name by the way."

Luciana blushed at the compliment. "Thank you chief," she said.

"Not to interrupt," said Sarah. "But it took me seven hours to summit Mount Marcy and that was when I was at my best. The rest of you are not habitual hikers and Marcy is the tallest mountain in the state. It will be a challenge for us to get to the peak in time. I am not even in the shape to go ahead of the group, in case you didn't notice. This will be a hell of a hike for all five of us."

Chapter 27

They had needed to administer a second dose of the sedative to Monica about halfway up the mountain. Not a full dose, they wanted her to be awake when she died, but enough to ensure she would not regain consciousness too soon.

Five thousand, three-hundred forty-three feet was a lot of mountain. They were well rested and had eaten a nutrient rich meal before taking her, but it was still arduous. They rationalized that all things worth doing were difficult. With this kill, they would catapult to the national news and be famous. Until this point, they had not understood just how badly they had wanted fame, or in this case infamy.

The e-mail that they had sent to Sarah had also gone out to the local news station. The footage must have made it on by now. That alone should garner them national attention, but the death of this reporter, which was going to be broadcast via YouTube and on a webpage that they had created would guarantee it.

The trap they had designed for Monica was going to provide her with a most brutal death. Even if she was rescued, a development they highly doubted, she would bear scars for the rest of her days, both physical and emotional. She would be placed on a cross that was constructed of aluminum and her hands and feet secured with pipe clamps. They would then attach a heavily modified bear trap to her ribcage. The razor blades that they had been hoarding would now be used. They would need to insert the teeth, tipped with the blades, through her skin, so it was very important that she be unconscious, lest she move wrong and die prematurely. They would then attach a simple kitchen timer that would trigger the trap, causing the teeth to remove her ribs and the flesh surrounding them. She would either die immediately or exsanguinate, either way it would be painful and terrible.

They smiled at their ingenuity. This would be their best trap yet. They began to feel giddy as they always did before a kill. The fatigue they were experiencing from the exertion of making such a difficult hike with the fifty pounds of supplies and the one hundred twenty pounds of person strapped to their back did little to dampen their mood.

Their thoughts shifted to Sarah and the two opportunities that they had had to take her life and chose not to. Last night had proved especially difficult. So soundly had she slept that they had run their fingers through her hair without her stirring.

The time was not right though. Sarah had more suffering to endure. Once the press learned that she had been unable to save Monica along with the other victims, she would be dragged through the mud and embarrassed. Once she was at her lowest and only then would they allow her to die.

They reached the summit after seven hours and were nearing the limits of their physical strength. They took a moment to rest and drink a liter of water before assembling the trap. They were not worried about being discovered. They had made sure no one else would be hiking this mountain today.

Having finished their water and recovering some energy, they unpacked the components and assembled the trap. They had gone with pipe clamps to hold the entire unit together to save on overall weight and assembly time. Were it to have to remain erect for more than an hour, they would have had to use stronger materials. They were fairly certain that the trap would hold up, but even if it failed, Monica would die.

Assembly took less than ten minutes which left inserting Monica into the restraints and then rigging the trap. She was right where they had left her, sprawled out on the ground in the fetal position. They rolled her onto her back and then withdrew a sharp knife from their pack. The knife sliced through her clothes with ease. Once her clothing had been removed, they picked her up and leaned her into the trap. This would be the second most difficult step, next to the hike. An unconscious person tended to flop about and made restraining them in a vertical position immensely annoying.

They used their body to hold her against the trap. Each time they tried to secure her hands though, Monica fell away from where they needed her. They could feel their frustration grow. They would need to remove the trap from the hole in the ground they had dug days before and lay it flat. They checked their watch as sweat poured down their face. If Sarah was as worthy as they thought, she would be three quarters of the way up the mountain by now. They had precious little time to lose.

They dropped Monica to the ground and pulled up the trap, laying it down next to her. Securing her into the trap was far easier this way but they were not completely certain that it would withstand the added stress of her weight when they stood it back up. Worse come to worse, they would have to leave her in the prone position. It would be less shocking but just as effective.

They used the remaining pipe clamps and a screwdriver to secure Monica's limbs exactly as they wanted them. When they were done, she resembled the representation of Jesus that was so popular in the Catholic faith.

They then carefully stood the trap back up and reinserted it in the hole. They were both surprised and relieved that it had held together. The last step was to set the teeth of the trap into Monica's flesh. First, they pressed the bear trap against her skin to mark where they would need to cut. Once that was done, they took the same knife they had used to cut off her clothes and made several cuts around Monica's ribs. They were careful not to cut too deeply lest they damage an organ. The game would not be any fun if she died from internal injuries before the trap could be sprung. Once the slits were finished, they secured the trap, inserting the bladed teeth into the slits. Lastly, they set the kitchen timer. There remained exactly one hour for Monica to be saved, which was the maximum amount of time allowed by the timer. It was serendipitous.

They heard Monica scream in pain and turned to face her. Blood slowly leaked from her abdomen where the teeth were inserted. It was a heavier flow than they would have liked, but not heavy enough to cause her to die before the hour was up.

"Do not struggle," they admonished her. "Should you strain too hard against your bonds, you will cause my device to go off and you will die horribly. You have one hour to be saved, well now it is only fifty-five minutes, but you get the point. Worry not, your rescuers should be well on their way. You will not die in vain though, should they fail. You will do exactly that which you wanted, help me gain fame."

Monica looked down at her body as best that she could. She recognized the source of her pain being the metal teeth inserted into her body. They could smell her fear and it was an intoxicating aroma.

"You sick bastard," Monica spat out. "I was going to make you famous."

"But my dear, as I just stated, you will," they said as they pulled a camera and tripod out of the pack. "This is going to broadcast your last hour over both YouTube and a webpage that I developed. People will be able to watch you suffer and then get ripped apart."

They set up the tripod a few feet in front of Monica so it would show her from the front. They did not want any viewers to miss the money shot. They then set the camera up and started to record and broadcast. They then pulled out a burner phone and dialed the local Fox station in Vermont.

"Hello," they said when someone answered at the station. "I am the killer you all are talking about. As you know by now, I took your reporter Monica Trudeau. She is now my victim and is set to be killed live via video stream. Don't you just love technology?

"I am uhhhhh, just the receptionist," the voice said back, trembling with fear. "Please hold."

To their surprise they were placed on hold and elevator music filled their left ear. They would have been amused had time not been an issue. After a minute someone else picked up the line.

"This is Jim Cantorez, station manager," said the voice.

"Jim, pleasure. I have Monica and she is not in the best of shape. Perhaps you would like to discuss her fate," they said, sarcasm dripping from every word.

"How do I know you are who you claim to be?" Jim asked.

"An excellent question. Please, go to www.todaykillz.com, kills with a z. I will wait," they replied.

After a moment they heard Jim curse. "What do you want, you sick-o?" he asked.

"What I want is simple. Monica has around fifty minutes to be rescued or she will die. Sarah Barney, the head homicide detective in Plattsburgh is on the case and should be well on her way here. I want you to broadcast my website, tell viewers it is also on YouTube, and let everyone know that it is because of Ms. Barney that Monica is where she is. Feel free to broadcast the feed live yourself," they said. They did not wait for a reply and ended the call and stood in front of Monica to address the camera. They had pulled their hood up over their head and made sure to face the ground, ensuring the camera would not show their face.

"My kind viewers, I am the evil lurking in the darkness, the taker of lives, the boogeyman if you wish. Behind me, secured in a trap of my own design, is Monica Trudeau. In less than fifty minutes, she will either be saved by the intrepid Sarah Barney, or she will meet a most terrible death. What you are about to witness is a fate that may be in store for any of you. I cannot be stopped, and neither shall I do so of my own volition."

They stepped to the side so that the camera would focus on Monica's bloody body. It was time to go. They were not certain that they could get to the deviation in the main trail in time to avoid Sarah. Marcy was quite treacherous towards the peak, lacking multiple ways down. This would force them to take the main trail until they reached the deviation that few knew about. They gathered up the now empty pack and started down the mountain.

Chapter 28

Jim Cantorez hung up the phone when the line went dead. He was in his sixties and close to retirement. He looked haggard and tired all of the time with large bags under his eyes. The news never slept and neither did he. His skin was marked with age spots and his white hair was so thin that his wife kept nagging him to just shave it off. His eyes had dulled with age from a vibrant blue to a washed out grey. He was dressed in khaki pants and a short-sleeved, button up plaid shirt, the same thing he wore every day.

He had started to record the feed as soon as he logged on to the website. He had a choice to make, ignore the killer's wishes and sit on what was perhaps the most salacious story to ever arise in this area, or broadcast the feed. It was not much of a decision. He looked at his watch and it was a quarter to six, the news would have to go on early. Jim picked up the phone and dialed the production office for the news.

"Steve, it's Jim. Listen get Jack and Molly in position now, we are going live," he said. Steve started to protest but Jim cut him off. "The killer that took Monica has her in a trap and is live streaming her murder, we are not sitting on that!"

Steve had been the nighttime news producer for this Fox affiliate since they had been formed, twenty-seven years ago. He had an eye on Jim's job, if the old goat ever retired. His hair was still jet black which was an achievement given his fifty-eight years. He perpetually had five O'clock shadow and a sad look to his brown eyes. Both his red nose and large gut spoke to the fact that he liked to drink perhaps too much.

The production office was where the camera angles were controlled, and the copy was sent to the prompters. It looked a lot like what the movies made mission control for NASA look like. Steve ran his hand through his thick, messy hair and leaned into the microphone on the console in front of him.

"Jack and Molly, out of make-up and into position. We go live in two minutes," he said.

That caused the small group of people around him to buzz. None of them were fully ready, but it didn't matter. Steve turned to the group.

"We all know that Monica was taken today. The person that took her has been confirmed as the one that has been killing everyone in the area of late. He is streaming her murder and Jim wants us to cover it. We will not be doing the news as usual," he said.

He looked at the set and saw an upset pair of anchors getting to their seats. He again spoke into the microphone, repeating what he had just told his crew. He added, "We need to let the audience know that what we will be showing is graphic in nature and most certainly not suitable for all ages."

His computer chimed that he had an e-mail and as suspected it was from Jim. The subject was "Recording of the stream". He opened it and watched for thirty seconds. Upon seeing Monica in her state of undress he turned to the graphics person, Shelly Hobart. Shelly was just out of her twenties and talented beyond words. She was indigenous and looked like one would expect. She had long, straight black hair with skin that looked perpetually tanned. Her brow was high and proud and her brown eyes full of soul. She was a little more than one hundred pounds overweight but wore it well.

"Shelly," he said. "We have exposed breasts and.....lady bits we will need blurred, think you can handle it?'

Shelly just nodded and waited for Steve to send her the feed so she could digitally blur out those areas. Steve sent it over to her and saw that there was only about ten seconds before they were to cut in live.

"Here we go everyone," he said.

After the breaking news graphic was sent out, Jack Spaulding was up. Jack was in his mid-thirties and always immaculately groomed, something he said that his husband insisted on. His short brown hair was styled with just the right amount of product to keep it from looking greasy and his face was always clean shaven without a hint that he actually ever grew facial hair. He made certain that his clothing always accentuated his bright green eyes.

Molly Tebbits was somewhere around fifty, though she never told anyone her age. She kept her artificially blonde hair cut in what some called a Karen style. Her signature feature was what some called a million-watt smile, though that was missing on this day. Her face was normally free of wrinkles but the somber look she wore aged her quite a bit.

"Ladies and gentlemen," Jack began. "We are sorry to interrupt your program, but we have just been handed some breaking news on the recent killings and our own Monica Trudeau. Please be warned, what you are about to see is not for younger viewers or the faint of heart."

The screen switched over to a frozen image of the killer just before they spoke. Molly took over talking. "As you all know, Monica was taken this morning. We have confirmed that the serial killer known now as Mountaintop Killer is responsible. He has placed her in one of his traps atop an undisclosed mountain. Homicide detective Sarah Barney is supposedly on her way to try and save Monica. The killer is streaming the event live from the mountain. We will begin playing the stream from when it was first broadcast around fifteen minutes ago. The link to the stream will be placed in the lower left corner of your screen. Please, join us in praying for her safe return. Once more, we urge any of you with children in the room to ask them to leave."

The control room started to play the recorded stream, starting with the killer addressing the viewers. The playback was on for two minutes when Steve's phone rang again. He answered on the second ring and did not get a chance to speak.

"This is Susan Day," the voice said. "If you are not aware, I am the head of Fox networks. Where the fuck did you get this video?"

"Susan, Steve Wilson here, producer of the evening news," he said.

Sue cut him off, "The fuck do I care who you are, answer my question!"

Steve was taken aback by her vitriol. "The killer called in and gave the address to Jim. We decided to run with it."

"Why did no one tell me?" she asked. "Never mind, it does not matter now. We are taking over your broadcast and the national news team is going to run with this story. Tucker Carlson is going to be lead anchor. You might as well send your people home, this is out of your hands now."

She hung up on Steve. He looked around the room at his crew and then leaned into the mic. "Jack, Molly, the network has taken over. That's a wrap for today." He then spun in his chair. "Shelly, I want you to stay here with me to make sure nothing goes wrong, the rest of you, see you tomorrow."

Chapter 29

At six hours into the climb, Sarah was impressed by both her ability to overcome her injuries and the rest of the group in keeping up with her. They were less than an hour from the summit and it did not look like they would make it before sunset. Sarah was not used to needing help from people, but she was grateful to have this fine group with her.

She noticed that Jessica and Luciana were hitting it off. She did not know if it was merely a budding friendship or if there was a possible romantic connection. She knew that Jessica had been married to a man before, but maybe she had an interest in dating a woman, one never knew.

Smith and Jones never allowed Sarah to get more than ten feet away from them before they doubled their efforts and caught back up to her. They were acting like overprotective brothers, and she found it endearing. Though, their actions were not without good cause. The killer had made it known that she was the ultimate target.

She could not get her mind around why then they had been close enough to kill her twice and not done the deed. She had been tossing around the question in her own head for long enough and decided she needed to talk it over with someone else. She looked back over her shoulder and saw that the chief and Luciana were far enough back to be out of hearing range.

She slyly motioned for her new brothers to get in closer and told them everything up to finding the picture of herself sleeping that was taken last night. The pair mulled it over for a while before Smith spoke.

"It seems to me that this guy is out right fucking with you," he said. "He wants you to know, without any doubts, that he is in charge."

Jones nodded. "Yeah, he also seems like he is trying to wear you down and break you. If you no longer feel safe in places where you should, like asleep in bed, then you will begin to lose focus."

"We all know that you are highly observant. He could be trying to put you off your game," added Smith.

"I've been off my game," said Sarah. "I've been stuck in a game of catch-up from the jump."

Jessica's phone rang and the group stopped. "Hello," she said.

They all watched her face while she listened and then ended the call.

"There was no one found on top of Whiteface," she said. "We appear to be on the right Mountain. Good call Sarah."

Sarah took little pleasure in the praise but felt more energized than ever. Knowing you are on the right path is vastly different than just believing it.

"There is more," Jessica added. "The killer is livestreaming Monica in a trap with the intent of showing her murder live. The Fox station started to show the broadcast and the other two local stations have joined in. That's not all. It also appears that this has gone national."

This news struck Sarah like a hammer and caused a renewed sense of urgency to come over her. She turned to resume the hike when something dark caught her attention from off to their left. She knew that there were a lot of bears in the area, and this was the time of year that they were trying to consume as many calories as possible before hibernation.

The four others saw where Sarah was looking and followed her gaze. Riviera was the first to speak.

"Someone is watching us," she said in a hushed voice.

Sarah knew at once that she was right. The shape was around fifty yards away, but it was too stationary to be a bear. She slowly reached for her gun, but the shape moved with alarming speed before she could get her hand close to it. It was a person, most likely the killer.

"I think that was him!" she yelled and began to give chase.

Jones and Smith passed her with ease. She was in no shape to be running, every impact of her feet on the ground jarred her broken collarbone and sent waves of pain cascading through her chest and shoulder. Jessica was next to catch her. She placed a restraining hand on Sarah's good shoulder.

"Let the boys chase him down," she said. "We have a reporter to save. Jones, Smith, we are proceeding without you. Catch that son of a bitch," she yelled.

Both men raised a hand to acknowledge that they had heard her. It did not take long before they vanished from view, the sound of them crashing through the brush was the only evidence that they were in pursuit. The three women were close to where the person had been trying to hide, so Sarah walked forward to the spot.

The dried leaves that had fallen from the oak tree behind which the person had lurked were crushed. That was clear evidence to Sarah that this was the correct spot. She did not know what she expected to find, but she still crouched down.

"Pen," she said without looking up.

Luciana handed Sarah one that she had in her breast pocket. With it, Sarah started to move the leaves around. This bastard was always toying with them, and she did not expect that to change. The pen struck something solid. Sarah looked up at Jessica and saw surprise in her eyes.

"I knew he would toy with us," she said as she used her hand to brush the leaves away. She uncovered a smart phone. It was nothing fancy, the kind one could buy at Dollar General. Uncertainty filled her mind before she decided to pick it up. She found it odd that there was just a touch of resistance when she lifted it. She realized a little too late that she had fallen victim once again to the whims of the killer. She had sprung a trap.

The phone had a thin filament line attached to it, leading to a small tree that had been pulled back, almost to the breaking point. When Sarah stood, the line released the tension in the tree, and it sprang forward with extreme force. The tree struck all three women, knocking them to the ground. Sarah's head found an exposed root and blackness followed.

Jones and Smith were fast on their feet. They were running after the suspect at top speed, and he was still slipping away from them. They could not understand how this was, yet the person that they were chasing grew smaller and more difficult to see with shocking rapidness. After ten minutes he had vanished.

"Little bastard runs like a jackrabbit," said Jones with heavy breath.

Smith nodded. "Should we split up?"

"No," replied Jones. "Whoever this killer is, he has overpowered every last person that he wanted. I think it is best if we stick together."

The pair had run across and down the mountain for ten minutes before they stopped. Jones strained to listen for the telltale sound of footfalls, but he could not hear anything besides his ragged breathing. He was out of steam and a quick glance at Smith let him know that his partner was as well. They would have to return empty handed.

They waited until their breathing slowed before backtracking to where they had started to give chase. The trip back would take far longer even though they were walking at a very brisk pace. They were both reaching their point of exhaustion, with the difficult hike and then the exertion of running.

Smith was an avid hunter and completely at home in the woods while Jones never hunted but still enjoyed the outdoors. As they walked back to the women, Smith kept his eyes on the ground. He was trying to uncover any set of tracks that the killer may have left when he fled from them. All he could see was their own sets of tracks. This meant that the killer had either veered off in another direction or that they had trampled any signs that he had left behind. Smith guessed that it was the former.

After twenty minutes of hiking back from wince they had come, Smith knew they were close, and he had failed to pick up any of the killer's tracks. The pair knew that the women would have gone on without them. It just did not make any sense for the trio to await their return.

By Jones' estimation, there was around twenty minutes left before the trap was sprung. It was because of that estimation that he was shocked to find the women almost exactly where they had left them. Sharah and Riviera looked pretty rough, like something had hit them.

"What the hell happened?' Smith asked.

Sarah just hung her head in shame. It was Jessica that had answered.

"Sarah had found where the killer had been watching us. They had dropped a phone, at least that was how it had seemed. Instead, it was a trap. We all got hit pretty hard by a tree but Sarah got the worst of it. Her had slammed into an exposed root and she was knocked out for around twenty minutes."

Sarah got unsteadily to her feet. "We don't have any time to waste," she said. "Monica has about fifteen to twenty minutes left, and we have just about that to reach the summit."

The tired and battered group resumed their trip up the mountain. The last leg was to be the most difficult part too, with many areas of loose rock and steep inclines. Sarah knew in the pit of her stomach that they had failed. She was not about to give voice to that thought though. They were still going to try.

Chapter 30

They were less than five minutes into their descent when they became certain that Sarah would cross their path. They did not have nearly enough time to make it to the place in the path where they knew they could safely diverge.

They would instead set a trap for their intrepid friend and be certain she failed to reach the summit in time. One thing that they always carried when they entered the woods was some fishing line and hooks. One never knew when they might have to fish for some lunch. They took several minutes to scour the area surrounding the trail and found the perfect sapling. It was a six-foot-tall pine and would have plenty of spring in the trunk. Using the fishing line, they secured the tree to a trigger. They then ran a line from the trigger and attached it to their burner phone. They knew Sarah would find it and spring the trap.

Once the trap was set, they crouched down next to the phone in eager anticipation of her arrival. They were positioned in such a manner that even the most obtuse of people would be able to spot them. They did not have long to wait for Sarah and her group to arrive. It seemed that they were not correct about lacking sufficient time to make it to the place where they could deviate from the trail. The trap and delay of Sarah were well worth the additional time spent on the mountain.

Sarah had called up the two very large black men and they were having a conversation in hushed tones. They could just barely hear their voices but not the substance of the conversation. The chief then received a call. They were so giddy that they could barely contain themselves. If only Sarah knew how close she was to them. Then it happened, Sarah saw them.

They knew that at least part of the party would give chase when they fled. They were not surprised by the fact that it was the two men. The pair was fast, requiring them to run faster than they had ever run before. Their speed coupled with their extreme comfort in the woods and on a mountain gave them the edge. It did not take very long for them to pull far enough away from the police that they had vanished from view. This was the opportunity they needed. With speed one might associate with a squirrel, they climbed the nearest large tree and hid among the branches and remaining leaves. Scarcely more than a minute after they had stopped moving, the pair of troopers ran past.

It did not take long for the pair to realize that they had lost their quarry and decide to head back to the trail. They waited in the tree for five minutes to ensure that the troopers did not double back before they climbed down. They were at a crossroads of sorts. They could return to where Sarah and her friends were left on the trail and see if their trap had been a success, or they could exit the mountain and continue on the path they had been walking. Tempting as it was to spy further on Sarah, they decided to leave the mountain. There were already five police officers on the mountain, who knew how many more would be joining in, especially since they had been seen.

Though this was not where their alternate trail was located, they decided to start their descent here. As they walked with slow ease down the back of the mountain, they wondered what the police had thought about the police tape that they had placed across the entrance to the parking area for the mountain. That would have to be one of the many questions that they asked Sarah before allowing her to expire.

The trip down the mountain went swiftly, their thoughts consumed both by the fun they wanted to have with Sarah and by their desire to get home so that they could watch the video of Monica being ripped apart. They turned towards where they had left their Jeep. They still had an hour to go before they arrived at their parking spot.

They continued their hike, uncharacteristically unaware of their surroundings. They typically prided themselves on their acute awareness of everything that transpired in their vicinity. This day, however, be it overconfidence, the thoughts of what was to come for Sarah or the deepening darkness, they almost walked into a man that was out hunting.

"Whoa," he said. "You need to pay attention to where you are going! What are you doing out in the woods during hunting season and dressed all in black?"

They were immediately happy that they had not removed the hood from their head. They looked at the ground as a child might when being scolded. Clearing their throat, they did their best to disguise their voice.

"I'm sorry mister," they said as they thought of a way out of this.

"Listen kid, where are your parents?" he asked.

The hunter must have assumed that because of their small stature, they were a teen. This helped them devise a false story to feed him.

"I, I, I don't know," they said. They started to speak hurriedly as a scared child might. "We were hiking, and I got separated. I have not seen them in hours."

"Shit," the hunter said. He stood up from the log upon which he had been sitting. He was average height and build. He was dressed head to toe in blaze orange, the only skin that was exposed was the small area of his face where his black beard and eyebrows did not cover. His eyes were a dull brown and it seemed more like they were looking into the eyes of a dumb animal than a man.

He pulled out a cellphone and said, "I suppose I should call 911."

"Oh, thank you," they said excitedly and rushed in like they were going to hug him.

The man did not expect what came next. They looked up into his face just before they would have embraced and pulled out the knife that they wore on their belt. In one swift move, they slit his throat. The knife was so sharp that with the momentum they had gained rushing in towards him they felt it scrape on his spine. Confusion spread across the man's face as blood gushed from his mortal wound. He fell, first to his knees and then forward so his face smacked into the ground.

What came next was the thing that movies and television shows never featured. As the man expired, his bowels and bladder emptied. His once orange pants took on a dirty brown hue in the seat and the air filled with a stench that they had not yet gotten used to.

While it was true that they had no compassion for other people, they almost felt bad for this guy. He was just out in the woods, minding his business and trying to secure some venison, even if it was past the legal hunting hours. Who were they to judge someone that was in the process of fracturing a law? He was not even on their radar. When he woke this morning and bid his significant other goodbye, he was blissfully unaware that it was to be a final goodbye. Now, he was to be found, if he was ever found, with a slit throat and pants full of excrement.

They bent over and wiped the blood from their knife on his clothes before returning it to the sheath. They chastised themselves as they continued on their way. They would need to be more aware of their surroundings, a thought that came not an instant too soon. They were getting closer to the road and in the darkness, they saw strobing red lights, a sure sign that the police were nearby.

They were now faced with a conundrum. They were five minutes from their Jeep. Either the police had discovered it, or they were simply being thorough and canvassing the area in hopes of finding them. They could keep walking and hope to avoid any police entanglements or turn towards home. It would roughly be a fifteen-hour walk if they stayed off the main roads. They had neither the time nor the energy for that kind of walk, so onward they pressed.

They crept up to the spot where they had left their Jeep. As they had hoped, it was still undiscovered. There was a cruiser parked in the road just beyond it. They had their plan, though it would delay their gratification of watching Monica die. They would enter their Jeep on the passenger side and wait for the cruiser to leave. Should they be discovered, they hoped that there was only one trooper in that car.

Chapter 31

Monica had silently counted the minutes passing. With each one, she felt her hopes diminish. She was so cold that her entire body was covered with goosebumps, but she fought the need to shiver as best she could. She knew that she was completely naked and that the entire world was most likely watching her suffer. This did not make her uncomfortable though, all modesty that she had was gone.

She knew that she had two choices. She could either remain mute and suffer in silence or she could muster up her remaining resolve and try to be the reporter she knew that she was.

She decided that, should she be saved, she would rather be remembered for being brave in the face of certain death. She slowly looked at the camera, wary of her movements triggering the trap.

"This is Monica Trudeau, reporting live from an undisclosed mountain, where I have been taken and inserted into a trap that is meant to take my life," she said as calmly as she could.

"As the killer said and as you can clearly see, I am in a trap that is meant to kill me upon springing. As you can also see that since I am covered in goosebumps, that I am quite cold after having been completely exposed to the elements."

"I have been hanging here, suspended by my wrists and ankles, for what is my estimation, at least half an hour, which gives me less than twenty minutes to be rescued. I am certain that the death awaiting me will be excruciating, so I am, of course, hopeful that detective Barney will get here and save my life."

"As we all know though, she was just unsuccessful in saving her partner's life. I guess that the question at hand is, is this killer smarter than the area's best detective?"

"As time creeps forward, I look back over my life and there are a few things I want to say. None of us know when we are going to die, at least I have this opportunity. To my parents, I want to apologize. In order to finance my immigration to the Unites States, I posed for some nude pictures that I am now certain will surface. As fate would have it, this serial killer was the photographer and they have plastered the inside of Sarah's house with them. Please forgive me for shaming you like that."

"I am not proud of the fact that I did whatever it took to get where I am now. I traded my body with the head of this very network in the hopes that it would further my career. Now that I stare down my mortality, I am certain that it was not worth it. All I wanted was to be famous, and I guess now I will be."

Tears started to flow from Monica's eyes, but she did not stop talking. "Unfortunately, I never got a look at the killer's face. They kept it hidden from me and used some instrument to alter their voice. They are around five feet, four inches in height and of slight build and definitely Caucasian. Unfortunately, that is all I can give you as far as a description. I do not know how they are capable of carrying so many people up the various mountains like they do."

A sound from behind caused her to stop talking for a moment. "I think I hear someone coming....."

Chapter 32

Sarah kept glancing at her watch and began to think that they might make it to the top in time to save Monica. The group was pushing themselves, perhaps harder than any of them had ever pushed before. Each of them was soaked with sweat.

Sarah was in the worst shape of the entire group. The impact from the sapling had undone any of the healing her body had managed on her collarbone. She now wore a large bump on her forehead where the tree had caught her, and its twin was at the base of her skull from the root. She was still in the lead and no one in the group could figure out how.

Jessica was the most concerned of the others. She had urged Sarah to slow her pace, thinking that there might be internal injuries. Sarah had scoffed at her, simply saying that Monica's injuries would be far worse if they failed. That statement prevented anyone else in the group from either trying to slow Sarah or complaining about their own fatigue.

Sarah could feel the tension in the group as they were feet from the summit. By her estimate they had three minutes left. She said a silent prayer to a God she no longer spoke to about not making her watch this woman die.

There was a grassy area amidst the rocks and that was where they saw Monica. She was fastened to a metal cross with her back to them. Sarah broke into a full run, ignoring the pain from what seemed to be her entire body. Though she was moving at a fast pace, Smith and Jones both passed her. They looked like marathon runners that saw the finish line.

Jones took the lead. As he reached Monica and slid to a stop, the trap sprung. He was bathed in a mix of blood and tissue. Her scream of anguish was something that no one in the group would forget. Jones fell to his knees and wept, screaming, "Nnnnnnnnooooooooooooooooooooooooooo!"

Sarah felt like a complete failure, she knew there was nothing she would ever be able to do that would undo all of the evil the killer had visited upon the people of the area. She too fell to her knees and felt tears stream down her face.

For the briefest of moments, she considered quitting her job, right there. She knew though that if she quit, the sick bastard responsible would get away with everything he had done and would continue to do. Her grief, as powerful as it was, was replaced with a fierce anger. She hated this person with every fiber of her being. There was no other emotion, just raw, unbridled hatred.

Sarah got back to her feet and stormed over to the camera and ripped it from the tripod. Before anyone could intervene, she looked directly at the lens and said, "I am coming for you fucker."

She then smashed the camera on the ground, ending the feed to the rest of the world. The game that this man was playing with her had gone too far. She knew that she needed to control her emotions and process the scene for clues. Sarah turned to the group that was with her. Their faces were a mix of fear and concern.

"I am alright," she lied. "I lost it there for a moment, but I am back. We know this sick fuck leaves clues as to what he is planning next at every scene, so let's split up and find it."

Jessica was unaccustomed to taking orders from one of her subordinates, but she knew that Sarah was correct. Sarah had already broken off from the rest of the group.

"Okay guys," she said. "Let's search the area."

The group broke up, each person going in a different direction. Sarah concentrated on the immediate area around Monica. She did not have any of the traditional equipment one would have when processing a scene like this, but she did not care. She did her best not to look directly at the carnage but found it difficult.

When the trap had sprung it removed all of the skin, muscles and ribs from Monica's chest. From her breasts down to her mons pubis was a terrible hole that exposed her organs, some of which had spilled out and onto the ground. Sarah was happy that the cooler weather was keeping the insects away. She could not understand why, but for some reason she felt extremely connected to Monica.

She did not find anything of interest on the ground, so she began inspecting the trap and body. The pipe clamps that were used to secure Monica in place were cutting into her flesh. There was dried blood on both wrists and her ankles that was intermixed with new blood. The trap itself was intelligently made, though she chided herself for giving that kind of credit to the killer. Sarah decided to start from the back of the trap at Monica's head and work her way down.

It did not take her long to discover the clue. Sarah moved Monica's hair aside and found a picture stapled to the base of her neck. It was almost like adding insult to injury, stapling a picture to her like that. She pulled it free and was perplexed. The picture was of a pair of green eyes. It was taken in such a way that the eyes filled the entire image, there was no hint of the brows or cheekbones.

"Out killer left us a partial picture of themselves," she deduced aloud. This caused a chorus of "What?" to come from everyone as they came to see what she had found.

"Those eyes belong to a woman," said Sarah after looking closely at the picture. "Look, there is eyeliner."

"Sonofabithch," said Jones.

"The person we were chasing was on the shorter and skinnier side," added Smith.

"Everything we thought we knew is wrong," said Jessica.

A silence descended on the group. Sarah once more felt like she was thirty steps behind the killer. At least now they knew what gender for which they were looking.

"I only ever arrested one woman," said Sarah, "and she was not white. This means that our killer is not a vindictive convict."

Sarah motioned for Jessica to walk off to the side for a private conversation.

"What's up?" asked Jessica.

"I really need to be alone," said Sarah. "I need to be able to just think. I want to see if there is any way I can start to connect the dots."

"I do not like you being by yourself," said Jessica. "Especially since we know that you are her target."

"I have not said anything, mostly because I did not want you to worry," said Sarah. "She had had two chances to kill me and passed on both. It seems like she is waiting for something. Give me a day?

Jessica begrudgingly nodded her agreement and Sarah turned away, starting her solo descent. Smith started to protest her walking away from the perceived safety of the group, but Jessica held up her hand and silenced him.

Sarah welcomed the relative silence that surrounded her as she left the group behind. She found that when the puzzle that confronted her was too large, then she needed to be alone. It was too difficult to piece things together when surrounded by constant noise. Her plan was to get in the cruiser and drive. Jessica had agreed to give her one day, so she would make the most of those twenty-four hours.

Chapter 33

The sun had risen on another day. The police never happened upon her as she hid in the Jeep. Samantha Ryan had waited until an hour before sunrise to pull out and head back home. She did not know when the cruiser that was parked in the road had left, but she decided to err on the side of caution.

Sam, as she preferred to be called, was anxious to get home and watch the footage of Monica's death. She knew that it would be easy enough to find recordings of it all over the internet, she had seen to it that plenty of people had access. Still, she was delaying her own gratification, wanting to watch it on a large screen rather than her cellphone.

As she drove, Sam's thoughts went back to second grade and the day that sent her on the path she now walked. Even back then she had known she was a lesbian, though it was far less acceptable then than now. That was most likely why she had never professed any feelings for Sarah.

Sam wished, as she had almost every day since that day, that Sarah had come to her rescue. She wondered how different her life would have been if Sarah had reciprocated her feelings, or maybe even just shown her the warmth of friendship.

To any outside observer, it was clear that Sarah had not even really known that Sam was alive back then. Sam was shy and quiet, not even finding the ability to talk to Sarah. When Tommy had beat her bloody though, everyone knew who Sam was, even Sarah.

Sam had wrestled with the notion that Sarah had simply been acting out of self-preservation. If Tommy had beat on her, what would have prevented him from beating on Sarah as well? Sarah had never checked on Sam though and that was the part that she had never been able to look past.

This last thought being her final as she pulled into her driveway. As always, she was relieved to find no police lying in wait for her. Sam had been a long-time resident of what the locals called the Villa. It was once a motel that the latest owner converted into small apartments. He had even bought four single-wide mobile homes and parked them in the back. There was the main motel as well as a dozen single room cabins on the property. The owner, Dick Shannon was as greedy as they came, charging almost one-thousand dollars for less than five-hundred square-feet.

Dick was next on her list. He was approaching sixty but could pass for forty. His head was shaved bald, and he kept his face clean shaven as well. He was five feet and ten inches of solid muscle, spending vast amounts of his free time in the gym. What used to get him all the ladies was his eyes though. They were a sparkling light blue with flecks of gold throughout. Sam had never met a woman that Dick had wanted to sleep with that could resist his eyes.

Sam was the first to reject Dick and that bothered him. He propositioned her every time he saw her.

Recently he had added "accidental" touches of her chest and butt. She had tried to tell him that she was a lesbian, but he did not believe her. She was more manly in build than feminine, with well-defined arms and shoulders, but that did no dissuade Dick.

Sam had always been short as a kid and that translated into her being short for an adult. She was a quarter inch taller than five feet. Her build was lean with a surprising amount of muscles. Her natural blonde hair was kept at just shoulder length and her green eyes were hard, like a person that had seen too much suffering in their life. It was her chest that Dick seemed to like so much. Whenever they were face to face, his eyes never left that area. She was small of frame and cursed with a small A cup. It was because of this fact that she never wore a bra. Since she did not care who looked at her, a lot of her shirts were skin-tight and left little to the imagination.

Sam was going to seduce him and lull Dick into a false sense of security before taking his life. His death would not serve her plan for Sarah, but it would be satisfying to her. She would make certain that his body was never found though, he would simply vanish.

She lived in one of the small cabins in the back. The only advantage to that was having your own driveway, for lack of a better term. It was only long enough to fit her Jeep, but it still counted in her mind. Sam entered unit twenty-three. It was not much but it was home. The living room and bedroom were one and the same with a small section to her left that functioned as a kitchen. There was a small row of three cabinets with a tiny sink in the center and a microwave on top. If Sam was not dining out, then she would eat something that was once frozen, Hot Pockets being a staple of her diet. The place lacked any sort of refrigerator, so she used a large cooler that required the ice to be refreshed every other day. There was a small door off to the left side of her bed that led to the bathroom. This too was small, featuring only a stand-up shower, sink and a toilet.

Sam did not even notice the dirty walls any more or the thin, worn-out yellow carpet. She sat on her double bed and grabbed the remote control for her thirty-two-inch TCI television. It was a smart TV, so she turned it on and went to the web browser. She accessed her website that had streamed the death of Monica and selected the file with the recording. Sam started the playback with thirty minutes left. She would watch the video in its entirety at some point but today was not that day.

She could not take her eyes off Monica's nude body. Even with the trap dug into her flesh, she was the sexiest woman Sam had ever seen naked. If she was truly a monster, then Sam would have had her way with Monica before killing her. Even with her skewed vision of the world, Sam knew rape was wrong. Monica was talking while sobbing. The action of sobbing made her breasts dance in a way that Sam found very alluring.

Sam's favorite part came at the very end of the recording, though she had no idea that it would be there. Sarah told her that she was coming for her, and she hoped that it was true. She replayed the last part several times, basking in the tortured look on Sarah's face. There was so much pain and anguish behind it that Sam knew she had won. It was just about time to begin the final phase of her plan and kill Sarah. It would have to be quite the spectacle in order to outdo Monica's death, but she was pretty certain that she could do it.

That would have to wait. It had been far too long since she had taken someone's life with her own hands for pleasure. It was time to go visit one Mr. Shannon. Given the fact that it was just before eleven in the morning, she knew that Dick would be in the office. Sam was not one that would normally dress slutty, not that she was incapable. She had a special outfit that she wore whenever her lust needed slaking. She went to her dresser and pulled out her ultra-low-cut tank top and what she called her micro-skirt. Neiter items of clothing left anything to the imagination.

It was pretty chilly outside, with temperatures in the low forties, so that would help sell the seduction. Her nipples would certainly be rock hard by the time she walked to the office.

It had been three days since she last showered, so she undressed and climbed into the cramped, wet sanctuary. As the steam and water washed over her body, she felt like she was on top of the world. She took her time, wanting to wash off any signs of what she had been doing the last few days.

After she was clean, she dried off with her only towel. It was once white but over time had turned a dingy yellow. She then got dressed, skipping putting on any undergarments. She knew that he would follow her anywhere if she propositioned him, but she wanted to be certain. With her skimpiest of clothes on, she did her hair, her make-up and put on a pair of three-inch black heels.

The walk from her cabin in the back to the office, which was located in the center of the long, white main building took only five minutes. By the time she walked into the office, she was covered in goosebumps from head to toe.

Dick was sitting behind the desk, watching something on his phone. Sam guessed that by the look on his face it was porn. One look at her and whatever was playing was swiftly forgotten. As she suspected, his eyes never left her erect nipples. She stretched nonchalantly, rolling back her shoulders so that the fabric of her shirt strained to contain her chest. She knew that when she did this, the fabric became ninety percent see through. Dick was visibly salivating.

"What can I do for you?" he asked, nervously clearing his throat.

Sam did not answer. She walked over as seductively as possible to where he sat and put her right foot on the arm of the chair. This afforded Dick an unobstructed view of her goods. He did not try to hide the fact that he was looking either. After she knew that she had his full attention, Sam pulled her leg down and bent over in front of Dick. Her shirt pulled away from her chest and he was given another unobstructed view.

"Listen," he said. "This day and age all I hear about is consent, consent, consent. If you are trying to tell me something, and I think you are, I am gunna need you to spell it out for me."

A sly smile spread across her lips; she knew the bait had been taken. "Why Dick, I want you to fuck me like I ain't never been fucked b'fore," she purred.

The color almost vanished from his face. "I will meet you at you place in ten minutes."

"Oh no," she said. "T'won't do. I am a dirty girl with one hell of an itch. I want you to do me outside. Meet me in the woods north of town. I will head there now, do not leave too soon. Don't want no one to know what we're doin'."

Dick had never been spoken to like that before, and he loved it. He watched her turn and leave, his excitement straining against the fabric of his pants. He had wanted her since the day she moved in, and now he was going to have her. Today would be a very good day.

Chapter 34

It happened after six hours of driving. The epiphany came to Sarah like an unseen slap in the face. It made total sense, she could not believe that she had not seen it before, though in her defense it was something that she had not thought about for over twenty years.

Back when she was in third grade there had been a younger girl that had developed a crush on Sarah. It had elevated to the point of obsession. Not knowing exactly how to handle the situation, because what eight-year-old did, Sarah had chosen to ignore this girl. Though this had not dissuaded her from following Sarah and her friends around like a lost puppy.

No matter where Sarah had gone when on recess, there this girl was. Every day before and during school, just lurking within ear shot, until the day that Tommy had beat her almost to death. As an adult looking back on it, Sarah now knew that she had been just as guilty as Tommy, because she was right there when it happened and had done nothing to stop it. If she tried hard enough, she could still hear the sounds of his fists striking her head, the crunch of her nose shattering.

Sarah could recall her face, but not her name. She did not even know if she ever knew it. She chided herself for being so callous as a child. She never thought herself better than anyone else, but she sure had acted that way back then.

Keeseville was a small town, one where everyone knew just about everyone else. If this girl, now a woman, still lived in town, Sarah did not think it would prove to be too difficult to track her down. Her first step would be to pull the old school records. Surely there was something on file about the beating. She pulled the car over and pulled out her cellphone. She dialed Jessica, who answered on the first ring.

"You have news?" asked Jessica.

"I know who it is," said Sarah. She then spent the next fifteen minutes telling Jessica about this girl and what had happened. Jessica said nothing during this time, she just listened. The self-reproach in Sarah's voice made her sad. It was like she was blaming herself for all of the murders that this person had committed.

"You're certain that this is the killer?" she asked when Sarah was done talking.

"It makes total sense," said Sarah. "I am close to Albany. I am turning around now and should be back in a little under three hours."

"Alright," said Jessica. "I will see about pulling the school records. Drive safe."

The call ended and Sarah pulled a U-turn. She turned on the emergency lights and accelerated to ninety. She was a few miles from an interstate entrance. She would make better time on that road, so she decided that she would take that route.

For the entirety of the drive back to Plattsburgh she chided herself about missing all of the clues. Tom should have been the one that screamed at her. Sure, he was a surly fellow with a checkered past marked by violence, but when you got down to it, who had the most motive to kill him? The answer was simple, the girl he beat and humiliated all those years ago. Maybe if Sarah had reached out to her, made any kind of effort at all, then things may have been different. All these people would still be alive. Maybe not.

When Sarah arrived at the Plattsburgh barracks, there was a throng of reporters in the parking lot. They swarmed her car like ants at a picnic. So many questions were shouted at her that she could not understand any of them. Sarah began to wonder how she was to get from the car to the entrance and decided to park the car right next to the section of sidewalk that led to the main door.

She turned the car off and got out to a chorus of people shouting her name. She was fairly certain one reporter accused her of being responsible for the death of Monica.

She entered the barracks and went directly to Jessica's office. For once Jessica was not alone in her office, the department psychologist was also there. Tim McEvoy had been the department shrink for 20 years. He was responsible for dealing with troopers that had gone through a traumatic experience. He was a short man coming in at just under 5 feet tall. His short gray hair was thinning and he had a comb-over on top. His bifocal glasses were always perched at the tip of his nose, his icy blue eyes peering into your soul. Today, Tim was dressed in a monochromatic suit. His black jacket and silk shirt nearly blended together. Were it not for the gleam of his buttons one might not know that there were two separate garments. His tie was even the same hue as his shirt. Tim's pencil thin mustache curled up to match the smile he wore upon his face when he saw Sarah enter the room.

"What the hell is going on?" asked Sarah. "Do you think I need a shrink?"

"Sarah," said Tim. "My presence here has nothing to do with our estimation of your mental capacity. Neither does it have anything to do with our concern about your mental well-being. I am simply here to try and help you remember the name of the girl."

"We could find no record of the fight," said Jessica. "It is almost as if that girl never existed. There were no references about any fight or a girl that was hospitalized at the end of your third-grade year. Whoever she is, she was smart enough to go erase herself from your past."

Sarah looked confused, which was starting to be the norm in her life. Once again it seemed as if the killer was one step ahead of them. Sarah finished entering Jessica's office and allowed the door to shut behind her. She started pacing back and forth in the small space in front of Jessica's desk. She looked at Tim as if to ask what the next step was.

"Please, have a seat and we will try to see if we can divine the name of this person," said Tim.

Without saying a word Sarah sat down in the proffered chair in front of Jessica's desk. Jessica took her seat and Tim sat beside Sarah. He took a moment to study her, trying to ascertain how susceptible she might be to hypnosis.

"Sarah, please close your eyes and take a deep soothing breath," said Tim. "We must relax your body to the point where we can access your hidden memories. Slowly breathe in through your nose and exhale through your mouth."

Sarah did as she was asked by Tim. As she breathed in and out slowly and deeply, she could feel the tension leaving her body. It did not matter how calm she got; she could not remember the name of the girl. Sarah could feel the calmness being replaced by frustration. The harder she tried to remember the name of the girl, the more frustrated she got.

To his credit, Tim was able to sense that Sarah was getting frustrated and that the exercise was futile. Before things got too tense, he rose from the chair and put a hand on Sarah's shoulder.

"That will do Sarah," he said. "It would seem that your mind has cut off this memory for some reason. You cannot achieve the level of calmness that one would need in order to be hypnotized, which in my estimation would be the only way to recall these memories."

"Then what will we do?" asked Jessica.

"That is the question," said Sarah.

"In a perfect world, we could try hypnosis, a method that I do not believe you are the best candidate for, or weeks or therapy, an approach that we have no time to perform. So, I have nothing to offer," said Tim.

Tim, sensing that he could be of no more help, excused himself from the room. The two women were now alone to try and puzzle together who the girl was, ultimately revealing the identity of the killer.

Chapter 35

Although everyone at the station had been in shock and upset over the murder of Monica, Meghan Goode had not shared in the misery. She had been the second choice every time there was a good story, Monica being the perennial favorite.

Meghan was not as striking of features as was Monica to be sure. She was six feet tall and quite skinny, to the point where people who did not know she had a rapacious metabolism thought she was bulimic. Her curly brown hair took a lot to manage, and if she was rushed, it would look like a rat's nest. Her grey eyes were dull, and her pale skin was covered so thickly by freckles that in spots that her skin looked patchy. This she hid with make-up the best that she could.

What she did have over Monica was a rapier wit and a keen nose for when someone was hiding something. When Meghan had started out, she worked for a local paper, The Burlington Free Press. She had broken several big stories, including the mayor's affair. That was what had gotten her the job at Fox, exactly two weeks before Monica came on. Since that day, Meghan had been relegated to research to utilize her nose for the truth.

With the removal of Monica, she was once again thrust into the lead reporter position and sent to the Plattsburgh barracks to await the arrival of Sarah. This story was too good to relent on. Viewership had gone through the roof with the livestream. As abhorrent as it was, murder made for great ratings.

She had gotten to the barracks at just after eight that morning, and so began her watch. She rode in with the cameraman, Les Wescot. Les was in his sixties and with skin the color of Mahogony. His face was free of any wrinkles except around his eyes when he smiled, which he did often. He was of both average height and build, and always dressed in jeans and a button-down shirt. Today's shirt was black, he said it was in honor of Monica's passing.

They had shot a couple of check-ins while they waited, but there was little else to do. This was the part that she hated, waiting. She had some hard-hitting questions at the ready, and given her height, she knew she would be able to talk over everyone else there.

There was a hum of excitement that rushed through the crowd of reporters just before eleven. One of the network guys that was closest to the road shouted, "She's coming." Meghan and Les jumped from the news van and made their way to the front of the group. She quickly talked into her microphone, knowing that someone at the station would be listening.

"We have a positive ID that Sarah is here. We need to cut in live immediately," she said.

Steve's voice sounded over her earpiece. "You've got it, going live in ten seconds."

Steve counted down in her ear while Meghan got herself ready to talk into the camera that was pointed in her face. When the countdown hit zero, she began to talk.

"Meghan Goode here for Fox 44. I am outside of the Plattsburgh State Police Barrack where Sarah Barney has just arrived. Her car is stopping now, we are going to see if we can get a statement from her."

Les, ever the competent cameraman panned over to the cruiser that had just stopped. A chorus of voices started to shout out questions at its former occupant. Sarah looked like she had been dragged through dirt for days as she glanced wearily at the group of reporters.

Meghan saw her opportunity to try and get her attention. "Detective Barney," she shouted louder than everyone else. "Meghan Goode, Fox 44. How does it feel to be responsible for the death of Monica Trudeau?"

Sarah paused mid-step at this but did not turn around. After that moment's hesitation, she continued making her way into the barracks. Meghan shrugged it off, at least she got a reaction from Sarah, no one else could say as much.

Les panned the camera back at Meghan. "It would seem that Detective Barney did not want to address our questions just yet. I assure you all that I will be waiting here for her to depart to see if she will be more willing. For now, I am Meghan Goode, Fox 44."

Again, Steve's voice came over her earpiece. "That's a wrap Meg. Good question."

Chapter 36

Dick arrived at the location 20 minutes after Sam had left his office. He had spotted her Jeep from quite a way away and accelerated to get there sooner. His body almost quivered with the anticipation of what was going to happen. Sure, Dick had been a man whore his whole life, but he had never before had sex in the woods with a woman.

Sam had not told him where exactly she would be waiting for him, but Dick saw a narrow path leading into the woods from in front of the Jeep. It did not take a rocket scientist to figure out that that is where he would find Sam. He started down the path unsure but excited. After a few steps, the sounds of the town were replaced by those of the woods. Dick heard the birds chirping and the small animals rustling through the brush. What Dick did not hear however was Sam sneaking up behind him, syringe in her hand.

She leapt on his back, wrapping her right arm around his forehead while her left hand jammed the needle into his neck. The cocktail acted swiftly, as it always did, and Dick fell to the ground with a thud. He was still semiconscious when Sam bent over to drag him away.

As Sam grabbed Dicks ankles, she looked around to be sure that there was no one watching. She dragged Dick further into the woods towards her secret location. His body was about to join the myriad others that she had hidden among the dead brush and branches. She would not be torturing Dick as she had her most recent victims, instead she would wait for him to regain consciousness and then take his life.

The traps that she had been setting were more for Sarah's benefit than her own. Although Sam could not deny that she took pleasure in watching her traps tear people apart, she found it much more pleasurable to end a life by her own hand.

As she dragged Dick along the trail, branches and exposed roots snagged against his clothes and skin, tearing holes in both. She did not concern herself with the injuries that he and his clothing were sustaining, instead she found her thoughts returning to Sarah and the police. Sam could not help but wonder how close they were to discovering her identity. She knew that she had taken enough precautions in the past to keep who she was a mystery. That did not mean, however, that Sarah would not have an epiphany and remember the little girl who was obsessed with her.

Ten years ago, Sam had gone through the trouble of accessing the school records via the internet and deleting any trace of who she was. She even went one step further and tracked down any mention of the beating that she sustained at Tommy's hands. She had long been meaning to go to the library and find out whether or not any microfiche existed with the story that the local paper ran. It had not seemed like a priority and given the fact that Sarah and the police were so far behind her now, she had still not done so. Now, the more she thought about it, the more worried she became that she had left the proverbial needle in a haystack. She knew that Sarah was of higher intelligence than most, and she was an exemplary police detective, but Sam could not decide if she was intelligent enough to find said needle.

Sam knew well enough that life without suspense and excitement was not a life worth living. She decided that the risk in which she had placed herself was acceptable.

Without realizing it, she had arrived at the spot where Dick would meet his end. She had been certain to give him a low enough dose of the drug cocktail that it would wear off within the hour. This meant that she had a lot to do and in very little time. As always, she had a pack slung over her shoulders that was full of all the tools she would need.

Sam released Dick's ankles and unslung her pack. She crouched down and placed the pack on the ground. Unzipping it, she removed a thirty-foot length of paracord with which she would tie up Dick. Located at what she liked to call the entrance to her killing grounds was a large oak tree. The tree had a unique feature, a large limb that branched off almost exactly a forty-degree angle. The branch was just far enough off the ground that it made the perfect place for Sam to hang a body.

She quickly bound Dick's hands together with the cord. She then threw the other end of the cord over the limb. Pulling on the cord, Dick slowly got closer to the tree and then ended up hanging in midair. Sam wrapped the loose end of the cord around the closest tree several times before securing it there with a Palomar knot. Once he was hanging in the air, removing Dick's clothes was easy.

She had time to kill and was still dressed to impress, so she took this opportunity to run back to her Jeep. She always kept a change of clothes in the compartment in the trunk. Given her activities, the risk of becoming covered in blood was high. One could simply not go around in public covered in blood and not raise any suspicions. It only took her a couple of minutes to change and head back down the trail.

Sam returned to her pack and withdrew her favorite knife. It was a six-inch long dagger that came to an almost needle point tip. She closed the distance between her and Dick and circled his helpless body. Although he was unconscious and would not feel the pain of what she did, Sam could not resist inflicting an initial injury. One thing about Dick that his parents got right was his name. He was the embodiment of a dick, and he was exceptionally well endowed. Knowing full well that the size of his penis was Dick's largest source of pride, Sam grabbed his limp member in her left hand and plunged the dagger through it.

To her surprise, the pain from the dagger ruining his genitalia was enough to rouse Dick from his drug induced slumber. He began to scream in agony and flail about at the end of the rope. Sam felt her adrenaline kick in at the thrill of causing him so much pain.

"Oh, my darling," said Sam, "you are about to learn the true meaning of pain. All these years I have had to suffer your advances, your unwanted touching, and you undressing me with your eyes. After today I will suffer you no more. I want you to know that I am going to kill you in a most heinous way, but first I'm going to make you hurt."

Dick began to scream for help. This elicited a round of laughter from Sam. She knew that there was no one close enough to hear him and allowed him to scream and cry like the bitch that he was. Accompanying the screams and the tears was an ample supply of snot. As Sam watched, Dick's face became soaked with both. She slowly started to circle him, like a pack of lions circled a downed animal, preparing to dive in for the kill.

She reached out with lightning speed and sliced a gash in the middle of his back. This caused Dick to flail about and scream with renewed fervor. Much like a cat that had played too long with the mouse, Sam began to grow bored with the sounds Dick made. She stopped circling him and stood facing him. She could see the horror in his eyes. Reaching out with her right hand, she plunged the dagger into the flesh where his right thigh met his belly. She swiftly dragged the dagger down towards his feet, the blade exiting at his knee. She did the same to his left leg, surprised at how much blood flowed from the wounds. She knew she had not hit the femoral artery, but also understood that at the rate with which he was losing blood, Dick would soon expire from exsanguination.

Sam rapidly and viciously lashed out with her dagger. The blade slicing through his flesh and muscle with ease. His screams became softer and before long, Dick had died. Sam had attacked with such viciousness that she found herself breathing heavily and her arms felt as though they weighed thousands of pounds. Covered in blood and gore, she collapsed on the ground, her legs unable to support her weight at the time. This death had been a long time coming, and she had exhausted herself while executing it. She knew she needed a few minutes to recuperate.

As Sam sat there waiting for her strength to return, she was overcome with a renewed desire to claim lives in person. Killing Dick had been an experience more pleasurable than any she had had in quite some time. Sam was unsure about how to proceed. She was not yet finished toying with Sarah, yet she knew that she had to give in to her desires. She thought, perhaps she could do both. Sam could see no reason why she would have to stop claiming lives by her own hand and stop toying with Sarah. She stood with her decision firmly in her mind. Sam would kill those she wanted and set traps to murder those associated with Sarah. She was, after all, unstoppable.

Sam untied the knot and allowed Dick's body to fall unceremoniously to the ground. It made a loud wet thumping noise as it contacted the firm ground. About forty feet from her killing tree was the spot where she dumped all of the bodies. Sam set about the task of dragging the body and all of the parts that had fallen to the ground to her cache. Dick's body snagged on every catchpoint there was between the tree and the dumping ground. Even in death he tasked her. When Sam arrived at the dumping spot, to vent the last of her frustrations with a human being that used to be Dick, she used her foot to shove him down the hole.

Sam gathered up all her tools and placed them back in her pack. As she did so her thoughts drifted back to Sarah. She knew now who would be her next victim. With a smile upon her lips, she headed back to her Jeep, she had so much to plan for. First, it would appear that she would need to redon her slutty clothes. She undressed and tossed her gore-soaked clothes down the hole behind dick. Returning to her Jeep, she pulled out a couple of bottles of water and used them to rinse his blood from the parts of her body that it had covered. It would not do any good to change her clothes but still have blood on her.

Once dressed and clean, she drove Dick's car as far up the trail as it would manage. She knew that she would have to return later to dispose of it properly. She could not leave it out in the open though, so this was her only option at this time.

Chapter 37

Dick's disappearance did not go unnoticed. Kevin Sevard had gone to pay his rent and found the office locked, which it never was during the day. Thinking that this was beyond odd, he went to the apartment where Dick lived, one door down from the office. He knocked at first and when he got no response, he tried the knob. The door was not locked.

Kevin was a small man at just over five feet tall. He was rail thin with less muscle than fat on his bones. His blue eyes were dull as was the mop of brown hair upon his head. His face was perpetually covered in a five o'clock shadow which did a pretty good job at hiding his sunken cheeks. He was wearing the same clothes that he had put on a week ago, a pair of jeans and a button-up plaid shirt. He was barefoot, which was the norm. Kevin was a long-time heroin user. With the exception of the exorbitant rent that he paid every month, all of his money went to support his habit. What little food he did consume was usually provided by whatever person was hosting a party.

Kevin looked around nervously, as this presented a unique opportunity. Dick's car was not parked in its usual spot. but he was not answering his door. This meant that Dick had left but forgot to lock his door. Uncharacteristic for sure, but not something that did not happen to people every day. An unlocked door proved to be too much temptation and Kevin entered the apartment.

Dick's place was no different from any of the other converted hotel rooms. Walking through the front door brought you to the living room/bedroom. There was a full-sized bed and a Loveseat in the room, along with a dresser upon which sat a flat screen television set. Both the carpet and the walls had seen better days. The kitchen was comprised of a microwave and a mini-fridge with one cabinet, a small sink and a stovetop. In the back, left corner of the room was a door that Kevin knew would lead to the bathroom.

Kevin was not interested in that room. He knew that if there was anything of value to be found, it would be in the small space housing the living area and kitchenette. He knew that he could get five dollars for the TV, and maybe the same for the fridge and microwave, he was after bigger game than that. He wanted to be the one throwing the next party. Maybe he could even get that slut Vanessa that always traded her body to their dealer to put out for him for once.

He went over to the dresser and began pulling out the drawers. They were predictably full of clothes. With carelessness born of a hunger that was never satiated, Keven ripped the clothes from the drawers and flung them onto the floor.

Kevin found nothing of value within the drawers. Desperate, he spun towards the love seat and pulled the cushions off, hoping to find something of value that had fallen from a pocket and secreted itself there. With the exception of a couple of quarters and three pieces of gum, there were no treasures to be found.

Sensing that his party was rapidly dissolving before it ever happened, Kevin went into a rage. How could a man that squandered so much money have absolutely nothing of value in his apartment? He punched the cabinet, shattering the cheap wood that comprised the door, kicked the refrigerator over on its side. His impotent rage then centered on the bed. Reaching exhaustion already, he barely had the strength to flip the mattress off the box spring. What lay hidden beneath the mattress was beyond his wildest dreams.

Kevin fell atop the box spring, surrounding himself with the piles of money that had previously been hidden there. He started to laugh and cry at the same time. There was surely enough cash here for him to throw many parties.

Kevin rolled over and started to gather up the piles of cash. He did not know exactly how he was going to get it all out of the apartment, so he stopped to search the place for something to carry it in. He was swiftly rewarded, finding several reusable shopping bags within the ruined cabinet.

He had three filled before all of the cash had been collected. He forgot about trying to take the appliances to fence and headed directly for the door. His mind was so busy planning the festivities for that night that he failed to notice the group of tenants that had gathered in front of the open door to Dick's apartment.

Kevin had become so excited about the large sums of money that he had discovered that he had begun to shout with joy. His faculties had been so diminished from years of drug abuse that he had not even realized that he was making so much noise. The shouts had caused everyone that was within earshot to come and investigate what it was that had elicited such a vocal display.

The small throng of people understood at once what had happened when they saw Kevin exit the apartment. As he made his way to his small domicile, he further failed to notice that Ken Jenkins had his cellphone up to his ear and was talking to the police.

Ken was the son of old Claudia Jenkins. He did not live at the Villa but was there daily to check on his mom. Standing at just over six and a half feet tall, he towered over most people. This fact did not make him stand out though, rather it was his albinism that caused anyone unused to seeing one so afflicted to take notice. Because of this condition, Ken wore hats that had a brim that went all the way around it and were wide enough to cast a shadow as far down his body as possible. Today, he wore a straw hat and his usual brown trench coat. His pale blue eyes that were run through with red blood vessels followed Kevin as he went around the building.

"Yes, I think that he may have killed Dick," he said to the officer on the other end of the phone.

Chapter 38

Officer Luciana Riviera had been in Peru grabbing lunch when dispatch radioed for her. It seemed like every time she had visited this specific McDonald's, she was interrupted before she could eat her food. Luck was almost on her side today as the call came through before she had ordered for once.

"Riviera here," she replied to dispatch.

"We have a call about unusual activity down at the Villa in Keeseville. Possible homicide. GPS says you are the closest to town, not to mention you assisted on the Mountaintop Killer case. This might be related," said the voice from dispatch. Riviera did not recognize who it was.

"Roger that," she replied. "I am about ten minutes out from there. On my way."

Riviera flipped on her lights and siren and pulled out of the line of cars that were awaiting service. She turned left out of the McDonalds parking lot and headed towards Route Twenty-Two. She knew that that was the quickest route. Since it was the middle of the day, the traffic was light, and she made good time to the Villa.

Riviera pulled into the front of the large parking lot and stopped where there was a large crowd of people. A tall, albino man approached her car with an almost excited look on his face. Riviera rolled her window down a couple of inches and instructed him to wait for her by the hood of the cruiser. He complied instantly and that put her at ease. She did not know who the Mountaintop Killer was, and this guy gave her the creeps.

Riviera shut off the engine and got out of the cruiser. She surveyed the crowd, looking for what exactly she did not know. Before she approached the man, she keyed on her microphone on her walkie to let dispatch know she was at the scene.

"Dispatch, this is one-ten," she said. "I am at the Villa. There is a man here that looks eager to talk to me, I am assuming he is a witness. Do me a favor, send a second unit. There is quite the crowd here."

Dispatch immediately responded, "Copy that one-ten. Be aware that the closest unit has an ETA of fifteen minutes."

Riviera replied with "Copy", before approaching the man.

"Before we get started, do you have an ID?" she asked.

The man pulled out his wallet, taking note that her right hand was resting on her pistol. He handed the ID to Riviera who looked it over thoroughly before handing it back.

"OK Mr. Jenkins, tell me what you know," she said.

Ken recounted everything that he had witnessed, including Kevin leaving the apartment with several shopping bags that were stuffed with what looked like piles of cash.

Chapter 39

Sam approached the Villa with a mind on showering again and then taking a nap. Noticing the cruiser parked by Dick's apartment helped drive those thoughts from her mind. She slowed down as she passed, recognizing the cop. It was the one that had helped Sarah more than once. This was too good to be true.

She ignored her instinct to flee and pulled into the main lot. A quick look in her mirror told her that her face was free of any signs of the carnage that she had just caused. She parked her Jeep and exited, slowly making her way towards the crowd. Sam was about to have some fun and capture her next target at the same time.

Sam stealthily made her way close enough to the trooper and the albino to overhear the conversation. The albino claimed that he saw Kevin leaving Dick's apartment with several bags full of things and that he even thought he might have killed Dick. In spite of herself, Sam snorted. This caused Riviera to look at her.

"Something amuses you?" the cop asked.

Sam rolled with the situation and said, "Well yeah, anyone that knows Kevin knows he is nothing more than a junkie and is not capable of killing anyone."

Riviera looked back at Ken and dismissed him before walking around the car to get closer to Sam.

"Who are you, exactly?" she asked.

"I am exactly Kevin's neighbor," she replied. "My name is Sam Ryan. I can take you to his place if you want."

Riviera looked Sam up and down, sizing up any possible threat and then glanced at her watch. Her back-up was still around ten minutes away. She did not think that this petite woman would be any threat to her, so she nodded and gestured with her hand for Sam to lead the way.

This was a dangerous game that Sam was about to start. If she followed through with her plan, she would not be able to return home. In anticipation of something like this, Sam had long ago made herself a bug-out-bag. That combined with what she had in her Jeep would make life on the run easier. She knew that she would need her Jeep close by though, there would be no easy way to move the unconscious cop from her place to the Jeep in the front of the lot.

"Mind if we drive around in my Jeep?" she asked.

Riviera nodded her permission and the two got in the Jeep. The drive around took less than a minute. Sam parked in her driveway claiming that it was Kevin's.

They exited the Jeep and Riviera turned to Sam. "Wait right here, I will go in and see if he is home."

Sam nodded and watched Riviera as she approached the door to her apartment. The cop was making this all too easy.

Riviera knocked on the door and announced who she was. There was of course no answer, so she knocked again. While the cop's attention was focused on the door, Sam pulled a fresh syringe from the mesh compartment in her door and crept closer. When Riviera kicked in the door, as Sam knew she would, she rushed forward and stuck the needle in Riviera's neck.

Sam had not counted on the cop having superior reflexes and was caught by Riviera's elbow on her jaw. This sent her flying backwards before she could depress the plunger and introduce the drugs into Riviera's system.

Riviera spun around with her weapon drawn and aimed it at Sam. "You bitch," she spat out as she reached up to ascertain what had caused the pain in her neck. Sam was trying to figure out how she would escape when the cop showed how stupid she was. Instead of slowly checking her neck, her adrenaline caused her hand to move hastily. She contacted the syringe with enough force to depress the plunger and snap the needle off.

A look of shock spread across Riviera's face as she fell to the ground. The clock was now ticking. Sam had to retrieve her bag and load the cop into the Jeep before any other police arrived. She scrambled to her feet and ran into her apartment. Her bag was right where she left it under her bed. She grabbed it and ran back to her Jeep, tossing the bag on the passenger seat. She then went to the cop and dragged her limp body to the trunk. Mustering up what strength she had left, Sam lifted her into the trunk and shut the glass and door.

Sam was now sweating profusely despite the cool temperature and the skimpiness of her clothing. She ran back into her place and gathered up some extra clothes, placing them next to her bag in the Jeep. There was one more calculated risk she had to take before leaving and she hoped that there was enough time to execute it.

She had been telling the truth about where Kevin lived. He was in the very next cabin, ten feet away. She covered that distance and burst through the door as she pulled a knife from her boot. It was small but would prove effective against the junkie.

Kevin looked up at the intruder with shock but did not have any time to react before the small blade slammed into his throat. His eyes went wide but the blade had punctured his trachea, making it impossible for him to utter a sound.

As she had suspected, Sam saw that the bags he had taken from Dick's apartment contained money, and a lot of it at that. She grabbed the three bags and ran back to her Jeep.

Sam had had the foresight to leave the Jeep running, so she climbed in behind the wheel and reversed out of her driveway. She started to drive around to the front of the Villa where she could access the main road when she saw the flashing lights that indicated the cop's back-up had arrived. She sighed as she knew she was leaving just in the nick of time. She would have to turn left and head towards Plattsburgh in order to avoid the new arrivals, but that did not matter.

With her next victim in the trunk, Sam drove as casually as possible and turned onto the main road. She would find someplace secluded enough to kill this cop. She would forgo the trap and just do it the old-fashioned way. This last thought brought a smile to her face. So deep in this fantasy was she, that she failed to see a pair of pale blue eyes watching her go.

Chapter 40

Jessica's phone began to ring and she glanced at it. Seeing that it was from dispatch, she picked up the receiver.

"Yes, what is it?" she asked.

Sarah could not hear what was being said, but from the look on the chief's face, it was not good. She waited as patiently as she could for the conversation to end.

"When did this happen?" Jessica asked. There was a pause before she said, "Alright, we will handle it."

Jessica hung up the phone and looked Sarah in the eyes. "We think that the killer has taken Riviera."

Sarah felt her jaw go a little slack as she listened to Jessica retelling what dispatch had just said. This was all getting to be too much.

"Did anyone find any clues there?" she asked.

"No," replied Jessica. "It would seem that the killer just fled the scene with Riviera. The trooper that showed up as back-up thinks that they left in a Jeep Wrangler, black and two-door. He asked around and we have a name. Samantha..."

"Ryan," Sarah blurted out. "Though she prefers being called Sam. I remember her now!"

Jessica looked pained to say what she was about to say. "I am happy that you do, but it is a little late for that now. Riviera was responding to a robbery with the possibility of a homicide. She is in the wind and we have no leads"

Sarah looked dejected. "We need to go there and see the scene for ourselves, well, at least I do," she said.

Jessica nodded in agreement. "First, we need to use that group of reporters to our advantage. You and I will go out, let them know another one of our own has been taken and give them a description of Sam. Anything you can remember would be helpful."

Sarah understood by that statement that Jessica would be the one doing all of the talking to the reporters, which was fine by her.

"I have not seen her in a very long time," she said. "But back then, she was shorter than average, had natural blonde hair and green eyes. The person we saw on the mountain yesterday looked to be around five-foot to five-five."

Jessica nodded and led the way out of her office, down the short hallway and out of the barracks. As they both anticipated, the group of reporters was still lingering, hoping for some bit of salacious information with which to further their careers. Did they have one juicy story coming their way.

Upon seeing the women come out, there was a chorus of shouts, all saying Sarah's name. Jessica took the lead and when they were within fifteen feet of the group, held up her right hand to silence them.

"For those that do not know, I am the chief, Jessica Momsen," she said. "We will be making a statement, but not taking any questions at this time."

With that, a murmur ran through the crowd. The only other sound was that of cameras snapping pictures.

"At approximately eleven-thirty this morning, a trooper by the name of Luciana Riviera was at the Villa in Keeseville to investigate a robbery. She had radioed for back-up, but before the second unit had arrived, she was taken. Riviera is of Latin-American descent. She has both brown hair and eyes. She is five feet, six inches tall with a stout build."

"We believe that the identity of the person that took her is one Samantha, Sam Ryan. It is also believed that Ms. Ryan is the person that you have all so eloquently dubbed the Mountaintop Killer. Sam is a resident of the Villa. She is believed to be around five feet to five feet and five inches tall, slight of build with blonde hair and green eyes. She is also believed to be armed and very dangerous. Trooper Riviera's weapon was not left at the scene, so we know that Ms. Ryan has at least this as a weapon."

"Ms. Ryan is believed to be driving a black, two-door Jeep Wrangler with New York tags."

"Now, despite her size, Ms. Ryan has been capable of overcoming and subduing many people, all of them larger than her, some substantially so. The M.E. has not been able to narrow down what, if any substance is being used to help her control these people. Ms. Ryan is clearly very strong for her size, as she has hiked up some very challenging mountains with these people, known to be unconscious in tow."

"It is because of this and the fact that she is armed that we ask anyone that sees her not to approach. Please call 911 immediately."

"That is all for now, please get this out on the air as soon as possible and help us find out trooper."

With her statement complete, Jessica and Sarah started to walk towards the car Sarah had been driving. There was a cacophony of questions being shouted at them, despite the fact that Jessica had said there would be no answers to any. One voice however, again rang out above all of the rest.

"Meghan Goode, live with Fox 44," she shouted. "Isn't it interim chief? Detective Barney, since this seems to be a personal vendetta against you, why not just give this killer what she wants and allow her to take your life?"

This question hit Sarah like a hammer to the chest. She was filled with an instant rage. She had already lost someone that she was close to, and now another person that she considered a friend had been taken and was most likely already dead. She shouted something unintelligible and turned to charge at the reporter. Luckily for both of them, Jessica had anticipated this response and grabbed Sarah by her one good arm and restrained her.

"She is not worth it," she said in as soothing a tone as she could manage. Sarah did not fight to free herself from Jessica's grip, instead shooting the reporter what she called her death stare.

Sarah allowed herself to be guided to the cruiser and climbed in behind the wheel. The engine fired after two cranks and Sarah turned on the lights and pulled away from the sidewalk.

"That fucking bitch!" she screamed when she had put enough distance between them and the reporters.

"How dare she presume to talk to me that way?" This was a rhetorical question, but it was one that Jessica felt the need to answer.

"Sarah, she was just trying to elicit a reaction from you," she said. "That is what reporters do. You are just so good at what you do that you have never had any bad press before."

Sarah knew that she was right and did not reply. Sarah chose to remain silent for the trip to Keeseville. Her head was not in a good place and she also knew that Jessica had more of an interest in Riviera than as an employee. Although Jessica never said anything, Sarah had known her for long enough to understand that there was something there. She did not know if it was reciprocal on Riviera's end, but that did not diminish what the chief felt. She decided against giving voice to any false hope statements about how Riviera would be alright.

They arrived at the Villa after twelve minutes of silence. Sarah drove the car around to the back where the trooper had indicated Sam's cabin was located. She pulled into the driveway and noted immediately that the door was still open. There were two pieces of police tape across the opening, but that was all.

Something here seemed off to Sarah, so she remained in the car and ran through everything she had seen while driving in. Some small detail that was missed by her conscious mind was tugging at her.

"Did you notice anything off when we pulled in?" she asked Jessica.

Jessica thought for a moment but ended up shaking her head in the negative. "Maybe I could talk you through it," she said.

Sarah nodded that this might work and closed her eyes.

"OK, we pulled in the main lot and drove to the side driveway, what did you see there?" asked Jessica.

Sarah thought for a moment before answering. "There was a door open in the center of the motel, also marked with police tape. Must have been Dick's apartment. Riviera's cruiser was still out front, lights flashing. There was nothing of any consequence in the side driveway."

"Alright," said Jessica, "What about the other dwellings on the way here. Was there anything out of sorts?"

Sarah started to recall all of the surrounding cabins and trailers. The one closest to Sam's cabin, the door was slightly ajar. Without speaking, Sarah exited the cruiser and pulled her weapon from its holster. Jessica followed her lead.

The cabin door was only ten feet from the door to Sam's place, the pair covered the distance swiftly. Sarah used hand signals to indicate she would open the door while Jessica covered it with her gun. Jessica nodded her understanding.

With as much speed as she could manage, Sarah leaned in and shoved the door open, pulling her body back and away from any potential threat. The doorway was empty, the ambient light spilled into the cramped living area.

Sarah felt her heart sink a bit when she caught sight of the body on the bed. She entered the cabin with her weapon trained in front of her and Jessica at her back. It only took a moment to search the rest of the cabin and confirm that they were alone.

"Kevin, I presume," said Jessica.

"Most likely," said Sarah. "My thoughts are that she knew Kevin here robbed Dick's apartment and wanted the cash. This will make it easier for her to stay off the radar."

Jessica nodded. "That is what I was thinking too. The question is, where do we go from here?"

Sarah thought for a minute before answering. "Well, we know that when Sam takes someone, they are going to be killed. We know that she enjoys setting people in these homemade traps, but that she also will take a life by her own hand. Kidnapping Riviera seemed like a crime of opportunity to me."

Jessica thought she knew where Sarah was going with her line of thought but still asked, "What are you trying to say?"

"I am saying that Sam is probably not going to place Riviera into one of her traps. There were no notes left behind, no clue as to where she would be taking her. She plans on murdering Riviera with her bare hands. We need to find her, and soon," Sarah concluded.

Jessica pulled out her phone and dialed the barracks. "This is the chief. We need an APB on that Wrangler owned by Samantha Ryan. We believe that she means to kill Riviera and soon. Alert all agencies and departments. I do not care what the plate is on the car, she could switch them. If anyone sees an older model two-door black Wrangler, I want it stopped and the occupants treated as armed."

Jessica ended the call and the two headed back towards the cruiser. Neither one knew where to start looking, but they both knew that action was far more productive than inaction.

Sarah stopped short of the doorway. Standing on the steps of Sam's apartment was a very tall, pale man. Her gun was still in her hand, but she restrained herself from taking aim at him. Though it was possible that Sam had a partner, it was unlikely as most serial killers worked alone.

"My name is Ken," he said. "I am the one that called in the initial call. No one will listen to me."

"Hi Ken, I am Sarah Barney, what do you want to say?" she asked.

"I know it's not much, but I know which direction Sam went," he answered.

Chapter 41

Sam had been driving for twenty minutes and she knew that she was pressed for time. There was no telling exactly how much of the drug cocktail had made it into Riviera's system, which meant that she could regain consciousness at any moment. She had lost some of her control over things, but that seemed to exhilarate rather than frighten her.

She found herself in the outskirts of the hamlet of Saranac. It was a small town in both size and population. Known as the gateway to the Adirondacks, Sam knew that there were plenty of wooded, secluded areas. There was an especially large swathe of woods behind the business Adirondack Hardwoods, located on Chazy Lake Road. If she remembered correctly, that was also the section of town where the Corners Brook flowed.

She knew that the brook would be the best spot to kill Riviera. Flowing water destroyed evidence and also afforded her a place to clean up. She would also be able to put on some real clothes, something she had not yet done.

Sam drove down Water Street until she saw the sign for Chazy Lake Road. She turned left and arrived at the hardwood store after three-quarters of a mile. Off to the left and behind the store was a field that would allow her to hide her Jeep in the trees. Sam just hoped that no one would see her drive over there.

The drive across the field was bumpy and although the Jeep was built for this kind of terrain, Riviera was still tossed around in the back. Sam saw the perfect opening in the trees where she could secret the Jeep. She pulled in, shut of the engine and raced around to the back to ensure that Riviera was still out. Sam opened the back gate, lifted the glass and poked Riviera in the ribs with her finger as hard as she could. The cop did not even flinch, allowing Sam to relax for the first time since taking her.

Sam reached into her trunk and retrieved some clothes that were more appropriate for the temperatures this time of year. She quickly slid out of the small top and skirt that she wore and pulled on a pair of Carhart jeans and a plain grey sweatshirt. The last item she strapped on was her belt, making sure to attach her sheathed knife before looping the end through the buckle. She then grabbed Riviera's sidearm. This she tucked in the waist band of her jeans at her back.

Sam then reached into the back of her Jeep and pulled Riviera's limp body out and slung it over her shoulder. This was an unexplored section of wood to Sam, so she made her way slowly towards the sound of water. Luckily, she had stumbled upon a path where other people had come through before, perhaps to fish.

Her luck held out and the area by the brook was free of anyone, fishing or otherwise. It was not good fishing weather anyway, but one never knew what they might stumble upon in an unfamiliar area.

Sam started to look around for the perfect spot to place Riviera when she felt a sharp pain in her right thigh. She stumbled and fell, dropping Riviera in the process. Somewhere in the back of her mind, she noted that there was no thud accompanying the body hitting the ground. She thought quickly and rolled away to the left and turned her head up.

Shock played across her face when she saw a fully conscious Riviera standing a few feet from her, Sam's favorite knife in her right hand.

"That's right bitch," Riviera spat out. "Today is not the day that I die."

Sam could feel the blood pouring from her leg. The wound was not mortal, but it would slow her down immensely. A smile spread across her lips before she spoke.

"I know something that you don't," she said.

Before Riviera could react, Sam reached into her back pocket and withdrew Riviera's gun. The cop had been too hasty in grabbing the knife and attacking her. Riviera started to turn away, but Sam fired three rounds in rapid succession. All three bullets hit their mark and Riviera was thrown to the ground from the impact. Her head bounced off the ground and she remained motionless.

Sam wanted to kill her, now more than ever. She needed to tend to her leg though. If the rate of bleeding was not slowed, she knew she would eventually pass out from blood loss. Shakily, she got to her feet and limped over to Riviera's prone body. She bent over as quickly as she could and retrieved her knife, returning it to the sheath.

"Perhaps you get to live another day," she said before turning to limp back to her Jeep.

The trip into the woods and to the brook took ten minutes, the return trip took almost thirty. By the time Sam climbed in behind the steering wheel, her right shoe was so soaked with blood that it made a squishing sound with every step. She was beginning to feel lightheaded and knew that there was not a lot of time before she lost consciousness. She was overcome by a sense of urgency, but not just about the bleeding. She knew that someone had most likely heard the gunshots. Even though it was hunting season, shooting this close to houses and businesses was not legal. That meant that the police were most likely on their way.

She first needed to stop the bleeding and had only one solution at hand. Unsheathing her knife first, she then dug around the compartment under the armrest and withdrew a lighter. Flicking the roller caused a small flame to be created. This she would use to heat the blade of her knife in the hopes that she could use it to cauterize the wound.

Sam allowed the blade to pass through the flame for five minutes before ripping the hole in her pants larger and placing the hot metal against her wound. The pain was both excruciating and exquisite at the same time.

It took Sam a few minutes to regain her composure enough to start the engine of her Jeep. She was about to back out of her hiding spot when some movement from her right caught her attention. Riviera had made it back to her feet and made it out of the woods. There was blood leaking from her lips and a large red stain on her grey uniform top. Sam had gotten lucky with at least one of the bullets.

Riviera watched as the Jeep backed out from the small pocket in the trees where it had been hidden. She realized that her radio was still clipped to her belt and shoulder. She reached up with her right hand and keyed on the mic, hoping that it would go through to dispatch.

"Dispatch, this is Riviera," she said. "I have been shot and need immediate assistance."

The last part she said as she fell to her knees. Darkness started to overtake her vision. She did not know where she was or how to direct help her way. She knew in the back of her mind that she was going to die, alone, and probably go undiscovered for months.

As she grew weaker from blood loss, Riviera fell forward, her face slamming into the hard ground. The part of her mind that was not clouded over was screaming at her to get her cellphone out and call someone, the call would allow them to triangulate her location. Her body would not comply. Darkness overtook her completely, her body stopped moving. Her mind never stopped screaming at her, though it did no good.

Chapter 42

Jasper Kennedy had lived in Saranac his entire life. His grandfather had built his house on Chazy Lake Road in eighteen-ninety-nine. When his father passed away five years ago, he inherited the house and lands. He had never moved out, so it was not a huge transition for him. He had never taken a wife either, so he had no kids and now at the age of seventy, no company.

Jasper was fit for a man his age, but he still carried an extra thirty pounds. He had worked hard his whole life in construction, which caused him to now suffer from pain in most of his joints. When he stood, he was just under six feet tall, but slumped forward from the pain in his back. He rarely saw a barber, so his stringy, white hair had grown down past his shoulders and his beard was almost as long. His moustache was stained yellow from the tobacco smoke he blew from his nose. His brown eyes were still full of life, though they were surrounded by skin that was deeply crisscrossed by wrinkles.

Jasper typically wore the same clothes for an entire month and rarely bathed. He figured that since he seldom left his house and had no one at home to impress, there was no need to change his outfit or worry about how he smelled. This month he had worn the same clothes every day and night, not even removing his shoes to go to sleep. He was dressed in a stained pair of overalls with a button-up shirt. It used to be red, but it was so old that the colors had faded to a muted pink.

Living across the street from Adirondack Hardwoods, Jasper had heard many different noises and learned to tune them out. True, he had a lot of spare time and could tell anyone that asked the comings and goings of anyone in the area, right down to the minute.

Today was a different story though. Jasper knew gunshots when he heard them, and he had heard at least three of them, in rapid succession.

Jasper was in his usual spot, sitting in his recliner in front of his huge bay window, watching the street. He must have dozed off for a bit before hearing the gunshots, because he noted that the shadows from the trees in his front lawn had moved considerably since the last time that he looked out the window.

The sharp report of gunfire caused him to sit forward in the chair and focus his attention anew on the surrounding area. He did not see anything that was out of sorts and was about to discount it, chalking it up to a dream, when he saw a Jeep pull out of the field behind the hardwood place. His curiosity was fully piqued now, so Jasper made the decision to go investigate. It would be a long walk for him, but he had to know what was going on over there.

He waddled over to his front door and pulled down his wool jacket from the hall tree. It took him more than a minute to get it on before he grabbed his cane and walked out the front door.

Every time that Jasper walked across his front lawn, he became upset. The road was only twenty feet from the steps leading into the house. When his grandfather had built the place, the road was more than one hundred feet away. The town had claimed eminent domain in the sixties and put the road closer to the house. Today, his anger was tempered with a slight feeling of happiness that the walk would not be as long as it could have been. The older he got the less Jasper enjoyed being ambulatory.

There was no traffic on the road today and no one was at the hardwood place, so there was nothing to distract Jasper as he made his way to the field. Crossing the driveway, it did not take Jasper long to locate the tire tracks in the tall grass of the field. These he followed to a small spot in the patch of woods where it had clearly sat for some time.

Jasper was far from a detective, but he had spent a fair amount of time hunting when he was younger. The grass where the tires had passed was already starting to spring back into place, while the grass here was matted to the ground. That meant to Jasper that the Jeep had sat in this one spot for some time. He felt his pulse quicken for the first time in ages. It was like he was twenty years younger. He knew that he had to keep investigating.

It only took a moment of looking around before Jasper saw a path leading away and into the woods from where the Jeep was parked. He was about to walk down the trail when a faint noise from somewhere behind him and to the right caught his attention.

Jasper turned towards where he thought the sound had originated and slowly moved forward. He chastised himself for not bringing a weapon before realizing his cane could be used as one. He made it to the other side of the opening for the path when he noticed a body lying there.

Jasper threw all caution to the wind and crossed the remaining distance with more swiftness than he had managed in a decade. As he knelt down beside the body, he realized that it was a female cop and she looked to be in bad shape.

For the first time in his life, Jasper wished he had one of those cellular phones that all the kids had. He decided to check the cop's uniform to see if she might be carrying one on her. He mustered up all of his strength and rolled her over on her back. He was shocked by how much blood had soaked into her shirt from under her vest. Her hair was also matted with blood from some impact he could only guess about.

Jasper quickly patted the pockets on her vest and though it made him feel dirty, he even checked the breast pocket on her uniform. He found nothing and scooted down her body to her pants pockets. In her left front pocket, he found what he was seeking.

It was a smart phone, something quite foreign to Jasper. Luckily enough, he had watched enough television shows to have a basic understanding of one. It took him a few moments to figure out that this was an Apple. He remembered that with an Apple, you could touch the logo on the back to make the screen appear.

From his various trips to McDonald's, Jasper was familiar with how to use a touch screen. He preferred to use that method of ordering over talking to some snot nosed punk. He touched the phone icon and the number pad appeared on the screen. The rest was easy, Jasper dialed 911. The emergency operator picked up on the first ring.

Chapter 43

Jessica and Sarah had arrived at CVPH before the ambulance. Riviera was listed by the paramedics in critical condition and an operating room was on standby for her arrival. Both women knew that this was not an episode of Grey's Anatomy though and neither held on to too much hope that she would survive. This was just a small city hospital and was not staffed by the best of the best surgeons alive.

Despite the fact that the two women were the chief of police and head detective, they were also not given any special access to the areas of the hospital that were relegated for the staff. Instead, they found themselves in the waiting room, pacing like expectant fathers.

The waiting room was like any other that the pair had been in before. It had white walls with light grey tiles on the floor. There was a window that looked out at the parking area in the middle of the longest wall and a television mounted to the wall. The news was on currently and the anchor was talking about the events of the day, most notably, the rescue of Riviera. How they got their information so quickly was boggling.

There was a row of chairs mounted to the floor along each wall, most of which were empty. The people in the chairs were all absorbed with their own sets of worries, and none seemed to be paying attention to Sarah or Jessica, with the exception of one man. He was staring at Sarah with hard, accusing eyes. On a normal day, Sarah would have been able to ignore this man, but today was far from normal and she felt her patience wearing thin.

The man was in his forties and looked like a mechanic. His clothes were stained with oil and grease as were the beds of his fingernails. He was dark complected, hinting at some mixture of races, with short, black hair that had flecks of grey. His brown eyes were hard, or maybe that was just the way he looked at her. His left hand was wrapped in a white paper towel, the spot nearest his middle finger soaked with blood.

She overheard the reporter mention her name and the man snorted. This was the proverbial straw on the camel's back. Sarah rounded on him, rage in her eyes.

"Did I do something to you?" she asked, just below a yell.

"It is all your fault," the man shot back, not missing a beat. "All these people dying, or almost dying. You should just pick a spot, let the killer know where you are and let him kill you."

"You son-of-a-bitch," Sarah started before Jessica stepped in between them.

"You do not want to push her," she said to the man before looking Sarah in the eyes. "We both know this is not your fault. Just let it go. People are going to think what they want."

It was purely out of the respect that Sarah had for Jessica that she acquiesced. She could not resist one last word though.

"You better never let me catch you speeding," she said mirthlessly to the man.

The pair turned from the man and saw a nurse waiting for them with a look of annoyance on their face. She was dressed in the blue scrubs of the hospital which really made her hazel eyes shine. He brown hair, which was highlighted blonde was tied back in a ponytail. Her look of annoyance swiftly changed to one of compassion which was probably her default setting. Her nametag identified her as Aubrey. She closed the gap between herself and the pair, her white sneakers squeaking on the floor.

"You two cannot cause a disturbance like that," she said softly yet firmly. "Don't let these guys bait you. We all support you guys here and know that your lives are always on the line."

This had an immediate calming effect on Sarah. She nodded like a scolded child. The nurse was right, of course. The entire situation continued to get the better of her.

"Riviera arrived ten minutes ago," Aubrey continued. She is now in surgery and as stable as can be. She was shot three times, but only two bullets made it past her vest. One was a through and through of her left shoulder. The other one is the one that has us worried. It entered just under her left armpit, nicked her lung and is right up against her aorta."

She paused so that this news could sink in. Sarah and Jessica exchanged looks before Sarah spoke.

"What does this mean? What are her odds?" she asked.

"Typically, we do not like trying to remove a bullet that close to such a major blood vessel," said Aubrey. "This case is not a typical one though. The bullet, while intact, is so close to the artery that the doctor fears any sort of hard impact would cause it to move enough to damage the aorta, which could cause her to bleed out internally before she even knew there was a problem. The surgery will be a long, slow process. I have to get back to the O.R. but will try and keep you all posted."

With that, Aubrey turned on her heels and left the pair. Indecision played across Sarah's face. She knew that Jessica would need moral support, but the urge to go out and find Sam weighed heavily upon her.

"Go," said Jessica. "You need to end this and the only way that is going to happen is if you find her."

Sarah was impressed by the chief's intuition once more. She hugged her and turned to leave. She made it to the door before stopping and looking back at Jessica.

"She is a strong woman, she will pull through," she said, even though she was not entirely certain that she believed her own words.

Walking out of the door to that hospital was one of the most difficult things that Sarah had ever had to do. Jessica was her boss but had become so much more than that during the events of the last few weeks. She climbed into the cruiser full of indecision. She needed to get into the mind of Sam and try and get ahead of her next move. As an afterthought, Sarah called Smith's personal cellphone. It would do the chief good to have him and Jones there as support.

Chapter 44

Sam had driven around aimlessly for a couple of hours. She stuck to the back roads, stopping at a Stewarts convenience store for food and water. She needed to recover her strength from the blood that she lost. She now found herself on the western side of Malone.

She saw a sign for a Holiday Inn Express and the idea of lying low until morning seemed logical. Turning left, the white building seemed like an oasis to her after being in a desert. She no longer found any excitement in being on the run, in fact it pissed her off.

She parked her Jeep beside another of the same color. Getting out of the Jeep, she went to the back and opened her bag. From an inside pocket, she retrieved her multitool. She was trying to look as casual as possible as she glanced around to see if she was alone.

She tried to crouch behind her Jeep but found that position excruciating, so, instead, she bent at the waist and removed her back plate before going to the front and removing that plate as well. Luck was still her ally as the parking lot remained devoid of people and the identical Jeep did not have an alarm. She quickly swapped those plates with hers and then mounted the pilfered plates to her Jeep.

She finished just in time, as she stood back erect, a car entered the driveway. She let out a sigh of relief as she returned her multitool to her bag. She glanced around furtively as she reached into one of the shopping bags and pulled out a wad of twenties. What she planned next would take the right kind of person behind the desk.

Sam limped over to the main entrance and found herself inside a spacious lobby. In front of her was the check-in desk, the darkly stained wood stood out nicely against the cream-colored walls. There were two computers set up on opposite ends of the desk, but only one person was working. Given the relative emptiness of the parking lot, that made sense.

There was an older man currently checking in. The way he was dressed informed Sam that he was most likely here on business. If she had to guess, he was somewhere in his fifties. He was taller than average, somewhere around six feet, and skinny. He was not remarkable in any sense of the word.

The woman behind the desk was in her late twenties and stunning. She had olive colored skin with jet-black hair and eyes that were so brown that they were almost black. She had the red dot just above her nose which confirmed to Sam that she was Indian.

The man checking in was doing his best to flirt with the woman, even going so far as to keep his left hand behind his back, the better to hide the fact that he was married. This was the sort of reprehensible behavior that made Sam angrier than anything else. It also caused her to change her plan on how to get a room.

Sam pulled her cellphone out of her left back pocket and pretended to take an important call. She casually walked past the check-in desk. Doing her very best to hide her limp and saying that she needed the documents by the morning. Neither the man checking in nor the woman behind the desk paid her any attention. Sam continued walking until she reached the elevators and there she waited, hoping that the man was not getting a room on the ground floor. While she waited, Sam looked over the area to confirm that the hotel lacked security cameras. She did not see any, though that only meant that there was a ninety percent certainty that none were hidden.

She did not have to wait long for the man. In less than three minutes, he walked by her and pressed the call button on the elevator, but not before undressing Sam with his eyes. She continued her façade with her cell phone and began to pace, shouting angrily into the receiver. She listened for the door to chime that the elevator had arrived and rushed in behind the man. He gave her a look of curiosity but did not pay her any extra attention.

She watched as he reached over and pushed the button for the third floor and smiled at him. "Same floor," she said before returning to her fake call and ending it.

The ride up to the third floor was brief. The elevator chimed and the doors slid open to an empty hallway. They both exited the elevator and Sam bent down to pantomime that she needed to tie her shoe. This hallway was like any other in every hotel in the world. It was a straight corridor, with equal lengths on either side of the elevator doors. Every few feet, on both sides of the hall and set into the white walls were doors that led to the rooms. The dark blue carpet was slightly worn and smelled mildly of mildew.

The man had gone right out of the elevator. There were no other people that way. Sam glanced to her left to confirm that they were alone. She stood and unsheathed her knife before following the man. He stopped at the doorway with the number three thirteen above it. Sam calculated the distance between them and was confident that she could close it before he fully entered the room. She waited to hear the sound of the electric lock disengaging before rushing forward as best she could with her injured leg.

The man never knew what had hit him. Sam slammed into him with all her might, propelling him fully into the room. The impact also caused him to lose his footing and he fell to the floor. This made very little sound as the floors were made of concrete for better stability. Sam did not hesitate, falling on top of him and plunging her knife into his neck at the base of his skull. Her aim was true, and his death was swift.

This all happened so fast that the door closing behind her made her jump up from the body and spin. Sam felt her heart rate slow as she realized that the sound that she had heard came from the door lock engaging. She turned around to survey her room for the night. She would have liked to stay here longer than one night, but she did not know for how long the man had booked the room.

The room itself was also typical of these chains. The king-sized bed took up a significant amount of the floor space. She cringed at the floral comforter that lay atop the bed. The carpet in here was the same blue as that in the hallway, the walls the same plain white. There was a worn loveseat next to the large window on the far side of the room. Across from the bed was a three-drawer dresser, made from what looked like fake cherry, a small flatscreen television sitting atop it. On the far side of the dresser was a mini-fridge and microwave oven. There was a door on her right that must lead to the bathroom, a fact that she confirmed by giving the door a push.

Sam stepped into the small room. Directly in front of her was the toilet, a metal rack was mounted to the wall above it, containing four towels. The left wall was mostly covered by a mirror with a vanity and sink. The pink vanity was the only thing in the bathroom that was not white. The right side of the room was where the tub was located. Sam pulled the white cloth curtain open and was happy to see that it was also a shower. The tub looked deep enough for her to be able to store the body. This, she would do later. She desperately wanted a shower, or to maybe even soak in the tub.

Sam needed to get to the Jeep and park it in the rear of the hotel as well as grab her bag and spare clothing. She did not want to bathe and then put on bloody clothes. She also did not want to walk past the front desk, so she looked at the back of the door where the emergency evacuation plan was located. She saw that at the end of the hallway, on this end of the hotel was a stairwell that would take her to a back door. It would require her to do a lot of walking, but in the long run, it would also save her any situations where she might need to explain her presence in the hotel.

Sam walked over to the body and pulled the keycard from the dead man's hand. She returned to the bathroom and gave herself a once over in the mirror to be certain that she did not look like a crazed killer. Satisfied with her appearance, she started the long walk to the Jeep.

Chapter 45

Darkness had fallen and Sarah was still out driving around in a desperate attempt to stumble upon Sam and her Jeep. She knew that the odds were against her, but she had nothing else to do. Fatigue was rapidly setting in, so she decided that it was time to go home for the night.

As she drove to her house, she ran through the names of everyone that had been taken and those that might be at risk. Her circle was small, most of the names she came up with were other cops. She would have to talk with Jessica about making it mandatory that anyone associated with her on the force be kept in pairs. Sam seemed to be able to easily overpower anyone that she chose, so Sarah was not certain this would help, but it was better than leaving everyone to their own devices.

Almost in response to thinking about Jessica, Sarah's phone rang. The caller ID signaled that it was the chief calling. Sarah pulled off to the side of the road and answered.

"Jessica, tell me some good news," she said.

"I am afraid that I have none to share," Jessica replied. Her voice was heavy with grief. "The surgeons were unable to save her."

Silence hung in the air while Sarah searched for appropriate words. In the end, she simply said, "I am so sorry."

Jessica was silent for a full minute before she spoke, her grief replaced by anger. "You need to catch this bitch," she said.

"I am doing my very best," Sarah replied. "We know who it is now, we have every cop in the state looking for her. We will catch her before she takes anyone else."

"While I have you," Sarah continued, "I think it wise that anyone associated with me, or this investigation be teamed up with another cop. That will make it harder for Sam to take anyone."

"Yeah, I will make the call," Jessica replied. "Then I am going home and getting some sleep."

Jessica ended the call without another word. The rudeness of this action informed Sarah more about her chief's mental state than any word could have. Sarah knew that she needed help, and she knew who exactly to call.

A few years ago, there had been an interstate manhunt for a murderer. They had started their spree in Massachusetts. They then went to Vermont and kidnapped an elderly couple and brought them to New York before murdering them. Since it was a multi-state investigation, the FBI had been involved. The lead on that case was a man named Francis Edenburgh. Special agent Edenburgh had taken an instant liking to Sarah, and it was the duo of agent and detective that had captured the man responsible. They had remained in touch, and he had always told her that if she ever was in need of help, that she could call on him, regardless of the time or the day. Edenburgh was based in Massachusetts, so if she called him now, he could be here before morning.

Sarah hesitated for just a moment before picking up the phone to call. Edenburgh always said that those that refused to ask for help when they needed it were either self-righteous or dumb. Sarah was neither. He answered on the first ring.

"Sarah, so nice of you to call, but what took so long?" he asked. His voice still had a hint of his British accent

The pair had grown close enough that Sarah referred to him by a nickname. "Ed, I know that you know what has been going on up here. We just lost another cop. I think I need you."

"I am so sorry for your loss," he said. "I see that you have decided you are neither dumb nor self-righteous. I would, of course, be happy to help, in an unofficial capacity. As it would happen, when that dreadful person broadcast the murder of the reporter, I took a brief leave and am already in Plattsburgh."

"Wait, you're up here?!" she said. "Why the hell did you not let me know?"

"Sarah, you are many things, not limited to being a brilliant detective. You are so good at so many things, but you do have a slight flaw, your pride. I did not wish to injure that. I figured that if you desired my help, you would call."

He was right of course. He always was. Among his numerous degrees was a masters in phycology. Ed could figure out what made someone tick in minutes after meeting them.

"Meet me at my hotel. I am staying at the Hampton Inn. Room 212," he said and then ended the call.

Sarah was neither upset nor surprised by the abruptness of him ending their conversation. That was how he was, time was a commodity to Ed, and he spent it greedily.

Sarah looked at the time, it was almost eleven O'clock. This looked like it was about to shape up to be a late night, again. She turned on her emergency lights and pulled a U-turn and headed to Plattsburgh.

Fifteen minutes later, Sarah was pulling into the parking lot for the Hampton Inn. The tan building was well lit. She found the first story being made of red bricks to be visually pleasing. She parked her car close to the front entrance and entered the lobby. The floor shone impressively, the Black and white tiles were set in such a fashion that they looked like diamonds. The green and brown area rug was the only thing that looked like it was old in the room. The brown check-in desk had what looked to be black granite sitting on top, and this too shone brightly in the lights. The brunet woman standing behind the desk smiled at Sarah as she entered. Sarah returned the smile and made her way to the elevators off to the right of the desk.

The doors looked to be made of stainless steel, and these shone like they were polished daily. Sarah had never been inside this hotel before, but if the rest of the place looked as nice as the lobby, she knew that she would recommend it to anyone looking for a place to stay.

The elevator chimed and the doors slid open with ease. Sarah entered the elevator and selected the second floor. The ride up was swift, and she soon found herself in the hallway. The floor here was covered with a muted red carpet which stood out against the white walls. She looked at the sign on the wall in front of her. Ed's room would be to her left.

Sarah walked past three doors and found Ed's room on her right. The door opened before she could knock. This did not surprise her. Ed always seemed to know when someone was approaching.

Ed stood in front of her, dressed in his typical black suit with a white, crisply pressed dress shirt and black tie. His hair was so blonde that it was almost white. His grey eyes sparkled, despite the fact that Ed was in his late fifties. He was tall and lanky, which caused many to underestimate his ability to defend himself. As part of his eternal thirst for knowledge, Ed had mastered five different forms of martial arts. He smiled warmly at Sarah and stood aside, indicating with his left hand that she should enter the room.

The room was impressive, as far as hotel rooms went. There were two queen beds with red comforters that matched the red carpet. The dresser, television stand and desk all looked to be made of Mahogony. There was a full-sized couch at the far side of the room, with a Mahogony coffee table in front of it. Ed's Apple laptop sat atop the table. It was open, but Sarah could not see what he had been working on. The television looked to be around fifty-five inches, which made it huge in a room with such limited space

Sarah heard the door click shut behind here before Ed said," May I get you anything, food, drink?"

"I'm fine," she replied.

Not sure of where else to go, Sarah headed to the couch and sat next to the arm that was closest to the far wall. She watched Ed follow her over, grabbing the black desk chair and wheeling it over on the opposite side of the coffee table.

"I have been conducting as much research as I could via the internet," he said. "Why don't you fill me in on the rest of the details?"

"Well, I suppose we would have to go back to elementary school then," she said.

Sarah spent the next hour recounting the events from school and then all the information that she knew about the murders, up to the still unannounced death of Riviera. Ed listened intently, stopping her several times to ask pointed questions and taking many notes. When Sarah was done talking, they both sat there in silence, Ed with his eyes closed. Sarah knew that this meant he was deep in thought and digesting every piece of information that she had provided to him.

"Well," he said suddenly breaking the silence, "I can assure you that you are to blame for none of this."

Sarah started to protest, but her friend and mentor held up a hand to stop her. "You have a huge heart, Sarah. You always have and clearly you have allowed this Samantha to cause you to feel so strongly that you are at fault here. Granted, you could have handled the events at your school with a bit more decorum, but you were in fact a child. Ill-equipped to deal with any kind of social disaster that unfurled that day."

"Now, let us get to the problem at hand," he continued. "Samantha is always at least one step ahead of you, as you correctly surmised. There has been a paradigm shift though, she is now playing defense instead of offense."

"What does that mean for us though?" asked Sarah.

"Well, one may logically surmise that without the ability to take the time to plan these elaborate abductions, followed by the ability to lay low within her dwelling, that Samantha is now more prone to make an error, such as she did when she took Riviera, rest her soul."

"You mentioned that you think she had a vast sum of money with her now?" he asked.

"All evidence points that way. We just do not know how much there was. One witness said that Kevin had three or four reusable shopping bags when he left the scene of the robbery. If that was even just ten-dollar bills, that would be..."

"Fifty thousand or so," Ed interrupted. "Which means that Samantha could essentially stay on the run for six to seven months, if needed."

"Or she could just vanish," said Sarah.

Ed scowled and said, "I think not. She has made it abundantly clear that she wishes to cause you harm. Most decidedly emotional harm. I am willing to bet that she would wish to inflict physical harm as well, perhaps even taking your life."

"You are right, of course," she replied. "So, we hunt her down."

"Yes. Though this all depends on if she has a plan in mind already. We might have prematurely forced her into her endgame, so to speak," Ed concluded. "I would highly suggest that you stay with me until we find her and find her, we shall."

"That is very gracious of you," Sarah said. "I could not impose."

"My dear, an invitation precludes any imposition," Ed replied. "We shall head to your place on the morrow and collect what you need to stay comfortable with me for the duration of the hunt."

That seemed to settle things. Sarah knew that he would give her no room to argue. "I guess I should get into bed then," she said.

"Capital idea," replied Ed. "Get yourself comfortable while I go shower and get ready myself. The bed closest to the couch is the open one."

Ed stood and left Sarah alone in the room. She had nothing to wear to bed, but she was not going to sleep in the nude. She compromised and pulled her jeans off. Luckily today she was wearing what she called her granny panties. She knew that Ed would be respectful and not leer, hell, he probably would not even glance, but she felt more comfortable in these than had she been wearing something more revealing.

Surprisingly, sleep found Sarah rapidly. She had been pushing herself hard the last couple of weeks but did not anticipate being able to fall asleep with such ease. Ed came out of the bathroom twenty minutes later and smiled. He climbed into bed and turned the lights off in the room. He grabbed his cellphone from the bedside table and continued his research into Samantha. He only typically slept three hours a night, so he had time to kill.

Chapter 46

The sun was shining in the window, signaling the arrival of a new day. Sam woke disoriented, forgetting briefly that she was on the run. Sleeping was such a rarity for her that when she got a chance, she slept longer than the average person. A glance at the clock informed her that it was just five minutes before noon.

With just under twelve hours of sleep, Sam felt young and vibrant once more. She felt a smile cross her lips despite the fact that she was out of her comfort zone. She was in an area where no one knew her, and she was fairly certain that she could move about the town freely.

Sam was certain that the police had figured out that she was the killer that they so desperately hunted. Even with that information, the best they would be able to put out for the public would be her DMV picture from her license. This represented the only picture she had allowed to be taken of her since school.

Sam was not stupid. On the days that she had to go for her photo, she always colored her hair or wore a wig. For her most recent visit, she had worn a wig that was dark black with long, wavy locks. Her normal hair was a super light blonde and kept short. She doubted that anyone would be able to make the correlation between her and that picture, even were they to be side by side.

Sam had showered the previous night and now there was a decomposing body in the tub. Because of those two things, she decided to forgo a morning shower. Sam slept in the nude, so her only tasks before leaving the hotel would be getting dressed and brushing her teeth.

Flipping the pile of covers off of her, Sam rolled out of bed on the left side. She walked the three steps to the large window that overlooked the parking lot. She opened the curtains, unconcerned about whether or not someone could see her. She did her best to take in all of the nearest businesses, seeking a place where she could secure sustenance.

Her leg was still quite sore, as one would expect from a stab wound. She had nothing in the form of a first aid kit, so she had used her knife to cut strips from one of the clean towels and fashioned a bandage that way last night. This morning, it was slightly stained by blood, but otherwise okay. She decided not to try to replace it and further anger the area.

Movement from off to her right caught her attention. A sheriff's car was parked behind the Jeep with her plates. There was one deputy standing between the two vehicles and another walking briskly towards the main entrance.

"Fuck," she said aloud.

She would have to forego brushing her teeth this morning. With great haste, Sam got dressed in the last clean outfit that she had grabbed before fleeing. She knew that she would not be able to leave in her Jeep. Once the cops understood that she had switched the plates, it would not take them long to figure out what the correct ones were for this Jeep.

The man had been carrying a duffle bag and a briefcase when he had entered the room the previous night. Sam began the search for his car keys. The odds that the police would discover the dead man before the maid came to clean the room were miniscule. Her best option right now was to use his car. She found the keys in the briefcase; they were to a rental car. The tag attached to the lone key said it belonged to a red Kia Niro, a mid-sized SUV.

With the key to her new vehicle in hand, Sam rushed from the room, pushing through any pain from her leg. She needed to get to her Jeep and retrieve her bag and the money if she was to stay mobile. She took the same set of stairs in the back of the hotel and found her Jeep right where she left it.

Sam wanted to be as inconspicuous as possible. She decided to stuff the stacks of money into her bag. This way, if the cops were looking for someone with shopping bags, which was a logical conclusion, she would be less likely to draw their attention. Before filling her bag, she withdrew a baseball hat that she always kept within it. This would serve to further disguise her. Before saying farewell to her Jeep, she also grabbed everything that would be useful to her from the various compartments within the cockpit, including what remained of her cocktail.

She could either reenter the hotel and exit via the main entrance and search for the Kia, or circle around to the front from where she was now. Deciding that the latter option would be the best way to avoid any interaction with the police, she made her was around the hotel. She kept her walk at a brisk but not rushed pace, fighting to hide her limp. She wanted to look like any other hotel patron leaving for the day. By the time that she made it to the main lot, there were two more cruisers parked by the Jeep.

There still remained just the one deputy standing guard. He did not seem to be looking in her direction, instead he was focused on the main entrance. The Kia was parked closer to her than the Jeep, so Sam casually walked up to it and got in. The black interior of the Kia still smelled like a new car and was hot from the sun beating through the windshield despite the crisp temperature of the day.

Her heart was racing as she adjusted the seat so she could drive it. She depressed the brake and pushed the button to start the engine. The sound of the engine coming to life did the one thing she had hoped it would not, it caught the attention of the deputy. She glanced to her right and saw that he was now looking directly at her and was speaking into his shoulder microphone. Before he could take any action, Sam put the car in drive and slowly pulled out of the spot. She did not want to look like she was rushing.

Her ruse seemed to pay off and she pulled out of the lot without having the deputy approach her or enter his car to give chase. Nothing to see here, she thought to herself. This certainly was not a black Jeep.

As Sam got further from the hotel, she had three state police cruisers drive past her. She had made it out in the nick of time. This development would hasten her final plans. There were still three people that she needed to kill before facing Sarah. She would have to take them all with rapid succession to keep Sarah on the defense and further wear her down. East was the direction she needed to head.

Chapter 47

Sarah and Ed had spent the morning trying to come up with a list of possible victims that were closely associated with her. In the end, excluding work colleagues, she had come up with four names. The next step was deciding what they should do with those names. Sarah was not sure she could advocate for police protection for them all and neither was she certain that she wanted to.

They were in the middle of eating lunch that was delivered by Doordash when Sarah's phone rang. The caller ID let her know that it was Jessica. She answered immediately.

"Jess," she said. "Has there been a development?" Sarah turned on the speaker function so that Ed could listen in to the conversation.

"They found her Jeep in Malone," said Jessica. There was a black Jeep parked at a hotel and the tags matched. Sam was smart enough to swap plates though and the Jeep was not hers. Deputies found her actual jeep in the back of the hotel with the pilfered plates on it, but there was no sign of Sam or any of her belongings in the Jeep. All that was inside that was worth noting were three empty shopping bags and one empty syringe."

"She must have been staying at the hotel and saw the cruisers and fled," Sarah concluded. "I am willing to bet that the syringe is the key as to how she gets control of her victims with such ease. She must be drugging them."

"'S'what I thought as well," Jessica agreed. "A woman vaguely matching her description was seen last night walking around the lobby and talking on a cell phone. She never checked in though. We are conducting a room to room search right now. Now for the bad news."

Sarah and Ed exchanged looks.

"There was one vehicle that left the lot before the state boys showed up. The deputy just let it go because it did not match the description of the vehicle we wanted and the driver was operating it in, and this is a direct quote, a leisurely fasion. It was a red Kia Niro."

"That's her," Sarah said without hesitation. "I would bet my life on it. Listen, Jess, we took her home, we took her ride, she is going to be desperate, but she has this other vehicle and a vast sum of money. I do not see her stopping."

Jessica sighed. "I agree. I will put out a BOLO for that Kia, but we do not have the plates. What are you going to do?"

"Follow my gut," Sarah answered before ending the call.

"And what does your gut tell you?" Ed asked.

Sarah was quiet for several minutes while she thought. She knew that there was only one way of stopping Sam, and that was catching her. She also knew that Sam would be going after her next target, the only question was who that would be.

"We have four options," she said. "I am fairly certain that Sam will be taking people that are closer to me now. What we have to do is try and outthink her."

Ed nodded but did not say anything. He knew that this would be Sarah's call. He hoped that she would not suggest that they split up. He did not want her out of his sight. He felt that he was the only person alive with the correct amount of training and experience to prevent Sarah from falling into Sam's clutches.

"If this woman has kept tabs on me our whole lives, then she knows about Jerry and John. John is dead. That leaves my once best friend Beth, though it is doubtful Sam knows that she is back in town," she concluded.

"I would not hazard to disagree with you, detective," said Ed. "To which person's rescue are we rushing?"

Sarah got up and started to pace. She had a fifty percent chance of being right, if Sam was as predictable as she hoped. "Jerry," she said. "We are going after Jerry."

She pulled out her cellphone and called the station. "I need a last known address on one Jerry Stevens," she said to the person on the other end.

Chapter 48

Meghan looked directly into the camera as her earpiece signaled that they were going live. Monica's death was perhaps the best thing to ever happen to her, at least professionally speaking. She was thrust right into the heart of the biggest story in the history of upstate New York. Each time she did a report, it made the national news, not just the tiny local station. The voice in her ear reached one and she began to speak.

"Meghan Goode here for Fox 44. I am standing in front of the Holiday Inn Express located on State Street in Malone, New York. It is believed that Samantha Ryn, known as the Mountaintop Killer, was here last night. It is also believed that she evaded capture by stealing a red Kia Niro.

Police are still warning everyone to avoid contact with her and to call 911 should you see her. She is armed and very dangerous, having taken at least four lives that we know of. I received an anonymous call earlier today stating that officer Rivera died on the operating table yesterday.

While the police want us all to think that they have the situation under control, I can tell you that they clearly do not. Three of their own have been captured by this emotionless killer thus far, with two of them perishing. Sarah Barney, the area's head detective has not yet shown up here, making me think that she is cowering in fear. It is this reporter's belief that Ms. Barney should just give herself to the killer before someone else falls prey to her.

Lastly, moments before I came on the air, another body was discovered. This one within the hotel behind me. Trevor Needle was here on business. When he arrived, he had no idea that this would be the spot where he met his doom. He was discovered in his room by the maid, dead in the tub, a single knife wound to his throat. This information has not yet been released by the police, instead I got it from a confidential source. So, remember, you heard it here first.

Before I go, I want to speak to the killer, to Samantha. Please, I beg of you, leave everyone else alone and just kill Sarah. I know that that is what you really want. You have proven yourself to be smarter than her and the rest of us. Also, if you ever want a real interview, call me. My number is five one eight, five five five, nine six two three.

Meghan Goode, Fox 44."

"And wrap," said the voice in her ear. "Great job Meghan."

Meghan felt more alive than she had in years. She hoped that Sam would take her up on her offer for an interview. So caught up in the moment was she that she did not think about how many people in the country now had her number. It was a small price to pay though. The five hundred that she had paid to the maid to talk only to her was also a small price in her book.

Her next stop would be back in Plattsburgh. She was going to pay a visit to the Rivera residence and see how her parents felt about her death. She was certain that they would be outraged by her being there and that made for great news.

Chapter 49

While it was true that for most of Sarah's adult life, she had avoided the messy entanglements that were interpersonal relationships, the same could not be said for when she was a child. As an adult she had not engaged in anything that would resemble a long-term relationship, though she had dipped her toe into the dating pool a few times. While in school she had found it difficult to deny her desires to be loved. As an adult, she had long ago decided that relationships were little more than a distraction that kept you from achieving your goals.

In school, Sarah had jumped from boy to boy like a dandelion seed danced in the wind. All in all, she had had only two serious relationships. The first was with a boy named Jerry Stevens in the fourth grade. The pair had dated, for lack of a better term, for almost the entirety of that school year. Sarah could not recall much about the boy now, just that he was goofy, and he made her laugh a lot. Her second serious relationship was from sophomore to senior year. It had been so intense that it was a foregone conclusion they would get married. His name was John Abbott, and he was the captain of the football team. He was six feet seven inches tall and nothing but muscle. His wavy hair reminded Sarah of the color of a hay field in the fall and his blue eyes were reminiscent of crystal-clear ocean water.

And if it had not been for the accident that claimed his life, Sarah was sure her last name would be Abbott right now. His death came just three weeks after graduation and Sarah went to a dark place for a very long time. Since then, she had had a few dates and even fewer trysts. Some people felt vast amounts of pity for Sarah because of her situation. Sarah was not upset about things though as her career skyrocketed.

Jerry Stevens was now a successful business owner living in Rouses Point, New York. He had turned a lifelong passion of playing video games into a company that designed them. His net worth was somewhere over twenty million dollars, and he lived a lavish life. He was now married to a senator and together they had three children. His house was the envy of anyone driving through Rouses Point. It was a large stone house with lake property included.

Jerry was a creature of habit, always leaving for work and returning home at the exact same time. He often joked that if someone wished to kidnap him it would not be difficult. Given his wife's vocation, Jerry was usually home alone. All but one of the children had moved out, his daughter Irene. She was two months shy of her twentieth birthday and still chose to live at home. His two oldest children, twin boys named Jayden and Jackson, were slightly more than a year older than Irene and both in college.

While making plans for what she would do to Sarah two months before leaving the body atop Poke-O, Sam had spent almost a week observing Jerry and knew his routine as well as she knew her own. It was just before five o'clock on a Wednesday afternoon, the time that Jerry always left for home. Jerry had bought a small building in the center of town. It was from there that he ran his business. The designing of video games did not require a lot of space, especially since he only employed four people. Directly across from his building was a Dollar General. Sam had parked there to wait for him to leave.

At exactly five o'clock, Jerry exited the building and went to his Porsche Cayenne. It was a flashy silver SUV with blackout tinted windows. It took him less than three minutes to arrive at his driveway. He never used the one on Lake Street, instead he turned right onto Pine Street and used the back driveway. Not being the most observant of people, Jerry did not notice the red Kia pulling in behind him.

Sam accelerated and used the brush guard mounted to the front of her Kia to push SUV into the shrubs that formed a natural fence around the property. Jerry was taken by surprise and failed to react with any kind of speed. Before he fully understood what was happening, Sam was at the driver's side door.

Her normal, calm demeanor failed her this time. Instead of using a syringe loaded with her cocktail of drugs, she unleashed a flurry of fists onto his face. Jerry was a good-sized man but the ferocity with which she delivered the blows coupled with the fact that he was seated and buckled in the car gave her an edge that he could not surmount. Before long, his face was bloody, and her knuckles hurt. It took every last bit of her self-control to stop hitting him once he had been knocked out. She desperately wanted to end this here, but that would make all of her planning moot, not to mention it would not force Sarah to jump through hoops in a futile attempt to save him.

Blood dripping from her knuckles, Sam dragged Jerry from the ruined SUV and tossed him in the trunk of the Niro. To ensure that he would not wake up mid trip, this would be a long one, she administered her sedatives before closing the trunk. The privacy afforded to her by the property meant that she did not have to worry about anyone having seen her take him. For the first time Sam felt completely at ease while performing a kidnapping. She returned to the Porsche and deposited the note on the driver's seat before getting in the Niro to leave.

The mountain was just under an hour and a half away and a good hiker could summit it at between seven and eight hours. She was running low of her drug cocktail and without a home base, she was not going to be able to make any more any time soon. She would have to push herself harder than ever before in order to get him to the summit and in her trap before he awoke.

Sam put the SUV in reverse and backed away from the ruined Porsche. Quickly turning around. She was taking a risk doing all of this in the center of town during daylight hours, but what choice did she really have? She also surmised that the police would have the description of the vehicle she was now driving, so taking the most direct route via the interstate was also a huge risk.

She felt her pulse race with adrenaline as she turned onto the main road and made her way to the interstate entrance in Champlain. The nine-mile trip would take her through some heavily populated areas for this part of the state. There was an old saying that Sam recalled hearing on a television show, though she could not remember which. It was, "May fortune favor the foolish". She hoped that she was just foolish enough for the god of fortune to smile down upon her.

Chapter 50

Sarah and Ed got off the interstate at exit forty-one, which was one shy of the exit for Champlain. She did not think Sam would be bold enough to drive through Rouses Point and into Champlain to get on the interstate and would most likely stick to the back roads. She thought the odds of them crossing paths was better this way. She had just gotten off the phone with Jessica as she took the exit ramp.

"The chief is happy that you have come on to help, even in an unofficial capacity," she said to Ed. "She is checking to see if the local police can swing by Jerry's house before we arrive."

"Very good," he replied. "Though I am not certain that either of us will be there in time."

Sarah knew that he was most likely correct. She was holding on to hope though. She wanted to catch Sam more than anything in the world and she knew that they were headed to the correct address.

They sat in silence for the remainder of the trip to Rouses Point. They were both contemplating what the next move would be. Surely if they got to Jerry before Sam, then they could set a trap. If she had gotten there in advance of them, then they would have to try and save Jerry of course, but they would also have to try and outthink Sam's next move.

"I believe that the chief will be her next target," said Ed. "It is logical. She is the next closest person to you."

Sarah did not answer at first. He was correct, he always was.

"So, let's catch her before it gets to that," she said after a moment.

As they drove past the Stewarts shop on the left side of the road, Sarah felt her hopes sink. In the dusk, she saw the familiar flash of emergency lights coming from the area where dispatch had indicated that Jerry lived. She turned onto Pine Street and knew that they were too late.

"Damn it," she exclaimed as they pulled into the driveway. The local police were there, checking out the wrecked Porsche SUV. Sarah put the car into park and the pair exited the vehicle.

"Whatever happened, you missed it," said the cop. "I am Corporal Desantis."

He was tall and rail thin, not what one might expect to see in an officer of the law. His blonde hair was a lot longer than one might expect too. His hazel eyes were wide with fear, as if this was the first time that he had been involved with something like this, and perhaps it was.

"Did anyone see anything?" asked Sarah.

"Doubtful," Ed chimed in. "Look at how secluded this back driveway is. She knew exactly what it was that she was doing."

"My partner is going 'round to the neighbors, but so far, nothing," Desantis said, confirming Ed's assessment. "I did find this on the driver's seat," he added, holding out a folded paper for Sarah.

She snatched it from his hand, a bit more harshly than intended. "You should have led with this," she snapped. "Our clock began the second that she took him."

The look of confusion that played across Desantis's face let Sarah know that he had no clue about what she said. To him, this must just have looked like an accident gone wrong, or even a murder scene. He clearly did not know that he had just become another piece in the game that Sam was orchestrating.

Sarah leaned in closer to Ed and unfolded the paper, positioning herself so that they could both read it together.

"Sarah, dear Sarah, our time to play is growing short. I commend you on being such a good sport. Soon there will no longer be any beanstalks for you to climb. Though there will be plenty of rocks for you this time. If you guessed this person, color me impressed. Though the thought of you catching me does not put me in distress. Now, hurry, hurry and come find Jerry. A hint in advance, my next victim will take a ferry. You have nine and a half hours."

"She fancies herself a poet," Ed said. "At least we know that she will be heading into Vermont to set her next trap. Tell me, what do you glean from this crude poem?"

"She always references a mountain in these things, so clearly the part about the beanstalk and maybe the rocks are the clues. I do not know of any mountain in the state that is named after beans though."

"Perhaps that is the point," Ed said. "Perhaps she is being more vague than normal, in order to put you off of your game, so to speak."

"Alright," she said, "what does a beanstalk have to do with a mountain?"

The corporal had been listening to the conversation and stepped closer to speak. "Maybe it is not the beanstalk itself, but what you find at the top of one."

Ed and Sarah exchanged looks. The corporal had figured out the clue, why couldn't they?

"Well, in the fairy tale, one finds giants," Ed said.

"Can't be Giant Mountain," Sarah said dismissively. "That is only a four-to-five-hour hike."

"So, then it is logical that the line about the rocks is the second part of the clue," Ed suggested.

"Of course," Sarah said excitedly. "There is a trail that goes from Giant to Rocky Peak Ridge. They are considered to be a set of twin peaks and most people do them both at the same time. That is one hell of a hike. The trip there and the climb will take almost the entire nine and a half hours."

She turned to Desantis. "Please, do not touch anything else. I am going to have my CSIs that have been working this case come and process the scene."

She did not wait for his reply. Turning away from the renewed look of confusion on Desantis's face, she walked back to the car, pulling out her cellphone and calling Jessica.

"What news do you have?" Jessica asked upon answering the call.

"Ed and I are heading to Giant Mountain. We believe that the trap will be set on Rocky Peak Ridge," she said. "And Jess, we both think that you will be the next target."

"I figured that I was on the list," Jessica said. "I will have myself guarded at all times. Get your asses to that mountain. I will have a team there to keep anyone from trying to hike, though it is late in the day. It will be dark before you get there."

Sarah knew that Jessica was correct. If there was more time, she would make a stop at her house to collect her night hiking gear, including headlamps. Unfortunately, time was a currency, and she was currently poor. She started the engine and took off, racing the clock once more. The only difference this time was that she was now on the same page as Sam and might even be able to catch her on this mountain.

"Hang on, Ed. This is going to be a fast drive," she said with a hint of a smile.

Chapter 51

Meghan was on her way to the Riviera residence when her phone began to ring. The Bluetooth system in her blue Jeep Cheroki showed the caller information over the radio display, showing that it was a restricted number. This could mean many things, though the most likely scenario was that the caller did not want anyone to have their number. Part of her wanted to ignore the call as it was most likely from a telemarketer, but the other half, the half that was all nose for the news, that half was screaming at her to answer. That was the half that won, it always did.

"Goode," she said after pushing the answer button.

"Meghan, I hear that you have the distinction of succeeding Ms. Monica, the poor darling," the voice of a woman purred.

"Yes," Meghan said slowly. "To whom do I have the pleasure of talking and how did you get this number?"

"Oh, ya know," the voice said playfully. "I just called the station and told them that I had a hot piece of news related to the Mountaintop Killer. They fell over themselves to get me your number. I do hope this is a phone that they pay for..."

"It is not," said Meghan. "And you failed to answer my first question. Please, tell me who this is, or I will end the call."

"Pity," said the voice. "I had hoped that you were smarter than Monica. It's me! The killer!"

Meghan felt her pulse race and her mouth go dry at the same time. How these brakes kept falling into her lap was beyond her.

"Sam?" she asked. "I mean, may I call you Sam?" The voice did not answer, so Meghan took that as an implied yes.

"Well, I am honored that you would call me. What can I do for you?" she asked.

"Honored? Really?" Sam said, still the playful hint to her voice, until she spoke again. "Who do you think you are fooling, bitch? We both know what happened to the last reporter that I called. Still, she did prove useful. My name is known from coast to coast and even across the ocean. I am, for all intents and purposes, immortal. As for what you can do for me, well you can help build my mythos."

Meghan was more scared than she had ever been in her life, but she did not let that affect her. "I am not sure how I would do that."

"Simple really," said Sam. "I am in possession of one Jerry Stevens. He is someone that Sarah had dated in school, and he will be the next to die. His body will be found on Rocky Peak Ridge. I just thought that you might want to be the first on the scene, maybe even be able to catch a picture of me."

Sam ended the call there. Meghan was unsure what to do. It was true that the last reporter to be alone with Sam died horribly, but this lead was far too good to pass up.

Meghan was currently on Fisher Pond Road, between Mineville and Moriah. This put her roughly twenty minutes from the parking lot at the base of Giant Mountain. She did not know from which direction Sam would be traveling, but she had a hunch that she would be able to get there well before Sam. She would have to use her new iPhone fifteen as both a still and video camera, but that should suffice.

She had just barely driven past Ensign Pond Road, so Meghan pulled a very illegal U-turn and accelerated back toward the way that she had just traveled. In less than a minute, she saw her turn approaching on the left. This would lead her to Route Nine and ultimately towards Giant.

"Siri," she said. "Call Susan Day." She wanted to have one of the techs link her phone up so she could broadcast live any time she wanted. This would ensure that she stayed at the forefront of the story. She could feel the Emmy in her had already.

Sue answered after the second ring. "This had better be important."

Meghan told her as quickly as possible what had just happened and what it was that she wanted. Sue, ever the ratings whore that she was, did not hesitate.

"It should take about fifteen to twenty minutes to establish the link," she said. "This story could land you a network position, so do not screw it up."

Sue ended the call with that, and Meghan leaned onto the accelerator a bit harder. This story would make her, she knew it in her soul.

As she drove, she began to wrestle with the fear that was growing in the pit of her stomach. Monica had died horribly at the hands on this killer, that much was certain. However, Sam had needed her to die. It was her way of getting herself known to the entire world. Meghan felt confident that she too was needed, but in a different capacity. Sam would use her to help keep her story in the news. She concluded that she had nothing to fear from this woman. It was not like she was dealing with a fictitious murderer like Jason Vorhees, someone that killed anyone that they encountered. Were that the case, then there would be a lot more bodies piling up. Instead, Sam seemed to choose her victims to further her agenda.

Before she knew it, the signs for the lot at the base of Giant Mountain came into her view. Dusk had fallen and this lent to the eeriness of the situation. Her car had automatic lights, which was good as she had been too deep in thought to pay enough attention to turn them on. As her lights illuminated the lot, she saw that it was empty. She sighed with the knowledge that she had gotten there before Sam.

Meghan parked her car and was about to get out when the phone rang. The caller ID let her know that it was the station. She answered and was greeted by the voice of Paul Lafountain. He was twenty-five and a new addition to the station's tech team.

His deep voice came across the car's speakers. "You are all set to go live. I sent you an email with a hyperlink. Click that and you will be brought to a webpage that I created which will interrupt any broadcast. As soon as you click that link you will be live so, make certain that you are ready to go. To end your live broadcast, just exit the webpage. I know this is not ideal, but it was the best that I could do given the time I had."

"No, no, that is perfect," Megahn said before she ended the call. She opened her email application and sure enough, there was the email. She opened that to have it ready.

Exiting her car, Meghan found herself in a small, paved area. This was one of the few lots for trail heads that was paved. It was large enough for roughly twenty cars, which was small considering the popularity of the mountain. The trees that lined the lot were all either at peak foliage color, or naked, having already lost their leaves. The entry for the trail was at the end nearest the road, and it was there that Meghan would set herself up. She had never done a live broadcast with a cellphone before. She assumed that the rear camera would give the best picture quality, so she decided to use that. She would have to flip the phone over with some rapidity to begin and conclude the broadcast, but that would not be difficult.

Sensing that time was running out before Sam arrived, Meghan made her way to the edge of the guardrail fence that lined the parking lot. The light was getting low, so she turned on the flash for the back camera. While she recorded, it would stay on, illuminating everything within a small radius.

She clicked the link, opened her camera app and pushed record. She then turned the phone over as quickly as possible and did her best to frame her face in the center of what the camera captured. Once he had the camera where she thought the view would be optimal, she began to talk, forcing herself not to squint in the harsh light from the phone.

"Meghan Goode here, broadcasting live from the trailhead at Giant Mountain. I am sorry to interrupt your program, but I have been handed a story that needs to be shared. Around thirty minutes ago, I received a call from the Mountaintop Killer, Samantha Ryan. She informed this reporter that she was coming here with her next victim. The chill that is in the air tonight does not come close to the coldness that inhabits her soul."

Meghan felt the eyes of the world upon her as she paused. From the corner of her eye, she saw headlights approaching from the road. She Realized that the lights belonged to Sam's pilfered vehicle. Meghan's pulse quickened with excitement. She was moments away from being face to face with a serial killer.

Without missing a beat, she began to speak again to the public that was watching her. "As I stand here talking to you, the killer has just arrived at the parking lot."

Meghan turned the phone around so that those watching at home would see the red Kia pull into the lot. The vehicle moved at a slow pace with what almost seemed like a purpose. There was no rushing, there was no panic, the Kia simply pulled into the lot and stopped in the space next to Meghan's car.

"As you can see folks, the mountain top killer is here. She is slowly leaving her vehicle and walking around to the trunk. I can only assume that that is where her next victim has been kept during the trip."

Sam went about her business, seemingly unaware that Meghan was even there, let alone broadcasting her every move. From what Meghan had gleaned about the killer though, she was fully aware of everything. Meghan watched and provided commentary to those that were viewing the event as Sam pulled a body out from the back of the Jeep. She watched in awe as there seemed to be very little effort behind anything that Sam did. It took only a couple of minutes for Sam to secure the person on her back and approach.

Ever the consummate reporter, Meghan took the opportunity to try and interview Sam. "Would you care to say anything to the people at home, watching you?"

Sam stopped and a small smile played across her face. "Jerry Stevens is about to become quite famous," she said slyly.

"Is that who is strapped on your back?" Meghan pressed.

Sam slowly shook her head, clearly not approving of the direction that the questions were taking, so Meghan changed tack. "Why Jerry?"

Looking directly into the camera, Sam said, "Because it will hurt her deeply." Without another word, Sam brushed past Meghan and began her ascent.

"You heard it folks, this is a very personal vendetta that the killer clearly has for Sarah Barney. It is clear to me that she will not stop until she has wounded Sarah deeply enough, or perhaps even takes her life. With this exclusive report, this is Meghan Goode for Fox news."

She swiftly flipped the phone over and ended the transmission. It was then and only then that Meghan allowed the fear that had crept into her body to take a firm hold. She had been inches from a merciless serial killer. Meghan's knees gave out and she slowly slumped on the ground. She sat there, ignoring everything around her, including the ringing of her phone, trying to compose herself.

Chapter 52

Sarah and Ed were well on their way to Giant Mountain, egregiously ignoring all traffic laws in an attempt to catch Sam before she was able to set the next trap. Ed had not spoken a single word in over thirty minutes and the silence had become an almost physical presence inside the car. When he did speak, though his voice was both low in volume and soothing in tone, Sarah jumped, in spite of herself.

"How many times have you played this part in this game?" he asked.

Sarah was confused at first, but quickly understood what it was that he asked. "Honestly, I have not been keeping track, but at least five times," she replied.

He nodded slowly, pensively. "She always has the advantage, she keeps you on defense," he concluded.

Sarah had nothing to say to that, Ed spoke the truth. She also knew that he was going somewhere with this line of thought, and it was best to allow him to get there in his own time.

"Another query, if I may," he said. "Why is it always you that runs up the mountain?"

Sarah was beginning to see where he was going. "She has me targeted," she replied, perhaps a bit more harshly than she meant. "There were two times when we had to split our efforts. On one occasion, there were two possible mountains and on the other, two victims in two locations. The second victim was not found in time."

"That point notwithstanding, you have also failed to save everyone," Ed added. He saw Sarah wince at that and continued. "You are my friend and I yours, but I also am your mentor. There was no malice in that statement. Please, do not take it to heart."

"You're right, of course," she said. Sarah removed her foot from the gas pedal and turned the car to the side of the road, coming to a stop before she spoke again. "So, we go on the offense, but how? She is in the wind but right now, we know where she is."

"Yes, but we also know, with a degree of certainty anyway, who she plans on taking next," Ed replied.

"We set a trap," Sarah said, making the leap to where Ed was steering her. "And, what of Jerry?"

"While we have been driving, I took the liberty of calling in a favor via email. There is currently a helicopter enroute with two very close friends of mine. They will arrive in the area with minutes to spare, however, I am confident that they will save Jerry. I am also quite certain that Sam will not linger as she had before. She knows that the entire state is now aware of the killer's identity, and I believe that she will make haste towards her next target."

"Then it is settled," Sarah concluded. "We will lay a trap for the spider and catch her in our web."

Ed smiled and nodded, "An apt analogy, if ever there was one."

Sarah had three cellphones, her personal cell, which was rarely used, her police issued, and one that only three people knew of, two of whom were in this car. It was a very old flip phone. Her friend at the FBI had had it upgraded internally so that it would function well on the more modern network. Sarah withdrew the black antique from the center console in the cruiser and flipped it open.

There was a chance, however slim, that someone had compromised the other two phones and anything that was said while they were in use would be heard by unwanted parties. Before making the call to the lone contact on the phone, she turned her other phones off. She did not want to take any chances that someone might have highjacked them with the ability to listen in on whatever was being said. She had heard that this was something that was possible.

"Any chance you've got a bug sniffer stuffed somewhere in one of your pockets?" she asked Ed.

He shook his head in the negative. Sarah unbuckled and exited the car. She was all done taking chances. Ed watched as she walked about a dozen feet in front of the cruiser and made the call.

"Sarah, if you are calling me on this phone, then something has gone terribly wrong," Jessica said.

"Quite the contrary, Jess," Sarah replied. "For the first time since any of this began, I think things are about to go right. Ed and I have a plan, and we need to let you know what it is, since you are the bait."

"Bait huh?" Jessica asked. "OK, you've got my attention. What is the plan?"

Sarah spent the next ten minutes pacing back and forth in a small area while laying out what she wanted. Jessica listened intently, not interrupting. When Sarah was done talking, Jessica knew that this was probably the best way to capture Sam.

"I will call a news conference in the morning. That should allow Sam enough time to have the trap set and have gotten off of the mountain. My only concern is whether or not she will see it," Jessica replied.

"Oh, I am quite certain that she will see, or at least hear it," said Sarah.

"One last thing," Jessica added before Sarah could end the call. "Meghan Goode may somehow be tied in with Sam. She was waiting for her at the parking lot and did a live stream of Sam lugging Jerry to the trailhead."

"Well, I suggest you make certain that that bitch is at the conference then," Sarah said as she hung up.

Sarah got back in the car and powered up her other two phones. Before they could fully boot up, she looked at Ed and said, "She's in."

Sarah looked in the mirrors before turning the car around and heading towards Plattsburgh. Time and surprise were now on their side, though how much time exactly, she did not know.

Chapter 53

The early morning November air was brisk and the light breeze that was blowing did little to help the throng of reporters stay warm. They were all clustered in front of the police barracks on Dunning Street, awaiting the chief to come out. She was late, which was uncharacteristic of her, so, there was a general consensus that something had gone wrong. The most popular theory was that someone else had died at the hands of the Mountaintop Killer.

Meghan Goode was the last to arrive. She looked like she had not slept in days. It was getting close to seven O'clock and even the time of the conference seemed dark and mysterious. Meghan had barely worked her way to the front of the crowd where her cameraman was waiting when Jessica exited the front door and looked over the reporters. She was flanked on both sides by three of the largest troopers the state had to offer. Meghan did not recognize any of them, which most likely meant that the Governor had sent them from other areas to protect the chief.

The six troopers were all at least six feet, five inches in height and almost as broad at their shoulders. Their features were equally hidden by the darkness of the early morning and their hats that they wore tipped forward on their heads. As best as Meghan could tell, they were an equal mix of black and white, but that was just a guess. Not that it mattered, they were all there to see what the chief wanted to say.

"May I have your attention," Jessica said. With that, a hush fell over the crowd. The only sound besides her voice was the clicking of cameras. "Yesterday afternoon between three and five, Jerry Connel of Rouses Point was forcefully taken from his driveway. We believed then and later learned for certain that Samantha Louise Ryan was the one responsible, thanks to Meghan Goode of the local Fox affiliate for breaking that story." Jessica paused and looked directly at Meghan with anything but appreciation in her eyes.

"Detective Sarah Barney was on the scene less than thirty minutes after the abduction and deciphered the clue in the form of a riddle that was left behind. She gave chase and arrived at Hurricane Mountain shortly behind Samantha. At some point during her ascent, we lost communication with Sarah. She is now believed to be missing, perhaps even falling victim to the killer."

This brought a rush of talking and questions from the reporters, all of which Jessica ignored. "We are not, I repeat not saying that Sarah is dead. We are simply stating that she has gone missing and until she is located, her current status is unknown. I ask that we all keep her in our thoughts and that everyone keeps an eye out for Samantha Ryan. I will now answer a few questions."

Meghan was the first to jump at this opportunity. "Chief, do you know if Detective Barney was alone?"

Jessica visibly stiffened at the sound of Meghan's voice. She recovered after the briefest of moments, but the change in body language did not escape Meghan's eyes. "She was alone, being the only officer in the area qualified to make the hike in the time required."

"Chief," a young man that worked for the local paper called out. Jessica did not know his name, but he resembled Christopher Reeve from the old Superman movies. "What of Mr. Connel, do we know his fate?"

While Jessica knew that he had been rescued by a small team of FBI agents, and that they had used jamming technology to prevent Sam's camera from broadcasting, she knew that she had to keep all of it from the public for now. "We do not. We also could not detect any sort of transmission from the area. As you are all aware, Samantha would set up a camera so that she could watch the kill or rescue as it happened. For some reason, it seems that she neglected to do that with this victim."

Again, Meghan jumped in, shouting over other questions. "What is the next step then?"

"The next step is that we locate our missing detective. As far as we know, Samantha has not yet taken anyone else hostage. There is a nation-wide APB out on her, so every cop, federal agent and security guard are looking for her. We must try to ensure the safety of the one person we know for sure is missing. Now, I have a lot of work to do, so I will be leaving here and working from my home. I ask that you all respect me and what I need to do to try and bring this case to a swift resolution with no further casualties. Please do not come to my home looking for answers, I will not speak to the press again until we have Samamtha in custody. Good day."

With that, Jessica turned and went back into the barracks. Her small contingent of troopers went with her, leaving the group of reporters with more questions than before. Some of them left while others finished up their live segments. Meghan was the first to finish her report and started to walk back to her car. Her camera man, Jeff Gooding following behind her. He was not her typical assistant but looked intelligent enough to Meghan. He was average height and build, with short black hair and bright blue eyes that stood out against his pale skin. His eyes were the only remarkable thing about him though, which helped him blend into the background. Even his clothes were plain, blue jeans, a plaid shirt and a black North Face jacket.

"What do you think of the last thing she said?" Meghan asked him.

"About working from home?" Jeff replied. "It almost seemed like she was sending a message out to someone."

"That is what I thought too!" she said excitedly. "We need to get an unmarked van and set up outside of her house. I think that she was letting Sam know where she would be in hopes of drawing her out. I want to be there when that happens."

"Funny how things work out," Jeff said. "My buddy just picked up a cargo van that has no windows in the back. It is white and pretty nondescript. We could park it byher house and set up shop."

"Jeff," Meghan said. "I think I love you. Let's meet up at the station around five tonight."

They parted ways. Meghan got into her SUV and Jeff into the Fox van. They drove away from the barracks, hoping that they were the only people that had figured out Jessica's plan.

Jessica had only gone inside the barracks far enough to refrain from being seen but she could watch the group of reporters. One by one they left and soon the lot was free of observers. She pulled out her phone and dialed Sarah's secret phone. She answered on the first ring.

"The trap had been set," she said.

"Great, let us hope that she takes the bait. What of Meghan?" Sarah asked.

"I don't know," replied Jessica. "She is smarter than we both thought. She might be an issue."

"We only need to worry about that if she is truly working with Sam. Maybe she was just being used as a pawn. Ed and I are in position at your house already. What did the feds do with Jerry?"

"They aren't saying," Jessica answered. "All I know is that they got him out of the trap, and he is alive and stable."

"Alright," Sarah said with obvious disappointment in her voice. "At least we know that she did not kill him. Be safe Jess."

Jessica ended the call and turned to Trooper Mackey. He was the head of her protective group and the largest man she had ever seen in person. When she first saw him, she was surprised that he went into law enforcement rather than a professional sport or even wrestling. He stood at six feet and eight inches. He was so broad in the chest that she was surprised he could find shirts that fit. The way in which he carried himself gave ample evidence of his former military career. His skin was the color of coffee, and his brown eyes were hard, almost too hard.

"I want only you to accompany me to my house. You have all been briefed on the plan. With the whole lot of you there, I am certain that Samantha will not try anything. We need her to think that you and I are the only people there," she said.

"Ma'am," he replied in a deep baritone voice. It was spoken with an inflection that allowed everyone to know he was agreeing. "However, I want to go on the record that I think this is a bad decision."

"Well Sargent," she said, "the decision is not yours to make."

"Ma'am," he said again.

Jessica went to her office to gather up the items she would be taking home with her. She was unsure as to whether or not Sam was currently watching her. She wanted to make certain that if she was under observation, that she fully sold the ruse.

Chapter 54

Samantha was parked in another stolen vehicle at a rest area between Keeseville and Plattsburgh. She had taken a late model blue Honda Civic. It was not as versatile as her Jeep, however; it was plain enough that it would be easily overlooked by the casual observer. She was in a fit of rage at the moment and struggling to maintain her composure. She had just tried for the tenth time to log into her server to watch the death of Jerry Connel. For the tenth time, she had not found a complete file waiting. It stopped twenty minutes after she left him on top of the mountain.

Something had gone wrong with her feed. She did not know if he was dead or if Sarah had rescued him. She needed something to calm her down, lest she end up having a tantrum and drawing much unwanted attention to herself. The lot was mostly empty right now, but cars came and went on a regular basis. She decided that she should use her phone to see if there was anything about her on the news. Given the fact that she had developed a relationship of sorts with Meghan, she decided to watch Fox.

She typed the URL into her phone's browser and saw a story on the top of the webpage that was about a news conference from earlier this morning. She selected the icon and waited while the phone buffered enough for the video to play. The Chief had held a conference about her and her best friend Sarah. As she watched and listened, her rage subsided and was swiftly replaced with joy and excitement. Not only had Sarah gotten herself lost, but that meant that Jerry had perished. It was the final statement by the chief that most excited her. She would be working from her home. She would be able to take the chief, and there would be no one to stop her, or rescue Jessica. This was the last piece she needed to complete her puzzle before ending Sarah's suffering for good, provided that she ever made it off of the mountain.

She would make her way to the chief's house after dark and abduct her. Jessica was small in stature, but Sam would not underestimate her strength. She was elevated to chief for a reason. Once she had Jessica, she would deviate from her usual plan and forego taking her up a mountain. Sam was thinking that something more in the public view was called for. This was her next to last performance, she might as well give the public their money's worth.

This next murder would not make her famous, it would make her infamous. Of this, she was certain. Sam only had a few hours to prepare and no home from which to do so. Her face was also well known in the area now, so it was not like she could go and get a hotel room. She needed to improvise, something that she abhorred doing.

The last location where she might find solitude was an abandoned trailer on the Highlands Road. It was part of a large piece of property that was owned by one of the larger, local families. The oldest surviving member of this family still resided in the main house, at the ripe old age of ninety-seven. His oldest son lived there with him, serving as a caretaker. The trailer was once the home of his oldest daughter. She had moved out twenty years ago. In that time, the trees and brush had grown up all around the property, obscuring the trailer from view on all sides.

Ten years ago, Sam had taken someone there to torture and kill. No one had heard the young man scream and this emboldened Sam to use it as a storage facility for some of her supplies. It was there that she would first head, in hopes that her cache held what it was she would need to ensnare and murder Jessica.

She was just over an hour away from the trailer, so she decided that she would use the time between now and sunset to perform some self-care. The town of Keeseville had several abandoned houses, most of which were in the advanced stages of decomposition. There was one house on Prospect Road that had just been foreclosed during the summer. The last that she knew, the power and water were still working there. Sam would head there, shower and cook some food and rest. She would have to park elsewhere and walk to the house. An unknown car parked in the driveway might pique the curiosity of the neighbors and give them cause to call in the police.

Luckily, there was a commerce park that was set up several years ago, and the entire place was empty. The developers had envisioned this as a way to bring a thriving business section into their small town yet had failed to sell a single lot. It consisted of a main road that split into a Y. The left branch of this Y had a small stand of trees, through which was a field. This field came out at the beginning of Prospect. No one really went into the commerce park, so she felt secure enough to leave her pilfered ride there for a few hours. The abandoned house was the third on the left, so this represented a total walk time of less than fifteen minutes.

Sam used the travel time to finalize her plans for Jessica. She would be the proverbial jewel in her crown thus far. Sam would humiliate her publicly before ending her life. These thoughts helped the fifty-minute trip pass swiftly and without incident. In fact, so deep in thought was she, that she did not notice the several police cars that she had driven past.

She turned left into the commerce park and then took the left section of the Y. Happily, there was no one there. She knew that people liked to take their dogs and children for walks in the park, mostly because there was little to no vehicle traffic there. She pulled the car into one of the lots and exited, making her way to the house on foot.

She swiftly found herself outside of the white colonial house. There was still a couple of hours before the sun would set and she was exposed to anyone that would happen to look, but she still took the time to peer in several windows to confirm that the house remained abandoned. Her slight worry abated; Sam made her way around to the back of the house. Although the lawn had stopped growing, it had not seen the attention of a mower in months. It was now a brown, tangled mess that snagged her feet as she walked.

The back lawn was empty of anything that spoke to whomever had lived here before. Nothing had been left behind. The front, far side and rear of the house had a wrap-around porch, which was in much need of care. It looked as though it had not seen a fresh coat of stain in a decade. There were several places where rot had started to blemish the wood.

The three steps creaked loudly as Sam ascended the small flight that led to the back door. Normally this would have given her pause. She was confident that there was no one in the house, so she moved boldly. The door was unlocked, as she expected.

The door opened to a spacious kitchen. The white cabinets that sat below the gray laminate countertop were all open, showing nothing but empty shelves. The same was true for the cabinets that hung on the wall above the counter. The refrigerator and stove were still in place as was the microwave that was mounted to the wall above the stove. Sam reached to her left and tested the light switch. She was relieved to see the lights mounted to the ceiling spring to life. She swiftly flicked the switch back to the off position and shut the door.

The gray tile floor was actually white, something she discovered as she ventured deeper into the house. There was so much dust settled on the tiles that they only appeared gray. It had indeed been quite some time since anyone had entered this house. Sam walked over to the counter and sat her pack down, unzipping the pocket where she kept a supply of food. She selected a package of instant noodles. This she could prepare in the microwave and slake her growing hunger. Sam set about preparing the food. When the microwave chimed to alert her that her meal was ready, she retrieved both the Styrofoam container and a fork from her pack.

The instant meal was flavorful, and the hot noodles and broth warmed her from within. She was once again reminded of the fact that she had no home from which she could select more appropriate clothing. The air outside was hovering around the forty-degree mark and her tee-shirt and Carhart hoodie combination did little to keep the chill at bay.

Once her meal was complete, Sam left the kitchen and entered what she assumed was the living room. The carpet was a lush brown, and the walls were finished with natural wood that was stained a tan color. The wall to her right featured a fireplace while the wall directly in front of her had a large double-hung window and the other entrance into the house. To her left was a staircase. The railing was the same color as the walls and the stairs were covered in the same carpet as the living room.

Sam ascended the stairs, divining that the bathroom must be on the second story. The stairs were quite sturdy and made no sound as she climbed. Sam reached the landing at the top of the stairs, finding a hallway. The second story was finished to match the living room. The hall stretched out on her right, offering four doors.

The doors to each room were open, so it only took the briefest of searches to discover that the bathroom was beyond the first door on the left.

The bathroom was plain, considering how nicely appointed the rest of the house looked. It featured a hardwood floor that had seen better days, a stand-up shower, an old, stained toilet and a vanity with a sink. All of the amenities were the same color, a muted blue. Sam surmised that whomever the former owners were, had been slowly renovating the house and had not yet reached this room before they lost possession. Sam reached into the shower and turned the temperature on the faucet to fully hot. She then went back down the stairs to get her pack while the water warmed.

With her pack in her left hand, Sam returned to the bathroom and delighted in the steam that was pouring from the small shower. Sam grabbed both a towel and a container of bodywash before she swiftly undressed and entered the haven of hot wetness. This was her first opportunity to shower since the night she had killed the man in the hotel, and it felt amazing.

Sam lingered in the shower until the water started to run cold. She was happy that she had had the foresight to close the door to the bathroom. This trapped the heat and humidity from the shower in the small space, preventing her from becoming instantly chilled when she got out. Sam used her towel to dry off and reluctantly pulled her dirty clothes back on. How nice it would have been to have a fresh set, but that mattered little in the grand scheme of things.

Once she was dressed and her belongings stored in her pack, Sam opened the door to the hallway. She almost had a heart attack as she came face to face with a young girl. The door had an old-fashioned knob with a keyhole set below it. This allowed anyone to spy on whoever was inside the room.

The girl looked to be around ten years old. She was maybe four feet tall with dark brown hair that was in a mess upon her head. She was dressed in pajamas and slippers. Sam guessed that she must have been from one of the neighboring houses, saw Sam enter and decided to check her out. This put her in a predicament. Sam, as cold as she was, had never killed a child before, unless one counted someone aged seventeen as a child.

The girl spoke, breaking Sam's line of thought. "You gots an owie on yer leg."

Sam was surprised by the poor English the girl spoke. It would seem that the public school system had not gotten better since she left.

Not sure how to proceed, Sam answered with, "Mmhhmmmm."

"You gunna live hewe?" asked the girl.

"No, I am just visiting," Sam replied. She needed to rid herself of this girl before her mother came looking for her. She decided that the only solution was to be rude and just gather her pack and brush past the child.

This tactic worked and Sam made it to the stairs before the girl turned to follow her. She did not wait to see her intentions and made it to the first floor as swiftly as her injury would allow. Sam entered the kitchen to find who she assumed was the girl's mother standing in the doorway, blocking her escape.

The woman before her was also dressed in pajamas. Her brown hair was long and unkempt. She wore a blank expression on her face, almost as if she was going through life without a clue about anything. The woman took a look at Sam and spoke.

"You seen a little girl?" she asked.

Before Sam could answer, the woman's brown eyes grew large with recognition. "You...you....you dat killer, ain'tcha?" she practically yelled.

Sam knew that her hands were tied. She could not be discovered. Almost reluctantly, she pulled the knife from the sheath on her hip and charged at the woman. Her prey started to turn to flee but was not fast enough. Sam reached her and plunged the knife directly into the woman's heart. From behind her, the girl let out a blood curdling scream.

Sam ripped the knife from the woman's chest as she collapsed to the floor and turned towards the girl. She saw that she was standing in a puddle of urine, her face a mask of terror. Sam knew what it was that she needed to do, but for the first time in her life, she did not want to do it. She took four quick steps and closed the distance between herself and the girl. To Sam's surprise, the girl ran to her and hugged her, sobbing uncontrollably. Sam stood there, hugging this child back and felt tears begin to fall down her face. This only lasted a moment before she gripped the girl's head and gave it a violent twist, snapping her neck. The now lifeless body fell to the floor with a thud. So much potential ended out of curiosity.

Sam spun on her heels and left the house. She made her way back to the Honda and started the engine. She wanted to put this place and those bodies behind her.

Chapter 55

Jessica lived at eleven Palmer Street in Plattsburgh, New York. It was a two-story house that was once converted to apartments. She and her late husband loved the location and house, so when they purchased it, they converted it back to a single-family residence. The exterior was white with black shutters. The lawn was small, but that did not matter to them, it was what one expected to find when living in a city. The only feature that they did not like was that they shared a driveway with the house at thirteen Palmer Street. In the winter, this had initially led to some disagreements over who bore the responsibility of removing the snow.

The interior remodel had been completed a month before her husband had been killed. The house held just over fourteen-hundred square feet of living space, equally divided between the two floors. They had the bottom floor set up to be used as living space and the second floor held four bedrooms and a full bathroom.

The living room was small by some standards, with only enough space for a five-seat sectional and the entertainment stand that held their fifty-five-inch flat screen. The kitchen and dining room combination took up the vast amount of the square footage. Jessica had once fancied herself a gourmet chef, though she stopped cooking when her family passed.

The kitchen featured natural wood cabinets with a light gray granite countertop. Set on the far end of them was a French door, stainless steel refrigerator. In the center of the room was an island, finished in the same natural wood with the stove and sink. The floor was tiled with white marble and shone like it was just installed yesterday. The hallway leading from these two rooms was short, interrupted midway by a doorway leading to the primary bathroom. This featured a giant clawfoot tub, a dual sink vanity and the toilet. All were gleaming white porcelain. The room at the end of the hallway was the study. This was a huge part of making life as a police officer easier. Whenever Jessica or her husband had been working on a difficult case, they would seclude themselves in this room. It featured no windows so there would be less distractions. The walls were covered in knotty pine and the floor was hardwood, with a tan area rug in the center. The only furniture was their Mahogony executive desk and the black leather office chair.

Since becoming the interim chief, Jessica had had no reason to use this room, until now. Although she was not really performing any work, she did not know the extent of Sam's abilities when it came to spying on people. Everyone involved had thought it made sense to have Jessica stay in the office.

The only other person within the walls of Jessica's house was James Mackey. He stood vigil at the beginning of the hallway. Their hope was that if Sam somehow was able to avoid being seen, that she would be forced to enter through the bathroom window and trap herself between the mountain of a trooper and Jessica.

Sarah and Ed had taken up residence at the neighbor's house at thirteen Palmer. The family that lived there was not happy about it but did not see the point in arguing with the detective and an FBI agent. There were two rooms that had windows looking out on Jessica's house from the second story. Two rooms and two people seemed serendipitous. From the second story, they were high enough to see the entirety of both the front and back lawns. As there were no ground floor windows on the side of Jessica's house they could not see, they knew that they would be able to spot Sam as she approached. Everyone, with the exception of Ed, was tense. He rarely seemed to get flustered.

The pair had arrived three hours ago, and Sarah took the window that provided a view of the front of the house. The room she was in belonged to one of the children that lived there. The girl was very into Barbie and the entire room was covered in posters and various paraphernalia. The walls and carpet were pink to boot. Sarah had taken a chair from the dining room table to make her vigil slightly more comfortable.

Several of the residents on this street parked in the road. Upon their arrival, Sarah had taken note of the make, model and plate of each. The only one that gave her a red flag was the white cargo van. It had no windows in the back half and was the perfect place for someone to lie in ambush. The van came back as belonging to Thomas Link. He had no priors, not even a speeding ticket. He also lived in Elizabethtown, forty minutes south of Plattsburgh. Why his van was parked where it was made no sense, but there was no probable cause to go and check it out either.

Sarah decided that it would be best to keep an eye on the van, since there was no reason that she would be able to produce for inspecting it. She was also reluctant to give herself up if Sam was hiding within the walls of that Van.

The sun had set thirty minutes ago but she and Ed were not concerned by the darkness caused by that event. The area was full of streetlights, and with the exterior lights on most of the houses lit, the area around Jessica's house was sufficiently illuminated.

Sarah and Ed had agreed to check in with each other every fifteen minutes. Prior to arriving at Jessica's house, they had picked up three burner phones, using a tactic employed by many criminals. They gave one to Jessica and kept the other two for themselves. They did not want to leave anything to chance, so they all had their primary phones off. Sarah left hers in the car that they parked two blocks away and Jessica had secured hers in her wall safe. Ed was the only one that still carried his, but that was only because it was federally issued and impossible to hack.

Sarah dialed Jessica's first and she answered on the first ring. They had devised a phrase for Jessica to say that would let Sarah know all was good but not tip off anyone that might be eavesdropping. "Anything to report Mack?" she said.

Sarah kept her reply short, "Copy," before ending the call.

She dialed Ed next. "Sarah," he said when he answered. "I have not seen anything nor anyone of interest since last we spoke."

"I have nothing to report either," she said. "The sun has only been down for about thirty-five minutes though."

"I did not mean to imply that we abandon our watch," he said. "Only to report on the lack of act..."

Sarah bristled at the way Ed stopped talking mid-sentence. She did not say anything, however, and strained her ears to hear something, anything. After several seconds without a sound coming through the phone, she pulled hers down to look at the screen. The call had ended. Either it had dropped and there was no reason for concern, or Ed ended it, which would be a reason for concern.

Sarah was torn. Ed was only one room over from her, and she could check on him in seconds, but that would leave the front of Jessica's house unwatched and vulnerable. She had to choose between her mentor or her boss and friend. Sarah quickly ran through everything she knew about Ed. It did not take but a second to understand that he would never just end a phone call, especially not mid-sentence.

Sarah rose from her chair with as much speed as she could and turned away from the window. She was both confused and shocked. Standing directly in front of her was Sam, a wicked smile on her face. Somehow this woman had entered the house where they hid, neutralized Ed and entered the room where Sarah sat, all without a sound.

"You make this too easy," Sam said.

Before Sarah could react, Sam came at her in a blur of motion, plunging a knife in the center of Sarah's right breast. The pain was excruciating, and she crumpled to her knees. With her left arm still in a sling, and the pain from the stab wound making moving her right arm nearly impossible, Sarah was at the mercy of the woman that wanted her dead.

Sam circled Sarah where she knelt on the floor like a predator. There was nothing but malice in her eyes. As Sam made her third trip around Sarah, she noticed the phone that had fallen from her hand. She raised her foot and brought it down upon the phone with all the force she could muster. It was destroyed with a satisfying crunch. Sam stopped in front of Sarah once more.

"You were supposed to be my greatest challenge, yet here you are, on your knees in front of me where you belong," Sam spat out.

Sam bent over at the waist and thrust the knife against Sarah's throat. To her credit, Sarah did not flinch.

"I could end this now," she said. "I should end this now. You are nothing, not even a thorn in my side. I cannot believe that I once loved you."

This last statement from Sam caused something to click in Sarah's mind. Every last piece of the puzzle fell into place. It had been more than a small crush to Sam back in school. She had developed a full-blown case of puppy love. Something in her brain was wired wrong though, and even after all of the years that had passed, Sam could not understand that the "love" she had felt for Sarah was not something that would have ever lasted. That did not matter though. Sarah knew she now had a slight chance.

"Sam, wait," she said through the pain. "I had fallen in love with you too back then, I was just afraid to admit it."

A mix of emotions played across Sam's face, from anger to confusion to rage to sadness, before ending on doubt. She withdrew the blade from Sarah's throat and paced once more, this time in front of Sarah. She was talking to herself, or perhaps to Sarah, it did not matter, she was off her game for the moment.

"Not possible, if you loved me then why did you not say anything? We could have been happy together. We could have been a great team. Now I have to kill you. I have no choice. But what if you still have feelings for me like I do you?"

Sam stopped talking and pacing with that last question. She strode over to Sarah and knelt in front of her. Sam set the knife down on the floor and gripped Sarah's head in her hands, pulling her in towards her. Their lips met and Sarah did her best to hide the revulsion she felt in being forced to kiss a cold-blooded killer. Instead, Sarah leaned into the kiss and injected as much passion as she could muster.

Sam lost herself to the moment, melting into Sarah. Sarah seized the opportunity and pressed into Sam, trying to cause her to lie down on her back. Sam was used to being the dominant one though and resisted. She reached down with her hands and pulled Sarah fully into her, causing Sarah to let out a grunt of pain. That was all it took to break the spell under which Sam had found herself. Sam recoiled from the tender moment and stood, grabbing the knife as she went.

"It is too late for that," she said with sadness in her voice. "Much too late. I cannot stop what I started, and you must die."

Before Sarah could react, Sam's left foot shot out and met her face with alarming force. Sarah fell over on her side, knocked out from the blow. Sam stood there, unclear as to how she should proceed. Once again, she was in the position to easily claim Sarah's life. She could end this now, or take Sarah hostage and torture her, or continue with her plan.

She had put too much time and effort into everything to simply stop now. She would take Jessica hostage and execute her publicly as she planned. The ball was in motion, so to speak. Unable to resist toying with Sarah, she knelt beside her limp body and used the knife to start cutting away her clothes. She would leave Sarah there bleeding and naked, one room away from a dead man.

Surprise captured Sam when a lamp crashed into the floor next to her. She spun away from Sarah, the knife still halfway through her shirt. Surprise was exchanged with shock. The man that was in the other room, that she had stabbed in the back and left for dead, was propped up against the wall, just inside the doorway. There were now two people in the room with formal training on how to defend themselves, and both likely armed. Almost in answer to this last thought, the man reached into his jacket, probably seeking out a gun. Sensing that things were spiraling out of control, Sam sprinted past the man and down the stairs, leaving the pair bloody and weak in her wake.

Chapter 56

Meghan and Jeff had been parked in the road across from Jessica's house for what seemed an interminable amount of time. The chief had arrived home hours ago, with one trooper as a guard. Neither of them could detect any activity within the walls of the house, and they were both growing bored.

Meghan was not sure what exactly she had imagined would transpire during this stake-out, but sitting in a van with a camera man and making small talk was not it. Darkness had fallen and it seemed as though nothing would happen. She was considering calling it a day when movement from the front door of the neighbor's house caught her attention. Against all odds, Sam exited the house and hurried across the lawn towards Jessica's. To his credit, Jeff saw her too and had the camera up and recording.

Meghan began talking into the microphone, narrating what she was seeing. "Meghan Goode here. I have been parked outside of twelve Palmer Street for the last several hours, hoping to catch a glimpse of Sam if she went after the interim chief. As luck would have it, she has just exited the residence at thirteen Palmer and is making her way across the lawn toward the Chief's residence. She seems to be quite hurried, as if something happened within the walls at thirteen Palmer. As you can see, she has reached the shared driveway and has stopped, looking in all directions."

A voice came over her earpiece, one that she did not recognize. "Meghan, you are now live, there is around a two-minute delay to play what you have already recorded."

Meghan felt a thrill at this, as she knew that she was live on the entire network, not just the local station. She went on with her narration. "Sam has clearly spotted the van in which my cameraman and I have been hiding. Perhaps I could get a word from her."

Without hesitating, Meghan opened the driver's door and got out of the van. Jeff was right behind her, ever the career minded individual. A deep frown crossed Sam's face at the boldness that Meghan was displaying. Such a display of hubris would not go unpunished. Sam started to walk towards the reporter and her camera man.

"Sam, a word if I may?" asked Meghan.

Sam did not allow anything else to be said. She struck Meghan with a solid backhand, causing the reporter to tumble to the ground. Before Jeff could react, Sam knocked the camera to the ground, shattering it. With her other hand, she plunged her knife into his throat, right above his Adam's apple. Jeff collapsed, choking on his own blood. Sam spun towards Meghan who was laying on the ground on her stomach. She straddled Meghan and grabbed a handful of hair, pulling her head up. Sam reached around with her knife and slit Meghan's throat before letting go of her hair. Meghan's forehead slammed into the pavement.

The small distraction removed; Sam made her way back towards Jessica's house. She did not know if the reporter was broadcasting live or simply recording for a later airing. If she had been broadcasting live, then her time before the police would be alerted was very limited. She refused to give up her plan now. She knew that she would not get another shot at capturing Jessica.

Unknown to everyone, apparently, and still undiscovered, Sam had set up video surveillance cameras both inside and outside of Jessica's house weeks ago. It was all part of her prep work. That was why she knew that she would win this contest, Sam had been playing the long game since before anyone knew that there was a game being played.

Jessica and her one bodyguard had arrived shortly after the news conference, with Sarah and the unknown man not long after that. Taking the pair out in the neighbor's house had taken more time than Sam had wanted, but it was unavoidable. She would have to outsmart and overcome the very large trooper that was standing guard at the end of Jessica's hallway.

She laughed at Jessica's imagined superiority, secreting herself in the study where there were no windows. With the trooper at the end of the hall, and Jessica there, this left Sam with only one option for entry, the bathroom window. She was sure that that was their plan, to trap Sam between the two. That plan would backfire, and Jessica would find herself in a room with only one exit. That exit would lead directly into Sam's clutches.

It was time to pull out another trick, her blowgun. Sam hoped that her entry through the window would be stealthy enough to go unnoticed and allow her to use the silent weapon to take out the trooper. She was not going to worry about sedating him, rather, she had found by happy accident a supply of hydrogen cyanide. The pale blue liquid, once injected into the body, would render the trooper harmless instantly and dead in minutes. It had taken Sam quite some time to develop a dart that would work in her gun that would hold a sufficient amount of the liquid to kill. She felt good about her chances, even given the large mass her target possessed.

Sam made her way into the back lawn as swiftly and as silently as she could and found herself looking at the bathroom window. There was no screen installed, whether by luck or design. She was not surprised to find it unlocked and slid it open. The bottom of the window was at waist level, so climbing through proved to be easy and Sam found herself inside a small, well-appointed bathroom.

On her left side was the toilet, gleaming in a pearl white and the double-sink vanity, also in pearl white. The cabinet itself was made of oak with a clear stain applied. On her right side was a narrow door that she assumed led to the linen closet and giant, white clawfoot tub. The complete absence of a shower curtain informed Sam that this was most likely set-up for Jessica, as most men abhorred taking baths.

Directly in front of her was the doorway leading to the hall. The door was open and there were no sounds making their way into the room except the ticking of some far-off clock. The only light in the bathroom was that which spilled in through the door from the hall. She was semi covered in darkness, but most importantly, she would see someone coming before they saw her.

Sam waited for a minute, which in her current state seemed like an eternity. She readied her blow gun and inched towards the door. She was hoping that the light blue tile floor was solid and would not betray her location. She reached the doorway and stopped just short of entering the hall. Again, she strained her ears and could not hear the sound of people. Furtively, she poked her head out of the doorway, just enough to look in the direction of the trooper. She saw him standing at the entry to the hall, his back to her.

Sam ducked back in the bathroom and sighed. She turned her body to face the office and repeated the quick glance, this time finding a closed door. This would be too easy. Sam turned and faced the trooper, raising the gun to her lips. She blew into the mouthpiece with all of her might and the dart exited the chamber. Her aim was true, and the dart struck the trooper just below his hairline.

His left hand shot up to where the impact was, but he made no sound. He ripped the dart from his neck with his left while he pulled his gun from its holster with his right hand. He started to turn in her direction, but the cyanide worked too swiftly, and he fell with a thud.

Sensing that that was enough noise to alert Jessica that something was amiss, Sam spun towards the office and practically ran to the door. She tried the knob and found it locked. Jessica was smarter than she looked. The door in front of her was not the typical hollow kind that one usually found inside houses. This was a solid pine door; she could not simply break through it. Her injured leg would prevent her from kicking it in as well.

The only answer was in the right hand of the fallen trooper, his gun. Sam walked over to where he was prone on the floor and plucked it from his hand. As she stood back erect, something grazed her left shoulder and was swiftly followed by a load bang. Jessica was shooting at her.

Sam immediately dropped to the floor and began crawling towards the door. This was taking far too long, and she was losing patience. Two more shots rang out and Sam was covered with splintered wood. Jessica was aiming too high and missing her mark. When Sam was two feet from the door, she aimed the gun at the knob and fired off three shots. The angle from which she shot precluded any risk that Jessica might be hit by a bullet.

The knob now hung loosely in the door and Sam knew that she could enter at will. There were two problems with that. First was that Jessica was clearly armed and Sam did not know how much ammunition was at her disposal. The second was that Sam could not think of any way to get in the room and subdue Jessica without killing her or getting herself killed in the process. An armed and ready opponent was not something for which Sam had planned.

Jessica sensed her hesitation and tried to taunt Sam into action. "You took out that mountain of a trooper with ease, but you were not expecting me to be armed. Were you cunt?"

Sam gave no reply, so Jessica taunted her some more. "I assume you also took out Sarah and Ed, so you are as smart as we all thought. How come you were not smart enough to foresee this?"

Jessica fired another shot, this one lower. The bullet hit the floor a few feet behind Sam. "I can do this all night," she spat out. "You only have one, or maybe two clips. My rescuers are already on their way. You should just leave now, or you will be trapped in here with me and half of the state police force."

Sam cursed under her breath. Jessica was right. It was time for action, either fight or flee. Jessica's office was one place where Sam had not installed a camera. She was guessing but figured that there was a desk beyond the door in front of her and hoped that that was where Jessica was standing. Sam slowly stood, hugging the wall on the left side in the hopes that if Jessica fired another shot that it would miss her. She put pressure on her injured leg to test out how strong it felt. Satisfied with the result she barreled forward, smashing through the door and into the office.

Once she had cleared the door, Sam dove to the floor, landing directly in front of the desk she had correctly surmised was there. The room was sparsely lit, but there was enough illumination for Sam to see Jessica from the ankles down under the desk. She did not hesitate and took aim with the gun, shooting Jessica in her right ankle. She fell with a scream, dropping her gun in favor of clutching her ankle. Sam got to her feet and circled the desk.

"Barely a challenge," she said to Jessica.

Before Jessica could respond or react, Sam fished one of her last three syringes from her pocket and injected the chief with her cocktail. The anguish that had taken over Jessica's countenance slowly faded to a look of peace as she lost consciousness. As Sam was bending over to grab her by the shoulders, she detected the sound of sirens approaching. They sounded far enough away that she knew she could make it out before they arrived, but just barely. Positioning Jessica in a fireman's curry, Sam made her way to the back door as swiftly as possible, dropping what would be her last clue on the kitchen table as she went.

Chapter 57

The night sky was awash with the red and blue strobe from the police and rescue lights. There was not a part of Plamer Street that did not have an emergency vehicle parked on it. Both ends of the street were blocked by state police cars to keep the media away from the grisly scene. It seemed like every single reporter in the state as well as from Vermont had arrived. Nothing like this had ever happened in upstate before and it was clear that everyone wanted to be the person that broke some snippet to the public.

Three hours had passed since Jessica was taken. She had been smart enough to send a text message to her friend Felix Lamountain, the chief of the state police in the Albany barracks. He had left for Plattsburgh immediately upon receiving the message and had taken over the scene.

Felix was approaching his retirement age, with only three months before his sixty-fifth birthday. He looked far older though, as the years were not kind to him. He was four times divorced but had no children. It seemed the women in his life could not commit to anything. He was still over six feet tall, but the years had caused him to hunch. His grey hair was thin, and his blue eyes had long ago faded to a dull grey. He was not in uniform but had thought to change from his pajamas to jeans and an NYPD hoodie. He could not decide though if it was the cold night air or the pair of bodies on the ground in front of him that chilled him to the bone.

He stared with a blank look on his face as the paramedics zipped the pair of body bags shut. The forensic team had finished processing the reporter and cameraman minuets ago and Felix wanted the bodies taken away. He had called in members of his own forensic team to help process Jessica's house and the dead trooper that it contained. He slowly raised the paper Stewart's coffee cup to his lips and took a long drink of the caffeine-rich liquid.

"Chief?" asked Sargent Lafountain.

Felix looked up from the bags, surprised. So deep in thought was he, that he did not notice the Sargent had walked up and spoken to him.

Sargent Mike Lafountain was from the Plattsburgh barracks. He was slim and tall, with an olive complexion and dark, black hair. His brown eyes were full of sadness. He was the only person that Jessica had let in on her plan before she left for the day. His specialty was burglary, but even he had known it was not a wise idea. He also knew that Sarah and her FBI contact Edneburgh were supposed to be in the area to keep a watch for Samantha.

"I said that I think we need to go door to door in search of detective Barney," he repeated.

"Yeah, that seems like our next step," Felix replied. "Though, if it was me surveilling this house, I would set-up shop there." He pointed to the house that shared a driveway with Jessica's.

Mike nodded and made his way to the front door. Thirteen Plamer Street was a two-story home that was sided in white vinyl. The front door was under the roof of the front porch. He slowly ascended the steps and opened the white metal storm door. Mike reached out with his gloved left hand for the knob while his right hand rested on the butt of his service gun. He did not have it pulled from the holster because he believed Samantha had long ago left the area. He was not foolish enough to completely dismiss that there was still a possibility of danger though.

He was not surprised to find that the doorknob turned freely. He pushed the door forward and pulled his flashlight from his belt. Aiming the light forward, he entered the living room. The room was a mess, though not because of a struggle. The people that lived here clearly had children as there were toys and clothes taking up a lot of the space. The brown carpet was stained and when his light found the small flat screen television, he saw that it was covered with small fingerprints. Directly in front of him was a door that led to the kitchen and to his immediate right was a stairway leading to the second story. Mike knew that when you were trying to keep watch of an area, height was to your advantage.

He climbed the wooden staircase, surprised by the fact that it did not squeak under his weight. He paid little attention to the pictures that adorned the wall and found himself on the second-floor landing in seconds. The hallway in which he found himself went both to his left and right. Clearly, if Sarah was keeping an eye on

Jessica's house, she would have taken up residence in one of the rooms to his left.

There were two doors, both ajar at that end of the hall. Mike used his flashlight to sweep the area to see if anything looked out of place. He saw blood on the blue carpet, forming a trail between the two rooms. Clearly, someone was hurt or possible dead. Shirking all further caution, he rushed forward to the closest door.

Mike entered a pink heaven, what was clearly a small girl's room. There were two bodies on the floor, one male and one female. Mike had only met Sarah once, and he had never met her FBI friend, but logic dictated that this must be them. Edenburgh was closest to Mike, so he stopped there first to see if he was still alive. Ed was on his stomach and there was a large blood stain on his suit jacket, with an obvious hole by his right shoulder. Mike placed two fingers on Ed's neck and detected a weak pulse. He got up from his crouch and approached Sarah.

As Mike crouched down next to Sarah, her eyes fluttered open. Her eyes met his and Mike saw relief in them. He grabbed his walkie and pushed the talk button.

"Lafountain here," he said. "I am upstairs in thirteen, I need medics ASAP. I have two officers down."

He got a copy back immediately. Sarah tried to move but he gently restrained her.

"Jessica?" she asked weakly.

Mike did not know what to say, so he shook his head. The chief was in the clutches of a madwoman. The only person that could probably save her was lying on the floor with a bleeding wound.

Chapter 58

To say that Sam was displeased with how events had unfurled while taking the chief hostage would be the understatement of the century. She had been rushed, which infuriated her, and she had passed on yet another chance to kill Sarah. But what of that kiss? Had there honestly been something there, or was Sarah playing her to buy time? Nothing leaves one so empty as unrequited love, and Sam's soul was a chasm of space right now.

Her only consolation was that she had gained some time, a thing that had been in so shorty supply for her as of late. Sarah was wounded, not critically but enough that she would require some time in the hospital. The man that was with her was also wounded, though not as badly as she had assumed. Regardless, neither of them would be hot on her heels this night.

Their attempt at trapping her had also given her an advantage. They thought that the four of them could capture her with no back-up anywhere near the house. Sarah and her friends had learned once more how dangerous underestiamting her could be.

Thirty-six hours was all the time that Sam had before her supply of sedative would run out. Thirty-six hours from when she had delivered the dose to Jessica, she would be fully conscious and not agreeable, to say the least. Sam would have to travel to Vermont, set-up the mechanism that would kill the chief and lay the trap for Sarah, where Sam would finally claim her life.

Sam already knew exactly how she would do it too. It would not be quick with a knife, nor would it be like the others she had killed lately. No mechanism for Sarah. She would beat her to death with her bare hands. Sarah would know what she felt like, all those years ago on the playground. Sarah would suffer excruciating pain before her body would give out and expire. This thought put a smile on her face, ending her sour mood.

For now, she would have to pick out a spot to lay low, to give Sarah enough time to be treated and continue their game. Sam did not for one minute believe that Sarah would give up, especially now that Sam had the chief. Sarah would see this through to the inevitable end.

Sam would be taking the ferry across the lake, which ran from Cumberland Head to Grand Isle. Technically the ferry did not deliver people fully into the state, but rather onto the islands that Vermont owned in the shared lake between the states. Lake Champlain, named after the French explorer Samual D. Champlain, was one-hundred-twenty miles long and ran almost the entire length of Vermont. Its waters were grey and cold, as one would expect in a body of fresh water this far north. Many people did not know that the lake was connected to the Atlantic Ocean, through the Richelieu River through Canada and then the Saint Lawrence Seaway and is often referred to as the sixth great lake. It had been the site of many battles during the revolutionary war. Those were just some of the useless facts that Sam had been forced to learn while in school.

Grand Isle would eventually lead her through the Heros, first North and then South. It was in South Hero where she would find a place to hide out. Route Two was the state road that she would follow and just before the bridge that would lead from the islands and into Milton, Vermont was a campsite named Apple Island. What made Apple Island unique was that it was the type of campsite that had permanent campers on it. Granted, they closed down every winter, usually by the middle of October, but everyone just left their campers there. A lot of people had built porches and other amenities around their campers to make it feel more like home during the summer months when they stayed there. Sam knew that since it was now the beginning of November, that all of the campers would be empty. At the far end of the property was Pike Circle, with most of the campers flanked by a small forest on their back lawns. There would be no one to see her come and go.

Sam arrived at the ferry dock without incident. She had half expected there to be some sort of police presence there, seeking her. It would seem that no one expected her to leave the state. She followed the booth attendant's instructions and parked in lane 2, one of several cars that were crossing the lake this night. Fifteen minutes later, the ferry arrived and the cars from the trip to New York started to disembark.

The whole process was efficient, as one would expect from an entity that had been transporting people across the lake for decades. As her line began to move, Sam followed the cars in front of her and had her boarding pass ready to hand off to the person in charge of collecting them. She had crossed here several times but did not recognize the young man performing the job tonight. He looked to be around twenty years old and was severely overweight. So much so in fact, that he was wearing only a T-shirt and shorts while the rest of the ferry crew was dressed in parkas, hats, gloves and jeans. His black hair looked like it had not seen a washing or brushing in weeks. His glasses had slid to the tip of his nose and snot was dripping from his left nostril. He leaned into her window instead of taking her boarding pass.

"Good evening," he said. His breath smelled like a garbage dump. "We perform routine and random inspections of the vehicles that cross here. Can you please open your trunk?"

Sam felt her blood run cold for a moment. She knew this was part of the process, ever since 9/11, but she had never been selected before. She could clearly not comply; the trunk was where she had placed the chief. She would have to try to bribe this guy and hope no one saw.

Instead of answering, Sam leaned over to the passenger seat and unzipped her pack. From it, she pulled out a wad of bills about three inches thick and placed her boarding pass on top. She showed the stack to the man and put the sweetest smile she could muster on her face.

"I would really rather not," she purred. "I have some pretty private things in there and I do not want anyone to see them. I am sure you understand."

The man's eyes went wide at the stack of cash, and he nervously licked his lips. Slowly, he reached into her car and took the offered money.

"You are good to go," he said and waived her forward.

Sam did not hesitate. She put her car back in drive and boarded the ferry, hoping that this was the last time she would come close to getting caught.

Chapter 59

Sarah woke up in what was clearly a hospital room, specifically an emergency room. Three of the walls were made of curtains. To her left, where the only solid wall stood a set of cabinets that contained all manner of medical supplies. Her right arm was wrapped in a blood pressure cuff and her index finger on that hand had the device that measured your pulse. She was alone.

Sarah took a mental assessment of her injuries. She could not feel the area where she was stabbed but her left side was sore. Her collar bone would never heal at this rate. She assumed the numbness in her right side meant that the wound had been stitched closed and that the result of being stabbed had not caused any major internal injuries.

Her bed was not set-up to lay flat but rather in a reclined position. Sarah sat up the rest of the way and swung her legs over the edge of the bed. Her head swam a bit, but she otherwise felt fine. She began to unstrap herself from the devices and located the bag that hung on the wall with the words "patient's belongings" written on it.

Sarah tested out standing before she walked over and claimed the bag. There was considerable stiffness in her right side, but she would have to deal with that. She dumped the contents of the bag onto the bed, removed the hospital gown and started to slowly dress in her own clothes.

"Leaving so soon?" a voice asked her from behind.

Sarah turned and saw that the nurse she had met earlier, Aubry, was standing just inside the curtain.

"I need to check on my friend," she replied.

"Agent Enedburgh?" Aubrey asked. Without waiting for her to answer, she pointed to the next curtained room over. "Luckily for you both, neither stab wound was mortal. His missed his heart by a fraction of an inch."

"I am not sure lucky is a word I would use in this situation," Sarah said gruffly. "That is mostly good news though. We have to safe the chief."

"Listen, far be it from me to tell you what to do, I am just a lowly nurse," Aubry said with a healthy dose of sarcasm. "But what you both need is a couple of weeks to heal."

She was right of course. Unfortunately, that would doom Jessica to die. "I'll heal when this woman is taken out of commission," Sarah replied before ducking through the curtain into the room where Ed was sitting on his bed.

He was already dressed and smiled at Sarah. "I knew that you would be joining me sooner or later," he said. "Your friend, Sargent Mike Lafountain dropped this off to me a few moments ago."

Ed handed a piece of paper to Sarah. "Her clue, I assume?"

"I do not know," Ed replied. "I wanted to await you before reading it."

Sarah unfolded the paper and began to read aloud. "What a wonderful game you have played, old friend. I do hope all of your injuries will mend. I took Jessica, without fail. I am Ahab to you, the whale. Think of our story, oh what a tail. Thirty-six hours is all you will have to save her. No more rhymes, no more games. Hurry, hurry. Rush to your death."

Sarah reread the note thrice before looking at Ed. He wore a look of puzzlement that matched her own. This was too cryptic to be solved in time. All of the other clues that Sam had left had at least hinted to the location where she was taking her victim. This time, it seemed as though that was not the case.

"Thoughts?" she asked.

"None, really," he answered. "All that we know is that the chief is in her custody, and from a former clue, that she would be most likely taking her to Vermont."

"I am not really sure what Ahab and the whale have to do with Vermont," Sarah said, clearly frustrated. "How long has it been since Jessica was taken?"

Ed looked at his watch, wincing slightly in pain. "Six hours, forty-two minutes and roughly thirty-seven seconds have passed already. This leaves us with just over twenty-nine hours."

Sarah had no time to spare, so she yanked open the curtain that led to the main hallway in the emergency department and almost ran into a man she had never seen before. Behind him was the nurse.

"Chief Lamountain from Albany," he said, introducing himself. "Jessica had called me in, long story."

"Chief", said Sarah. "To what do I owe this pleasure?"

Felix looked strained as he answered. "Well, I am kinda assuming command of this situation. This nice nurse here just informed me that you two think you are going after this Samantha."

Sarah glared at Aubrey. "As good as her intentions might be informing you of my plans, I do not see how you think you can stop us," she said, gesturing at Ed.

"Special Agent Francis Edinburgh," Ed said to Felix. "I have been working with Detective Barney on this case for the last few days. This is now officially an FBI case as we suspect that Ms. Ryan has absconded with the chief to Vermont. Before you try to relieve the good detective here of any of her duties, I am assuming command of her as she is vital to this case."

Felix knew that there was no way he could pull jurisdiction on the agent, so he simply nodded. Typically, the feds would work with the local police, but it seemed as though Edinburgh had covered that by keeping Sarah on the case. In any event, Felix was too old and too damned tired to fight it. "Keep her safe," he said as he turned to walk away.

"Chief," Sarah called out. "We will be needing a vehicle."

Felix paused a few feet from the pair but did not turn to look at them. "There are several cruisers out front, just take one of them."

Free of all local restraints and federal ones too, the FBI had not yet announced they were working on the case, Sarah and Ed made their way out of the ER and towards the lobby. Time was against them once more.

They exited the building and found several troopers at the front door, keeping the press from entering. Sarah saw one she knew and shouted his name.

"Rodrigues!"

Trooper Jose Rodrigues was new to the Plattsburgh barracks, having freshly graduated. He was dark in both skin tone and hair color, with probing brown eyes. He was shorter than the average trooper, at just five feet eight inches tall. He turned when he heard his name and smiled as he walked over to Sarah.

"Nice to see you on your feet detective," he said. "How can I help?"

"You and your car are coming with us," she said. "We have to get to Vermont. This agent and I have a lot to discuss, so having a driver will be helpful."

"Indeed," added Ed.

Rodrigues nodded and led the way to his cruiser, which happened to be the first in line. As the trio made their way, the large crowd of reporters shouted questions, none of which were acknowledged.

Rodrigues assumed the driver's seat and Sarah and Ed got into the back to facilitate their conversation. Rodrigues started the engine and took off from the hospital.

"Ferry or bridge?" he asked.

Sarah and Ed exchanged looks before she answered, "The ferry."

"Logical," said Ed. "Should our quarry have wanted a speedy exit from this state, that was certainly her best bet. Now, to the problem at hand. Where will she be taking the dear chief?"

"That is the million-dollar question," Sarah replied thoughtfully. "We know that she enjoys the spectacle of these traps of hers, and that she wants, no craves the attention of the masses. I know little enough about Vermont though to make any connection to whales. The only thing I can think of is the Echo Center, which is a nature and science museum. But, if I am not mistaken, there were never any whales living in the lake."

"That is not entirely true," Rodrigues chimed in. "Sorry to interrupt, but sometime around eighteen-fifty there was a Beluga whale skeleton found buried in sediment in the town of Charlotte. It is believed that during the last ice age that the Atlantic Ocean made a direct connection via the Saint Lawrence and the area was salty enough to support whales, or something along those lines."

"You seem quite well educated on this matter," Ed said with a hint of surprise.

"Not really, sir." said Rodrigues. "I dated a girl who was going for her degree in geology. They have the skeleton on display at UVM at the Perkins Museum of Geology. That was her idea of a fun date, spending hours there."

Sarah chuckled mirthlessly at this. "I do not think a museum on geology would be a public enough of a place for Sam to kill the chief."

"That and the fact that setting people into her contraptions takes time, something she would lack in that sort of environment."

"What we do now know though, is that there is a history of whales in Vermont, though how that helps is beyond me," he concluded.

"Mind sharing what you are trying to figure out?" Rodrigues asked.

Sarah saw no harm in another set of ears hearing what was written, so she pulled out the paper and read it aloud. When she was done, silence descended on the car as everyone tried to think.

"Rodrigues, are there any stories about the whale, that you know of?" Sarah asked.

He shook his head in the negative. "Out of curiosity, how did she spell the word tale?" he asked.

Sarah had noticed that the word was spelled to indicate the appendage associated with animals. "T A I L," she spelled out.

"As in whale tail?" he asked more to himself. "Of course!"

Rodrigues continued with clear excitement in his voice. "On Interstate eighty-nine, the northbound side, just north of Williston is a sculpture. Care to guess what of?"

"By the excitement in your voice, I would hazard to say whale tails," Ed replied.

"You would be correct," Rodrigues said in answer.

"Do we put all of our eggs in that basket?" Sarah asked.

"I believe we do," Ed said.

Things might just work out in their favor this time. They knew well in advance where Sam would be going. They just needed to outthink her. She had clearly known that Sarah and Ed were watching from the rooms, how else had she been able to find and neutralize them? It was an established fact that Sam was tech savvy and had on multiple occasions employed the use of cameras.

"She is gonna see us coming a mile away," said Sarah into the silence.

"I was thinking the exact same thing," Ed agreed. "She will most likely have the area under surveillance via cameras. That would also explain the ease with which she discovered the two of us within the walls of the house."

Sarah was happy that her mentor was thinking along the same lines as she. They could jam the equipment, something that they had already done, but this would only serve to alert Sam. Sarah was going to have to use herself as bait. She pulled out her cellphone and dialed the barracks. When the call was answered she asked to be patched through to Chief Lamountain.

"Chief, Sarah Barney here. I need you to release a statement to the press. Tell them that I have been released and am working on tracking down Samantha Ryan but the mystery man that was with me had to undergo surgery and is in the ICU."

No one in the car could hear what Felix had to say, but the look on Sarah's face told them it was not what she wanted to hear.

"I do not care if you are unaccustomed to taking orders from subordinates. If you do not do as I asked, Sam will be expecting the two of us and Jessica will surely die."

After another brief pause Sarah said, "Thank you, sir." and ended the call.

"It would seem that you have a plan," Ed said.

"I do," Sarah agreed. "If she thinks that I am the only one coming, then that will provide an opportunity for me to distract her on one front while you two can approach her from the rear. We will need another car and a bit of luck, but I think this will work."

Ed pulled out his phone and made a call. When he was done, he addressed the car. "I have just secured a rental at Enterprise, located on the Williston Road in Burlington. Mr. Rodrigues and I shall use this as our mode of transportation, whilst you can employ the cruiser. Now, let us hear the rest of this plan of yours."

By the time they reached the booth at the ferry landing where you paid to board, Sarah had laid out the entirety of her plan. It was not without risks, but Ed could find no fault in it.

Almost as an afterthought, Sarah called up a picture of Sam on her phone. It was a drawing done by a sketch artist as the DMV photo they had gotten looked little like the woman that they were after.

"Has this woman come through here tonight?" she asked as she handed her phone to the attendant.

The woman working the booth was in her forties, her brown hair run though with greys. She looked as though sitting in a booth and collecting ferry fees was the last thing she wanted to do in life. Her face lit up a bit when she saw the image though.

"Yeah, she said with a voice that gave away the fact that she smoked heavily. "She was one of the first people through at the start of my shift."

She handed the phone back to Sarah who thanked her.

"Not sure if it's connected or not, but Gary, the guy that collects the boarding passes, well he quit right after she got on the boat."

"Thanks," Sarah said. "We will keep that in mind."

Chapter 60

Sam had been watching the time tick by, waiting to administer the second dose of her cocktail to keep Jessica unconscious. The trailer she had selected to hold up in was equipped with a heater and since it was also connected to the power that the park provided; she had fired it up. She saw no sense in being cold while she waited to execute her plan.

To pass the time, she had been keeping an eye on the local news sources. She enjoyed hearing the fear mongering that was being broadcast about her. The top story on all three networks was about the murder of the reporter, the cameraman, the trooper and the kidnapping of the chief. There were blurbs here and there about the injured detective and her companion, but they failed to delve deep into their injuries or status.

She was about to shut off the television when the advertisement that was playing was cut off by the news anchor. "I have just been informed that there is a statement about to be made by the Plattsburgh state police. We go live to the barracks."

There was no reporter that appeared on the screen to confirm what was just said. Instead, the camera was focused on a lectern that had been placed in front of the barracks. Slowly, an old man that Sam did not recognize approached and took his place behind it.

"For those who are unfamiliar with me, my name is Chief Felix Lamountain, from the Albany barracks. Last night, I received a text message from interim Chief Momsen. She and I had formed a friendship and she had been keeping me apprised of the situation up here with the so-called Mountaintop Killer. The message had said that she was about to be taken by the killer and the department could use my help."

"As you are all aware, three people were killed last night by Ms. Ryan and Momsen was kidnapped. Detective Sarah Barney and one of my detectives who was on loan to this area, John Cline, were both attacked by Ms. Ryan and stabbed. While Detective Barney was released from the hospital last night, Detective Cline had to undergo surgery to repair the injuries he sustained. He is listed in critical condition and is in the ICU. Detective Barney left for Vermont immediately upon her release in an attempt to track down and apprehend Samantha Ryan. She adamantly refused to take any help with her, as she did not want another one of her brothers or sisters in the department to fall victim to the killer."

"People of Vermont, be on the lookout for Samantha Ryan, as she is known to be armed and is very dangerous. If you see her, do not attempt to approach her. Dial nine-one-one immediately and tell the operator what you have seen. I have already reached out to the governor of Vermont and he, with his state and local police are working in conjunction with us to help apprehend Ms. Ryan and to bring both the interim chief and Detective Barney home safely."

"I have no other information at this time, and neither will I be taking any questions. Good day."

With that, he turned and walked away from the lectern. Sam shut off the television before the feed cut back to the studio. If Sarah had left at some time during the night, she was most likely already in the area. It was time to get things moving.

The whale tail sculpture was in a field of sorts, and because of this Sam had found an area where she could hide the parts that she would need to construct the device that would kill Jessica. All that was required of her for now was for her to transport Jessica to the location.

There was a large construction project on Community Drive in South Burlington. From that, she would be within walking distance to the sculpture. She would have to wait until later in the day to ensure all of the workers had left. Sam walked down the short hall of the trailer and entered the bedroom.

The queen size bed was the only actual furniture in the room. There were drawers built into the walls where Sam assumed the owners kept their clothes while staying here. The bed itself was covered with a paisley comforter, which in turn was covered with a sheet of plastic. It was upon that sheet where Jessica was deposited and remained. Sam injected her with a second dose of the drug cocktail and then scooped her up.

Sam walked back down the hall and just before she entered the kitchen area, there was a door on her left. This door led outside, she opened it and descended the two metal steps to the brown grass surrounding the camper. The smell of the lake flooded her nose as it was carried on the strong wind that had swept in a couple of hours ago.

She walked over to the Civic and dropped Jessica on the ground by the rear end. Walking over to the driver's door, she opened it and pushed the button that would release the trunk. Returning to the chief, she roughly collected her from the ground and inserted her into the compartment before slamming the lid shut. All of this seemed dull and boring to her now. It felt like it had been far too long since she had claimed a life. The need to kill was becoming a daily thing to her now.

Sam knew that just down the road from the park was a grey house and that a single woman lived there. She could easily break in and overpower this woman and claim her life, slaking her desire. As strong as the need to kill was though. It would only serve as a distraction to her. Sam had a goal and if she stuck to her plan, she would be killing Sarah in just a few short hours.

Renewing her resolve, Sam climbed behind the wheel of the car and started the engine. She had another need that had to be addressed, hunger. Sam had not had a proper meal in more than a day. Having frequented the area often when hunting for victims, she knew the area well. There was a small town about fifteen minutes away called Colchester. Seconds away from the interstate was a Mcdonald's and a Burger King.

The trip to Colchester was uneventful, with a fair amount of traffic. The trip ended up taking her twenty minutes, but she had nothing but time to kill right now. It was just before eleven O'clock, so she decided to go to Mcdonald's for their breakfast. Her face had been broadcast over every news report for the last few days and most likely on the front page of every paper, so drive-through was the only logical choice.

Sam placed her order and got into the long line of cars waiting to pay and receive their order. McDonald's had been at this game a long time, and they were pretty efficient at it, so her wait was less than five minutes before she arrived at the first window. The woman working there was in her late fifties and haggard looking. She confirmed Sam's order before telling her the amount owed. Sam handed her a twenty-dollar bill and as the woman accepted it, she paused and looked hard at Sam.

"You look familiar," she said.

Sam had expected something like this to happen, so she just replied to the comment as nonchalantly as possible. "Yeah, I come here every day, cannot get enough of your Mcsandwiches."

The woman chuckled at this and started to make change. As she leaned out of the window to hand the money to Sam, she said, "No, that's not it. Are you famous or something?"

"Not yet, but hopefully someday soon," Sam replied as she pulled forward. Her nerves were now wound tight. She was certain that the woman would eventually place from where she had known her face. What was worse was the crew wore headsets and could communicate with each other. As expected, when Sam reached the second window, there was a small group of employees doing their best to look inconspicuous as they watched her pull up.

The person that looked to be working at the second window was dressed in the blue uniform that signified they were a manager. He was somewhere around forty and looking at Sam critically. He handed her the plastic cup and straw for her drink before turning to grab the brown paper bag that contained her food. Someone in the group of employees said something to him and he looked at Sam again. His face became a mask of fear.

"Here you go," he said handing her the bag and pulling his arm back a little too quickly. She had been made, and there was nothing that she could do about it. They were certain to call the police, but by the time they arrived she would be long gone. They would have the color and type of car she was driving but she hoped that the popularity of the Honda would make it difficult to spot. She did not have the time to steal another car.

"Off to Stowe I go," she said as she pulled away, trying to sound like she was talking to herself. The man at the window looked dimwitted enough to maybe buy it.

She had a lot of options as to where she could go and hide in plain sight. The Burlington and Williston area were meccas of shopping, with Burlington having a mall and several shopping plazas and Williston having two plazas in the same vicinity. The Dorset Street mall was notoriously difficult to exit with any sort of rapidity though. Whomever had designed the parking area did not understand the way that traffic flowed. Sam remembered once around Christmas several years ago she had gone to the mall, looking not for goods to purchase but rather a potential victim.

The mall that day was packed with people. The walkways were difficult to navigate as they were choked, and the parking garages and the surrounding lot were so full that it was difficult to even find an open spot. After spending a few hours there without locating anyone that looked to be alone and an easy mark, she had left. It took her almost an hour to finally make it out of the lot and onto Dorset Street. For that reason, she immediately discounted the mall as a place to lay low. Should the police happen upon her, she would not be able to make any sort of getaway, let alone a quick one.

Maple Tree Place in Williston was home to a lot of big box stores. There was Walmart, Best Buy and a slew of others, not to mention one of the area's largest movie theaters. Maple Tree Place was set on both sides of Route Two A, locally known as St. George Road. The parking lots on both sides also exited onto other main roads, most notably Route Two. This would make for an easier exit, should she be forced to run.

As Sam left the road that held both the McDonald's and Burger King, she turned right towards the entrance to the interstate. She would take that to exit twelve to Williston. She had decided to go to the half of the plaza where Walmart was located. The parking lot for this store was huge and heavily used, so she felt this would be her best bet to hide for the next four or five hours.

Chapter 61

Unlike the state of New York, most Vermont towns and cities had their own police departments. The state police and the sheriff departments also had a heavy presence in a lot of the towns. As such, Vermont was a relatively low crime area. This also lessened the amount of time one would wait for a response to a call that required an officer.

Corporal Dave Hicks had been with the Colchester police for five years now. He had gotten his undergraduate degree in criminal justice from Champlain College in Burlington, Vermont. Hicks was born and raised in Montana but had wanted to travel for college. Once he was in Vermont, the decision to stay here after graduating was easy. The people and the scenery were both equally nice. Since he was at the top of his class, the job offers came fast and in abundance.

Hicks was five feet and ten inches tall. He was single so he spent the vast majority of his free time at the Colchester Health and Fitness gym. Being a young man with motivation he had packed on fifty pounds of muscle swiftly. When he joined the department, he was one-hundred-eighty-three pounds. He now tipped the scale at just over two-hundred-thirty pounds. He was referred to as being shockingly Caucasian, his skin was so pale he almost looked albino. This made his jet-black hair and hazel eyes stand out. He also looked like he was always in need of a shave.

He had just left the Barracks and was still on Blakely Drive when dispatch radioed him. He picked up the handset and keyed the microphone on.

"Car twenty-one here, what's up Mike?" he asked.

Mike Myers was three years older than Hicks. He had long suffered jokes about his name and the tie-in to the Halloween movie franchise. He was a quiet person and held his feelings inside, which had caused him to gain a substantial amount of weight. Hicks was the first person he had met that did not make a joke about his name and they had formed a quick friendship. Hicks also defended Mike to anyone that dared make any joke about how differently they appeared. Mike was just over five feet tall with thinning blonde hair and a bushy beard. He carried the majority of his excess weight in his gut, so the pair could not look any different if they tried.

"Dave, we have a possible sighting of that Samantha Ryan from the Plattsburgh area at McDonald's by exit sixteen. Go and take some statements," Mike's voice came across the speaker.

"Copy that, on my way," Hicks replied.

It was probably a wild goose chase but given the number of lives that she had claimed already, it was definitely worth checking out. Every single police officer in the state had been given a color picture of Sam. The picture was a still image taken from a news broadcast that had gotten a good look at her face. It was to be kept with them at all times, and Hicks had his on his clipboard.

He spent the ten-minute drive thinking about Lena, a woman that attended the same gym. Although they had been flirtatious with each other, Lena was ten years his senior and that made him reluctant to ask her out. She was in a different place in her life, divorced with two kids. Hicks had never even really been in a serious relationship before.

There was just something about her that he found irresistible. She was average height with a slight mom-bod and long, curly red hair. Her pale skin was an art gallery of tattoos. None of those were his type. As he pulled into the McDonald's parking lot, he decided he would ask her out. Life was too short to waste on missed opportunities.

Hicks parked his car in a spot that was closest to the door on the side of the building. He exited the cruiser and walked to the glass door. The smell of burgers and fries practically slapped him in the face as he opened the door and entered. The lobby was like every other McDonald's lobby he had been in, with the newly added self-service touch screens immediately in front of him.

Before he could proceed any further, a man came rushing out from behind the counter. He was dressed in the manager's uniform and his name tag identified him as Steve. He was middle-aged and slightly overweight. His skin was far darker than most of the African Americans that lived in the area. His dark brown eyes were wide with excitement.

"Thank god you are here!" he exclaimed. "Follow me."

Without waiting, Steve turned and headed back to the counter. Hicks followed him, past the pair of registers, through the kitchen and past the two drive through windows to the small manager's office. It was little more than a desk, a chair and a computer.

"The order screen for the drive through takes the picture of everyone that orders," said Steve. "It helps the crew keep track of which order belongs to which person, since there are two order screens. When I recognized the Mountaintop Killer, I ran down here and saved the picture."

This last part he said while indicating the computer screen on the desk. Hicks pulled out his hard copy from his clipboard and got closer to the monitor, comparing them.

"Sonofabitch," he said. "It really is her. Did you happen to notice what kind of car she was driving?

Steve smiled at this, like he was some kind of hero. "Of course, officer. She was driving an older, blue Civic. She also said something that I am not sure I was meant to hear. She said she was heading to Stowe."

Hicks thanked the man for the information and swiftly made his way back to his cruiser. He pulled out his notepad, wrote down the time, where he was and all the other information that Steve provided him. He then picked up the microphone.

"Mike, this is twenty-one, come back."

"Go ahead Dave," came the quick reply.

"I have confirmed that the manager did in fact see Samantha Ryan at this location. She was last seen in an older blue Honda Civic, most likely with New York tags, possibly headed to Stowe. I am going to drive around and see if I cannot find her," Hicks said.

"Dispatch to twenty-one, copy that. I will alert the other local PD, especially Stowe. Dispatch out."

Hicks started the engine but did not back out of his space. He had to think. If he was a criminal, with a hostage, where would he go to hide out? Samantha was clearly an intelligent person, she had evaded capture this long and had managed to capture and kill some very large, highly trained troopers. He immediately discounted the Stowe lead. She had probably figured out that the manager had recognized her and was trying to create a false lead.

Except for the outskirts, Colchester was an urban area with a high population density. She would not do well if she tried to break into a house in town, so she would want to stay mobile. On a hunch, Hicks backed out from his spot, left the McDonald's and headed for the south bound entrance for interstate eighty-nine.

Chapter 62

Rodrigues had driven past the whale tail sculpture three times, and they were approaching it for the fourth time. The SUV that they were now in looked like many others on the road, so, if Sam was watching, she would be hard pressed to discover them. On each drive-by, Ed was taking pictures and notes about the area surrounding the sculpture. Everything he was gathering would be passed along to Sarah.

It was Sarah's plan to park along the side of the interstate, navigate over the safety fence that ran along it and approach the whale tails directly. This would be bold and most likely unexpected by Sam, allowing the pair of Rodrigues and Ed to approach from the rear. It was a quite solid plan.

As daylight savings had ended for the year, as the hour of five O'clock was approaching, so too was the darkness. Ed was studying the area immediately behind the sculpture when he spotted movement. It was difficult to be certain, but he knew that it was Samantha. He pulled out his cellphone and sent Sarah a text, alerting her that the time had come to set their plan into action.

"The time has arrived for us to head to Planet Fitness," Ed said to Rodrigues.

Rodrigues simply nodded and stepped on the accelerator. They would need to drive to the next exit, number thirteen, and make their way through the heavy traffic to arrive at their destination. They had made a dry run earlier in the day, and it had taken twenty minutes, while obeying all traffic laws.

Granted, they were a New York state trooper and an FBI agent, but they were not in an official vehicle and getting pulled over would still add valuable time to their trip. It would take time to assure whatever law enforcement official that pulled them over that they were on official business. To that end, Rodrigues kept the SUV under seventy-five miles an hour, the posted limit being sixty-five. The distance between the two exits was just over four miles, so they reached theirs in under five minutes.

They would need to now merge onto Kennedy Drive and then take a right onto Kimball Avenue, all heavily traveled roads. The current time would not help them either, it was rush hour in the city of Burington. The exit ramp was backed up almost all of the way to the main road of the interstate and the pair sat through three cycles of the light before they were able to get onto Kennedy. They both sat there, helplessly watching the minutes tick by.

"We shan't make it in time," Ed said to himself.

Rodrigues nodded in agreement. There would be no way of warning Sarah either. Part of her plan was to have her cellphone in do not disturb mode. This would prevent an unintended call from alerting Sam that Sarah was close. They were all still in hopes that Sarah could surprise her.

"I suggest you make haste, as much as is possible," Ed said after they had sat in the same spot for six minutes.

Rodrigues understood the meaning of his words but saw no way of hastening their progress. There were not even any lawns that he could cut through. "Open to suggestions," he said.

Ed pulled out his cellphone and used the GPS to pull up a map showing where they were. Immediately to their right was Twin Oaks Terrace. They would have to force their way in between the vehicles lining the road beside them to get on that road, but it looked like they could cut around the traffic and get to Kimball from there.

"Signal right, please," he said. "We are going to take a shortcut. Do not be tame, force your way through, this vehicle is insured."

Rodrigues smiled at the last part. Ed had gladly paid the extra fee for insurance at the rental place. He flipped on this directional and was met immediately with a chorus of horns. The entrance to the road that Ed wanted him to take was to their right and about thirty feet in front. The roadside of Kennedy featured an extended shoulder in the area, so he just needed to get in between the Ford pick-up that was slightly in front of them and the Mazda Six that was behind it. Clearly the smaller vehicle would be the easiest to move.

Rodrigues turned the wheel as far as it could go and stepped on the gas. The SUV shot into motion, the right side of the bumper slamming into the fender of the black Mazda. Pushing down harder on the gas, the SUV started to push the much smaller car out of their way. He could not see the driver, but she was screaming obscenities at them. The screams were mixed in with the sounds of horns, rubber screaming against the pavement and the terrible sound of metal moving in protest.

After a minute of shoving, the Mazda had moved enough for them to fit through and reach the shoulder of the road. Within moments, they were on Twin Oaks Terrace. It was a largely residential area with both sides of the road lined with what looked to be condos or apartments.

There were a few cars on the road, mostly people returning home from a day's work. It took very little effort for Rodrigues to navigate around them, even at the heightened speed he was driving. In order for everything to work with their plan, they could not afford to arrive late. He had decided to throw caution to the wind and speed as safely as possible.

They arrived at a four-way stop where Twin Oaks met Forrest Park and Hayes Avenue. At Ed's direction, Rodrigues turned right onto Hayes. This road too was mostly residential and lightly filled with cars. The SUV reached fifty-miles-an-hour, the tires screeching as they kept right at a Y in the road.

So focused on driving and avoiding an accident was he, Rodrigues did not notice the Colchester police cruiser as he shot past it. It was not until they had reached the intersection of Hayes with Foxtrot and Kingston Streets that the sound of a siren behind them alerted them that the cruiser had given chase. Ed looked at Rodrigues and sighed.

"We had better pull over and handle this now," he said. "Lest the strobing lights and sirens give us away."

Rodrigues nodded and slowed down, eventually stopping on the right shoulder of the road. Being a trooper himself, he knew the drill and shut the engine off. He was about to step out of the SUV but was stayed by Ed's hand on his forearm.

Rodrigues watched as the officer exited the cruiser and slowly approached the rear of the SUV, his right hand on his gun. With his left hand, he shone his flashlight into the windows as he walked up to the driver's door. Rodrigues rolled down his window and had both his license and badge ready. Hicks ignored the proffered items and looked Rodrigues in the eyes.

"Care to explain the reckless driving, sir?" he asked.

Before Rodrigues could answer, Ed spoke up. "I am a federal agent, and this man is a New York state trooper under my command. We are on a mission of the utmost importance. I kindly request that you return to your vehicle and allow us to continue on our way," he said.

Hicks turned his attention from Rodrigues to Ed and then back again. He noticed that Rodrigues was in uniform. Slowly he grabbed the items that were still being held out of the window for him. Using his flashlight, he examined the badge carefully before shining the light at Ed.

"You have any ID, sir?" he asked. "How do I know that just because this guy looks like a trooper and is in uniform that he is not impersonating one and that you are who you claim?"

Ed slowly pulled open the left side of his suit jacket with his left hand and reached in with his right, withdrawing his FBI credentials. These he handed to Rodrigues who in turn gave them to Hicks.

Hicks examined them but still looked at the pair incredulously. "This have anything to do with the call from McDonald's?" he asked.

"I promise you that we do not know about what you are talking," Ed replied. "You need to understand, we are pressed for time. I should like to show you the respect that your position deserves, however, I am more than comfortable in instructing Trooper Rodrigues here to drive away and leave you standing in the road."

Hicks knew that he was serious. He handed back their identifications and stepped back from the SUV. Rodrigues did not waste any time. He started the engine and pulled away, leaving Hicks there to watch them go. He knew in his gut that this had to have something to do with the Samantha Ryan case. There could simply be no other reason for a New York trooper and an FBI agent to be in Chitenden County, let alone in the same area as she was last seen.

He knew that he should just let it go and resume his search for the blue Honda, but they were driving like they knew something that he did not. While Hicks was young, he was not naïve. It would be an immense boost to his career if he helped bring her in. Making his decision, he ran back to his cruiser before the SUV vanished from sight. He would follow them, but from far enough back that they would not notice.

Chapter 63

The sun had set, and the construction crew was gone for the day. The last time Sam visited this site, the only work that had been done was grading of the ground. As she pulled into the lot, she was happy to see that there was one and a half stories fully framed and covered with plywood in place. This would allow her to hide her car from view.

Sam navigated the rough pseudo-road that circled the project. It was comprised of packed dirt and full of potholes, not the kind of road upon which the owner of a Civic would drive. She bottomed out a few times and reduced her speed to avoid causing sufficient damage to the car and stranding herself. Regardless of whether she succeeded in killing Sarah or not, she would need to get away.

She reached the rear of the building, parked the car, shut off the engine and got out. This would prove to be the easiest of all of her traps to set up. All she needed from the car was Jessica. With that thought in mind, she opened the trunk and roughly grabbed the chief by her hair, sitting her up as best she could to facilitate placing her in a fireman's carry.

Once she had Jessica secured across her shoulders, Sam made her way across the uneven terrain that comprised the field between the construction site and the sculpture. It was an arduous and slow trip, but she made it there without falling. She dropped Jessica on the ground and oriented herself. The ground beneath her feet was covered in old, dry mulch and crunched as she turned in place. In the darkness, she spotted the large bush where she had hidden her components and started towards it. The mechanism was simple. It would attach at four points to the sculpture with large springs and paracord. The springs would be secured to each of Jessica's limbs, with a lever holding them tight. Once the lever was triggered, the springs would pull away from the trap at such a velocity that it should also take the associated limb with it. This was a design that she had never tested, so she hoped it would work.

Along with the supplies to construct the trap was another camera that could broadcast over the 5G available in the Burlington area and two flood lights that were one-million candela units each. This would ensure that the night would be turned into day and the people on the interstate would be able to watch the show.

It took her three trips to her hiding spot and back before she had retrieved everything. The first order of business would be to set up the camera and start recording. Her website that she had used to showcase Monica's death was still in operation and she was certain that the news networks still monitored it. The last time she had checked, it had almost one-million visitors per week.

Sam went about the task of setting up the two lights and then the camera on a tripod. She had included in her stash several batteries to power the lights. Once the three things were set up and the camera was recording, Sam stood in front of it to address whoever was watching.

"Hello friends," she said cheerfully. "We are back at it, playing another game. Tonight, I will be killing at least two of New York's finest. Behind me and quite unconscious is the Plattsburgh chief, Jessica Momsen. If I am not mistaken, Sarah Barney will be joining us shortly. What you may or may not know is poor Sarah has some pretty serious injuries, inflicted by mine own hands." This last part she said with an evil grin.

"As you watch, I will be placing Jessica into a device of my own making. Unlike the other devices that I have employed over the past few weeks, this one has no triggers, so it can be disarmed. That is how confident I am that Sarah will once again fail. This particular device will have a simple timer that, when it reaches zero, will trigger it into action, removing all four of Jessica's limbs."

Her phone made a chiming noise in her pocket. She withdrew it and smiled widely. She had subscribed to the local channels for alerts to breaking news, and she had just received a notification from all three. She opened her web browser and selected Fox. Once it had finished loading, she saw a news anchor and in the bottom right corner, herself.

"It looks like we are live on the networks now. Alright kids, it is time for mommy to get to work. Enjoy the show."

Sam turned from the camera and started to construct her device. It went together in less than ten minutes. She paid no attention to anything that was happening around her until she was finished. Before she went to retrieve Jessica, she glanced over her shoulder and saw a line of cars parked on the interstate. It seemed that it had not taken long for her to attract a crowd. She walked the five paces over to where she had dropped the chief and bent to pick her up when a voice from behind started her.

"Put your hands up and step away from her, you bitch." The voice belonged to Sarah.

Sam turned around and smiled. "You are early, old friend," she said. What Sarah had not noticed was that as Sam had stood up, she had removed a small device from her jacket pocket.

"Happy to surprise you," Sarah said. "Now, walk to me."

"I think not," Sam said. "You want me, come and get me."

This put Sarah on alert. Sam was not running, she did not even look worried. Perhaps it was from the fact that Sarah was pretty beat up, or perhaps it was from something more nefarious than that. Whatever the case might be, Sarah had a gun pointed at Sam, so she had the advantage. She advanced three steps and stopped, waiting to see what happened.

"I should just empty my clip into you," she said with anger. "You killed so many people, you launched an attack on me, my friends, my co-workers. Over what? A perceived slight from elementary school."

Sam knew that Sarah was baiting her, but she could not help herself in replying. "Perceived? You walked away while that fucking asshole beat me to a pulp. You might as well have done it yourself. I was in love with you. I just wanted to be a part of your world. Yet, you ignored me and allowed him to humiliate me."

"I was a child!" Sarah yelled at her. "I knew no better. I am sorry, truly, for what he did to you, but that does not give you license to murder."

Sarah decided this was enough talking and started once more to close the distance. As she got close to the camera, she heard it click and a fine mist sprayed her in the face. It was pepper spray, instantly blinding her. Reflexively, she fired off two shots, hoping that her gun was still aimed at Sam. Her hopes were dashed when she felt someone crash into her with alarming strength, knocking her to the ground. She then felt three fierce kicks meet her ribs, shattering several. Her breathing was now labored. She was blind, with several broken bones, and she was once again at the mercy of a cold-blooded killer. The only difference was that this time, she knew something that Sam did not.

"We could have been great!" Sam screamed, kicking Sarah in the ribs again.

She coughed and it was wet, meaning her lung had most likely been punctured. All that she kept thinking about was where in the hell Ed and Rodrigues were. She curled up into the fetal position, doing her best to shield her injuries from further assault.

"Look at you," spat Sam. "The great and powerful Sarah Barney. You are beaten. You are a mess. Covered in blood and snot. And who is it that has beaten you? That little girl you took no notice of or pity on. It is truly funny how life works. But enough editorializing from me."

Sarah heard the sound of footsteps retreating and she knew that she would at least how some reprieve from the onslaught of attacks. Her mind was racing. Something had clearly happened to Ed and Rodrigues. It was going to be up to her to save both herself and the chief.

Sam started to whistle her favorite song as she scooped up Jessica's limp body and set her in the trap. This took some effort, but after ten minutes, Jessica was secure, hanging there like a limp noodle, and the timer was set.

"You have been granted fifteen minutes more of your pitiful, miserable life," Sam said. "After that time has elapsed, Jessica will be dead, and I will take your life."

The short amount of time made sense. It would not take long for anyone watching to figure out where they were and get to the area. She heard Sam approach again and braced herself the best that she could for another blow. It never came though, and Sarah divined that Sam had probably taken her dropped gun.

Slowly, as the minutes ticked by, Sarah's vision started to clear. She knew that pepper spray took up to thirty minutes to naturally clear from your eyes, and she did not have that much time. She rolled over on her back to facilitate getting to her feet when the time was right.

"Tsk, tsk, tsk," said Sam. "You are not planning on trying to do anything heroic, are you?"

Sarah ignored her, not wanting to elicit another beating. She was both surprised and relieved that Sam had not searched her. Squinting through her painful eyes, she tried to keep an eye on her to see if she turned her back. When the killings had started and Sarah discovered that she was not even safe within the walls of her own house, she had started carrying an ankle holster with a small twenty-two caliber pistol.

"Ten minutes left," Sam taunted. "My viewers will delight in the show that is about to happen. How should I kill you? Slowly with a knife, letting you feel everything, until you beg for death? Or, perhaps swiftly, with your own gun?"

Sarah was getting sick of hearing the sound of Sam's voice. "I'll pay real money for you to shut the fuck up," she said.

"Spirited, to the last," Sam said. "I commend that, but you also helped me to decide. Slowly it shall be. Then we will know just how spirited you truly are!"

Sarah blinked hard and by a miracle that she did not understand, her vision cleared to almost normal. Her eyes still burned, and the tears were still flowing, but she could see well enough to aim at her target.

"NYPD!" a voice from behind Sam shouted. "Put your hands up and get on your knees."

The voice belonged to Rodrigues and Sarah felt a wave of relief. She was about to shout a warning to him that Sam was armed, but the woman was too fast for her. Sam spun around with shocking speed and fired a shot in the direction of the voice.

She missed her target, but this gave Sarah the opportunity she had been needing. Ignoring the screaming pain from her ribs, she sat up and reached for her hidden gun. In a blur of motion, she retrieved it, aimed and fired two shots at Sam. The first one went wide, and she hoped that it did not strike her companions. The second shot found its target though, striking Sam in her left shoulder.

Sam spun slightly from the impact but proved to be unflappable. She turned and dove for the ground, hiding behind one of the whale tails. Sarah could not see her, and the silence from Rodrigues made her nervous. She also was beginning to wonder what had become of Ed.

"You bitch," yelled Sam. "You actually shot me!" This was followed by an unaimed shot towards Sarah, missing her.

Sarah rolled to her left, hoping that she would be far enough away from her original position that Sam would not get lucky with any wildly aimed shots. She was so focused on the area where Sam had taken refuge that she did not hear Hicks approaching. He touched her shoulder and scared her half to death. She let out an involuntary scream of surprise and almost shot him in the face.

"Ma'am, name's Hicks," he said to her. "Are you alright?"

Sarah reached up and yanked Hicks to the ground. "Are you trying to get shot?" she yelled at him.

He just stared at her, clearly out of his element. Sarah scanned the darkness surrounding them, hoping to catch a glimpse of Sam. Instead, she saw Ed Approaching from her left. They basically had Sam surrounded. Rodrigues, if he had not been shot, was to her right. Sam had nowhere to go. Time was running out for Jessica though. She was still in the trap and had less than eight minutes left before it sprung. The time to act was nigh. She leaned closer to Hicks and whispered into his ear.

"Listen, you stumbled onto something bigger than anything you have probably ever encountered. That is the Mountaintop Killer over there. Me and two others have tracked her here and are trying to apprehend her. I need you to do exactly what I say, and maybe, just maybe you will walk away from today alive and a hero."

She paused, making sure he was looking into her eyes and understanding what she was saying.

"This woman has killed my colleagues, my friends and who knows how many others. She has overpowered large and formidable men with ease. Now, for the first time since everything started, we have her surrounded and outnumbered. I want you to circle around to my left, and I will go right. I am the one she wants, so, logically, I should be her first concern. Try to stay out of her line of sight, she has a gun. If you see an opportunity to shoot her, take it, but I want her alive. Do you understand me?"

Hicks looked like he was on the verge of a panic attack, but he nodded that he understood what she was saying.

Sarah held up her hand, hoping that Ed would see her. He mirrored her signal. Sarah did her best to indicate her plan with hand gestures. Ed nodded his understanding and started to slowly move in on Sam. Sarah tapped Hicks and nodded. He slowly got to his feet and walked in the direction Sarah had indicated. She too got up and walked to her right, staying as low to the ground as possible.

Sarah had walked about fifteen steps when she heard Hick's speak and terror gripped her.

"Colchester police, you need to drop your weapon and come out with your hands up," he shouted. "You have ten seconds to comply."

Sarah did not know what he was trying to accomplish but thought better of yelling at him. She slowly inched forward, keeping the sculpture between her and Sam when a gunshot rang out. She heard Hicks hit the ground with a thud. The idiot had gotten himself shot. She sensed that the time was right to make her move and ran forward towards where she had heard the gunshot.

Sarah rounded the whale tail and surprised Sam. She was still leaning around the far side of the base of the tail and taking aim at Ed. Hearing Sarah, she was spinning as fast as she could to get a shot off, but Sarah kicked the gun from her hand.

Sarah ached from head to toe, her body signally her many injuries to the point where simply thinking hurt, but she now stood over her quarry, victiorious. Her gun was aimed at Sam's head and Ed was rapidly approaching from the other side, his gun too trained at Sam.

"This is over," Sarah said. "You have lost. Now, free my boss."

"I will die first," Sam said. Sarah knew that she meant it too.

"Ed, hurry. I need you to free Jessica, and we only have minutes left."

Ed sprinted past the pair and went to inspect the device that held Jessica. He started where it was attached to her body and followed the lines to the machine.

"I cannot simply free her, it will trigger the device," he said. "I shall have to disarm it."

He studied the switch and timer, concluding that it was safe to stop and disarm there. With thirty seconds left on the clock, he stopped the count down. After a minute's more inspection, Ed discovered how to disengage the tension and Jessica was free. Her limp body fell to the ground with a thud, causing Sarah to glance back over her shoulder. That was all the time Sam needed.

Sam pulled her knife from its sheath and like a cat, leapt at Sarah. As her knife was about to plunge into Sarah's throat, a gunshot rang out. The bullet struck Sam in the left temple and the force caused her body to topple over, narrowly missing Sarah. Everyone spun towards the sound of the gun and saw Rodrigues. He was on one knee, his pistol still out in front of him in a two-handed grip. Sarah could see where her stray bullet had struck him in the right arm. It looked to have either grazed him or been a shallow through and through.

She felt both a wave of relief and nausea as the adrenalin in her system wore off. Her body was battered in many ways, and she was tired to her core. Before she knew what was happening, the ground rushed up at her as she collapsed. Ed rushed to her side and knelt beside her.

"Are you alright?" he asked.

"I need a vacation," she quipped as blackness overtook her.

Chapter 64

Sarah was staring out of the window in the chief's office. It was December, with Christmas rapidly approaching. Normally, Sarah was excited about the holiday as it had been her favorite her whole life. The outside world was awash in white as the snowstorm that had been raging for the last four hours continued. Already, seven inches had fallen with another eight to ten promised.

Her body was still healing from the myriad injuries that she had sustained in ending Sam's reign of terror. Her mind and heart would take longer to recover though. Many good people had died because of an action she took, or rather did not take when she was a child. Ed had stayed with her for two weeks, helping her with mundane tasks like cooking and cleaning. She had protested, but he would not have it. The last thing he had said to her before leaving for Boston still tugged at her heart.

"I never married and neither did I sire any children. I think of you as my daughter."

He had not waited for a response. Sarah did not expect him to. The man was typically quite stoic, so she understood how difficult this small look into his heart must have been. Although she had had a father, she did look up to and admire Ed, almost like a second father.

The Mountaintop Killer case was just barely fading from the news storis. CNN had tried to get Sarah to do an interview, let alone the constant calls from the local networks. She had even heard that Netflix was in the works of doing a docuseries about the events that happened. For the sake of accuracy, Sarah had decided if they contacted her, she would participate. She was loathe to stay in the spotlight though.

"There, that looks much better," Jessica said, breaking her train of thought. She had just finished moving the new plaque on her desk for the fourth time.

"No more interim," Sarah said. "How does it feel to officially be the chief?"

"It feels good, though I am not sure the cost to get the title was worth it," Jessica answered.

"Hogwash," Sarah said. "You earned that title."

"How are things going with your new partner?" Jessica asked.

Sarah smiled before answering. "Great, actually. Rodriguez is very smart. He keeps telling me though that he cannot wait to remove the word junior before his title of detective."

"All in good time," Jessica replied. "Though, with you as a teacher, I assume that will be sooner rather than later."

Sarah decided to change the subject. "Going tomorrow night?" she asked.

The mayor and governor had arranged a ceremony to honor those that lost their life to Sam. It was to be held at the West Side Ballroom and there were rumors that the President was even going to attend.

"Yeah, my first act as chief cannot be avoiding that," she said.

"Great, I will pick you up at seven," Sarah said.

"Oh, no! I am driving," Jessica said.

They both laughed at that, given Sarah's record over the last few months. It was the first time either of them had laughed in months, and it felt good. Things will return to normal, Sarah thought to herself as she returned to looking out the window at the white flakes.

Prologue

He had watched the news unfold about the case in New York with great interest. This Sarah Barney had proved herself to be a formidable opponent to the one they called the Mountaintop Killer.

He had been in the business of taking lives for the last twenty years, and no one had been smart enough to even connect any of the murders, let alone decipher that the three-hundred lives he had taken were all the work of one man. Sure, he had moved from state to state over the course of those twenty years, but still, one would think someone would have enough brains.

Yet here he was, unknown to the world when he should be famous. Perhaps he had found the one that would make him so. Plattsburgh, New York was a Podunk city, but it would serve his needs. Google informed him that it was only thirteen hours away if he drove.

He turned to the woman that was tied to the pole in front of him. She was clad only in her underwear, her body full of bruises and open cuts as he had toyed with her for days. Her once blonde hair now looked red from the blood that it had soaked up. She no longer looked afraid of him, resigned to death.

"I guess that I am done with you," he said as he reached out and slit her throat. "I am leaving tomorrow for bigger and better things."

Before he left the abandoned house he had been using to torture and kill this woman, he decided to see what he could do to kick things into gear. He ripped off a piece of the wallpaper that was already hanging loosely from the tattered walls. He walked over to the dying woman and dipped his gloved finger in the copious amounts of blood that flowed from the gaping hole in her neck. On the back of the paper, he wrote a number, 301, and then set the paper on her lap.